Handyman

—

Linda Nichols

DELACORTE PRESS

Published by
Delacorte Press
Random House, Inc.
1540 Broadway
New York, New York 10036

ISBN 0-385-33437-0

Cataloging in Publication Data is on file with the publisher.

Manufactured in the United States of America
Published simultaneously in Canada

Book design by Virginia Norey

January 2000

10 9 8 7 6 5 4 3 2 1

BVG

To Ken, John, David, and Steve—my safe harbor

Acknowledgments

———

Thanks to my husband, Ken, who sacrificed time and money so I could write.

To my agent, Theresa Park, who picked me out of the slush pile; Jackie Cantor, a wonderfully encouraging editor; Kathy Keller, my teacher, friend, and mentor; and the members of the TCC Advanced Writer's Workshop. Thanks also to Howie Sanders, Richard Green, and Scott Schwimer, traveling companions on a wild ride.

Thanks also to those who answered questions and aided me in research: Priscilla Lane, Agricultural Biologist for the Sonoma County Agricultural Commission; Judy Walters Blakefield of Petaluma Visitor's Services; Sandy Lazarz, Jennifer Swan, and Melody Hardesty of the Petaluma Chamber of Commerce; the Faith Dairy in Tacoma, Washington; and Karen Barker, Special Occasion and Dress Specialist at Nordstrom, Tacoma. And finally—many, many thanks to Maggie McDonogh, skipper of the *Bonita,* who took pity on me and made an unscheduled trip to Angel Island in the rain.

Monday, April 20
NYU Medical Center
New York

Dr. Jason Solomon Golding, member in good standing of the American Psychological Association, and author of *The 21-Day Life Overhaul* and *Tuning Up for Love*, couldn't imagine lousier luck.

"Of all the lousy luck," he repeated, feeling very sorry for himself, and very solitary in a romantic, pining sort of way. He felt solitary much of the time, he realized, distracted briefly by the insight. Maybe he should write a book on it, call it *The Solitary Man*. He stared into space for a minute or two, thinking about chapter headings and alternate titles, before he remembered his lousy luck, and annoyance won out over melancholy. He gave the hospital table a calculated shove—hard enough to wobble the bright green Jell-O and to let Monica know he was suffering—but not hard enough to tip it over and cause a real mess.

"Oh really, Jay." Monica glanced at him briefly over her thin shoulder. She was staring out the window onto the traffic below, probably mourning the loss of shopping, and lunch at the Four Seasons. As he lay dying.

"Of all the lousy times to have a heart attack," he said again. He had been recounting his lousy luck to the paramedics, to his wife, to the emergency room nurses, to anyone who would listen, from the moment he had clutched his chest and fallen dramatically to his knees on the speaker's podium at the Tenth Annual Symposium on Stress Reduction, where he had come all the way from San Francisco to give the keynote address. He had just received the introduction—he smiled again, remembering it—and had thanked the APA president for his kind words, was just clearing his throat to begin his speech, when pain, like a vise—no, that wasn't a strong enough image. It was more like a hot vise—that was it. Pain, red-hot and searing, had crushed his chest. He had fallen to the ground, hands over his heart, face grimacing from that pain, which, though real, was now gone. At least he had really had a heart attack, he thought. How humiliating to have been carried off to the hospital in front of all his colleagues only to be diagnosed with gas or indigestion.

"There'll be other conferences," Monica said now without even bothering to turn around.

Jay had already comforted himself with that thought, but it irritated him to hear Monica say it. Still, he had to admit she was right. It wasn't as if this conference were the pinnacle of his career. It was more like the latest in a series of pinnacles. It was like climbing a mountain range, he thought, warming to the analogy. Just when you got to the top of one peak you sighted another off in the distance. He should write that down.

"Monica, bring me some paper, for crying out loud."

Monica tore herself away from the window, arranged herself in the chair by his bed, and began a languid search of her purse. He didn't know how she could do anything with those nails. It exasperated him almost beyond endurance to watch her picking through her things with the tips of her fingers. She began transferring the contents of her purse to a slithering pile on her lap, pausing every now and then to brush a strand of determinedly auburn hair from her face with a French-manicured finger.

Jay sighed deeply, nobly, and resolved not to take out his frustrations on Monica, even mentally. He picked up the conference brochure from the bedside table and studied it, allowing himself to fully experience the depth of his disappointment. His own face stared back meaningfully from the pamphlet. He had taken a somber pose, chin cupped thoughtfully in his hand. He noticed again how well the transplant and Rogaine had filled in that troublesome spot on his forehead. Not bushy, but not thin. Definitely not thin. Now that he could see the impact the photograph made he was glad he'd let his editor talk him into putting it on the jacket of his new book.

"Too shallow," he'd initially protested, wondering if the Rogaine had had time to work. "Not me. Not me at all."

"I respect that," she'd argued, "but isn't the point of *Celebrating Me* self-acceptance? I mean, isn't it your responsibility to lead by example?"

She'd had him there. He nodded and gave the picture another close inspection. His hair definitely did not look thin. He ran his fingers through the new growth now and was struck again with regret at the wasted opportunity. Here he sat while life went on around him. And even though Monica was right and there would be other conferences, missing this one was a painful blow. Monica had been dead wrong when she'd insinuated his reason for accepting the invitation was to show off in front of the graduates of the schools that had rejected him. Still, being asked to give the keynote address was a vindication of sorts. He had finally gotten it right. Two books, six months each on *The*

New York Times Best Seller List, and a third due out next month. He, Jason Golding, invited to speak at one of the APA's most prestigious conferences. And now this. It was so unfair.

"Your coronary arteries are eighty-five percent occluded," the cardiologist had told him.

"What about the balloon, or the Roto-Rooter thing?" Monica asked.

Jay shook his head, never ceasing to be amazed at the way Monica blatantly revealed her ignorance. "There are too many blockages for that, Monica," he said slowly and clearly.

The cardiologist had agreed. Jay's bypass surgery would take place tomorrow. Here. In New York. When he should have been finishing the keynote address. When he should have been enjoying the high point of his career. Really. It was always something.

Another wave of suffering washed over him, and he spent the next few minutes recalling the trials of the past year. First there had been the house in Pacific Heights that wouldn't sell. Then that trouble with his book. And now this. Even though Monica had spent the past half hour reminding him of the house's eventual sale, the book's overwhelming success, the fact that the convention had chosen him to be keynote speaker, that they had each other, and that, really, at a time like this he ought to be thinking more about his health, it was little comfort.

"Here you go," Monica said now, finally handing him a dull pencil and a scrap of paper hardly big enough to write an address on.

"Oh, for crying out loud, Monica," he said. "It's too late. I've lost the thought."

"Sorry," she said.

Jay gave her a piercing glance. Her lips had that little purse to them, as if they were being tightened with a string, and even though the taut skin of her face never registered much emotion, he could tell she was annoyed. It was the tone. The exaggerated politeness. He looked around for a place to set the pencil and paper, but he had shoved the rolling table out of his reach.

"Here," Monica finally said with the same excruciating tone. "Let me."

Jay gave her the paper, wiped his forehead with his palm, and ran his fingers through his patchy new crop of hair. It had to be eighty degrees in here. He'd raised hell to get a private room, and it looked like he was going to have to do it again to get the damned air-conditioning turned on.

"Monica, get somebody in here to adjust the air. I'm sweltering."

"It's already on, hon," she said. "Just lie back, and you'll cool off in a minute." She never looked at him, just unclipped the tethered remote from his bed, turned on the television, flipped through a few channels, and began watching *Hollywood Squares.*

Really. She was so like a child. You had to stay on her all the time or she just drifted off. Here she was watching the damned television while his life hung in the balance. He recalled the two or three matters he'd left up to her in his last-minute rush to prepare his speech and pack. What had he been thinking? Now he added another item to the list of his misfortunes—his entire practice was probably going to hell in a handbasket as he languished here.

"Did you take care of the things I asked you to, Monica?" he snapped, determined to focus her attention where it belonged. "Did you hear back from that contractor?"

"Which one, hon?" She crossed one long leg over the other with the graceful ease that had first attracted him. Before he began wondering if mispronouncing words was a valid reason for divorce.

"The one Metzger recommended out of Petaluma." He could almost feel his blood pressure begin to rise.

"I think he's taking a look tomorrow." Monica clicked the remote. Whoopi Goldberg's square was replaced by a foreign drama. Monica watched intently, her pink lips slightly parted, as two women carried on a tearful conversation in what sounded like Hindi.

"Well, find the hospital's fax machine and tell him to fax me back the estimate right away. His is the last bid, and I want to get started on that thing."

Monica gave a half lift of her chin that passed for agreement without taking her eyes from the television. Jay shook his head. Just like a child. She had no conception of where the money came from. Her only interest was in keeping the St. John suits on that size six back of hers.

"The sooner we get the office done the sooner we can start the seminars," he clarified, and was rewarded with another chin tilt. She flipped the channel to *Ricki Lake*.

He thought about the seminars, finally cheered. They would multiply his income exponentially. "Think of it, Monica," he said, mostly to himself, since she was apparently engrossed in the confessions of partner-swapping identical twins, "instead of seeing one patient at two hundred dollars per hour, I can see ten or twelve at a time and charge them all." And no listening to individual problems, he reminded himself. That was the beautiful thing. They would all listen to *him*. No more crises. No more phone calls in the middle of the night. He frowned, remembering another last-minute detail he had left to Monica, definitely an unusual occurrence, but he'd been busy. Preparing the speech he would never give. Another surge of suffering crested and broke. He sighed, then barked out another question.

"Monica. Did you tell Angie to change the voice mail message?"

"Um-hum." The twins were finished confessing, and Ricki Lake was winding up. Monica began flipping channels again. Really, her attention span was shorter than a four-year-old's.

"I called the office myself to check," she said. "The greeting says emergencies should call Dr. Hammond, and everyone else should leave a message. Angie said she'd check them every day from home."

"Sure," he said, not believing it for a minute. Still, it was the lesser of two evils. Pay Angie full salary to sit around for three weeks while the office was being remodeled or trust her to return a few phone calls. He wondered for the hundredth time why the New Beginnings Clinic couldn't just hire a service like everyone else. But some genius had come up with the idea of subscribing to a voice messaging service, and here they were. Not that Jay would be personally grieved by missing a few phone calls. For humanity as a whole he felt a profound compassion. He envisioned them as sheep without a shepherd, bedraggled, huddled masses, that sort of thing. But when they called one at a time and whined into his ear, that was something else.

That's why groups were such a beautiful idea, he thought, and felt the excitement bubble again. *The Genesis Experience,* he would call his workshop. Begin your life again. He'd gather them around in a circle to start with, then pair them up to work on exercises or do rebirth imaging in the hot tub. All he had to do was cruise the room and make sure there were no psychic emergencies. And the sooner the interior walls were knocked out and the spa installed, the sooner he could begin moving them through.

"What's that guy's name again?"

"Who?" Monica turned her eyes toward him. Once he had thought they were hooded and mysterious, but now they just looked droopy and dull.

"The *contractor*," he said, annoyed that she couldn't follow the thread of a simple conversation.

"Oh." She sounded slightly surprised, as if they hadn't just been speaking about him. "They're partners—a man and a woman," she said, beginning another sojourn through her purse and making the shifting piles on her lap again. "Here it is." She pulled out a business card and handed it to him.

He squinted, patted the breast of the hospital gown for his glasses, and held out his hand with an expectant look, prompting Monica to sigh and fetch them from the pocket of his suit jacket, hung in the closet. He put them on and held the card at various distances until he could read it: JAKE COOPER AND ETHELDA JACKSON, COOPER-JACKSON CONSTRUCTION AND GENERAL CONTRACTORS, it said, and under a tasteful logo of a builder's square, the motto in flowing script, LET US TURN YOUR DREAM INTO REALITY.

"Hah." He gave a little bark of laughter. "I wonder how much they'll gouge me to turn my dream into reality. It's criminal what they charge to put up a few walls."

"Actually you're knocking down walls, Jay," Monica corrected him. "And adding a hot tub."

"I *know* that, Monica." Jay felt another wave of annoyance pass through him and settle as an ache in the middle of his chest. This time even the bedside monitor seemed to register it, and began giving off a high-pitched beep that brought two nurses into the room at a trot.

"What's going on?" he asked the blonde. She didn't even answer him, just lowered the head of his bed, none too gently, and began doing things to his IV. The other one was adjusting the oxygen controls. Monica's face, when he glimpsed it behind their heads, was finally looking concerned.

"Call my office," he said, his words coming out muffled and thin-sounding. "Make sure that contractor gets over there tomorrow. I want that remodel finished before the *Examiner* interview."

"Oh, Jay, really," Monica said again. "I can't believe that's what you're thinking of at a time like this." He couldn't see her anymore. The two nurses were in his face.

The blond nurse with the brown roots went out to the hall and rolled in a cart. The heavy one ripped his gown off. If the elephant would get its foot off his chest, he would share a few thoughts with her about the way she treated patients. He looked over at the monitor to see what all the fuss was about. The EKG was looking more like a lowercase *w* than the capital *V* it had resembled before. One of those moron nurses had probably knocked off a lead, he thought, though he was feeling a little tight.

He remembered one more thing to say to Monica, but he couldn't tell if he was saying it, or just thinking it. He tried to get the words out. *Call Angie and tell her she needs to cancel one more patient.* The check and registration had come in Friday's mail, and when he'd seen it he recalled with a start that he had indeed scheduled the woman, but must have been distracted before he'd written her down in the appointment book. He'd tossed her registration on the top of a stack of mail and had taken it home. He intended to call her and cancel before he caught the plane to New York, but he'd forgotten. It was some friend of a former patient in for a *21-Day Overhaul.* He would cancel them all when he got back. No more Overhauls. They were money losers—yesterday's news. One person tying up two sessions a week for three weeks and all for a lousy thousand bucks.

He tried to tell all this to Monica, but the words seemed to stick in his throat, and then suddenly his chest was crushed, incredible weight forcing his ribs in place. He couldn't expand them to get a breath, and the pain was excruciating. He forgot what he'd been trying to say, and the edges of the room began to break up and disappear.

"Call a code," barked the heavy nurse, and the blonde ran to the phone.

More people came in running, and then everyone was talking at once. Someone squirted some goo on his chest. It was cold and landed right where the elephant had its foot. Someone else stuck something down his throat, he began to gag, and just when he thought the pain in his chest couldn't get any worse, the elephant reared up on its hind legs.

"Clear," said the frowsy blond nurse.

1

Just tell me one thing." Ethelda was bent over the plans she was drafting for Dr. Jason Solomon Golding's office remodel, her pencil poised in the air. She looked right at home at the secretary's desk, though Jake knew better than to tease her about it. "What on God's green earth," she asked him, "is a psychologist going to do with a hot tub this size, and smack in the middle of his office?"

Jake shrugged. "Not our job to ask," he said, and went into the doctor's inner office to finish measuring. "Maybe he likes the open concept," he called over his shoulder.

"Uh-*hunh*," Ethelda answered back.

Jake thought it was strange, too. The doctor's present arrangement of L-shaped waiting room, reception desk, and small half bath with walled-off inner office seemed perfectly adequate to him, though Ethelda, with her designer's eye, said the architect could have done more to maximize the view. But who knew what went on in these guys' heads? These celebrity thera-

pist types were odd ducks, all of them, and from what Bob Metzger had told him, this guy was the king of nutcases—always
coming up with some new way to bilk people out of their cash—
his latest offering being some sort of birth therapy where you
got into a hot tub and pretended you were being born again.
Jake shook his head, incredulous at the idea of people paying
money for such a thing.

He went back to work measuring the room that would not
exist in a week or so when the doctor's plan was implemented,
and opted not to share what little he knew about the hot tub
with Ethelda. She would have an opinion, and the ensuing discussion would probably last all the way back to Petaluma, and
the truth was, he didn't really care what Dr. Golding was going
to do with his hot tub. In fact, he didn't even really want this
job, and was tempted to put the bid high enough to ensure they
wouldn't get it. Petaluma was a long way from San Francisco, a
good thirty minutes if he drove and forty-five or so if Ethelda
took the wheel. He'd done the estimate only because Bob Metzger was a good customer and had asked him to, but there were
plenty of jobs closer to home. He thought about the people he
knew who got on the bus at four A.M. to be in San Francisco by
eight for the start of the business day, and concluded again that
they were crazy. Jake was even sorry they'd agreed to do the estimate, regardless of the fact that the money was better in the
city than it would be for the same job anywhere north of Marin
County. Golding was already proving to be a pain, leaving
phone messages and sending faxes, trying to get them to hurry
things along. Well, he'd give the guy his estimate. Today. Five
more minutes and they'd be on their way, Jake told himself. And
then, with any luck, he and Ethelda would never see this place
again.

His Stanley steel measuring tape snapped back from its twenty-five-foot extension, giving that satisfying little *schwaap* that he loved, and he bent over to note the last measurement on his chart, actually a page in a frayed three-and-a-half-by-five-inch spiral notebook he carried in his pocket. A door opened and closed. He looked up, thinking it was Ethelda, but it was not Ethelda he saw coming through the doorway of Golding's office. It was someone else—a small woman, a *girl* Jake would have called her if he hadn't learned not to—and he could tell with just one glance that she had been crying hard, and recently. Her face was mottled—little red splotches all the way down her neck to her chest. Her nose was bright red, and she stabbed at it savagely with a crumpled-up tissue.

He remembered the little cloudbursts his sister, Shelley, would treat them to from time to time when they were growing up, but this was nothing like those. Even he, a failure where everything about women was concerned, knew this woman had been doing a different kind of crying. He thought about Shelley's sniffling histrionics and shook his head. This woman's crying had been no mere cloudburst. It would have taken a thundering gully washer of tears to leave her in such a state.

Jake dropped the measuring tape onto the chair behind the doctor's huge desk, beside his jacket and frayed blue Cooper-Jackson Construction cap. He straightened up and tried to think of what to do. Ethelda stood behind the woman in the doorway, arms over her chest, her face a familiar cross between humor and suspicion.

The crying woman seemed oblivious to both of them, to everything but the cause of those tears. She looked sad and tight, and after a second or two she spoke, but hesitantly, as if she were afraid that making any sound would cause her careful control to wash away. She stood there, just inside the door, all blotchy and red, and said, "I'm Maggie Ivey. I'm here for the *21-Day Overhaul.*"

Jake felt rooted to his spot by the desk. His mouth opened and closed, but no words came out. The crying woman—Maggie Ivey—didn't seem to notice. She walked over to Dr. Golding's little love seat and crossed her arms over her chest. Jake could see a new crop of hives beginning on her neck, right before his eyes. She glanced toward the seat, and then back at him, and he realized she was waiting for an invitation to sit down.

"Please." He gestured toward the little couch.

"Thank you," said Maggie Ivey in a polite, tight little voice. She sat down on the love seat and dropped her purse into a heap at her feet, then pulled out a fresh tissue from her pocket and looked around for a place to put the used one. Jake looked around, too, a little wildly, but he couldn't locate the trash can. Maggie Ivey finally put the Kleenex on her knee.

She took a second or two and seemed to be gearing up to say something. Jake watched her face go from stiff to crumpled to scrunched, and then she began crying again, so hard that the words she tried to say came out as rhythmic groans, the same sound his engine made when the battery was dead and he tried to start it. Ethelda still stood in the doorway.

"I can't do this anymore," the crying woman said, but taking much longer than normal and each word interspersed with the dead battery noises.

Ethelda, who seemed to be much better at architectural planning than sign language, was motioning, and mouthing things Jake couldn't decipher. Tell her something.

He motioned himself—that Ethelda should come in and talk to the crying woman—but she waved him away and walked back out toward the waiting room, leaving him alone. Jake felt foolish just standing there by the desk, so he pulled a chair from the corner and dragged it over to the love seat. He positioned it to face the crying woman, but he wasn't exactly able to face her, since her face was now on her knees. Her arms were around them, too, and her shoulders shook with the force of her sobs.

She stayed that way for quite a while. It seemed like hours to Jake, though it was probably only five minutes or so. But five minutes was a long time, he thought, when you were heaving those great, gut-wrenching sobs as Maggie Ivey was doing. And through it all, he sat there. He was afraid to touch her, so he just rested his elbows on his knees, leaned forward, and waited for her to finish, his heart pounding from all the emotion in the room. At first. But then, oddly enough, after a while he forgot all about his own discomfort, and instead felt pity stirring somewhere in the vicinity of his tight chest, that someone so young and pretty could be carrying burdens that would bring her to such a state.

He wished he could think of something to do or say. He murmured something from time to time. "It's okay," usually. He gave up on "What's wrong?" after the first minute or so, when he realized that Maggie Ivey wouldn't be able to tell him right then even if she had known. Finally, after what seemed an eternity of listening to her tearing cries, the sobs diminished and came further apart. Jake looked around the room again, more calmly this time, located a box of Kleenex, and rose up from his chair long enough to get it, prompting Maggie Ivey to lift her wet face. He handed her the box without speaking. She mopped her eyes, and with an embarrassed glance at him, blew her nose. Jake shifted on his seat.

"I'm sorry," she finally said, sounding as if she had a bad cold.

"No need to apologize." Jake shook his head and examined his shoes, then couldn't help noticing hers. She had tiny little feet, and she wore loafers, old and a little run-down at the heels, but carefully polished, and a bright new penny in each.

She straightened up, and so did he, but neither one of them looked at the other for another minute. When he glanced at her, Maggie Ivey was dabbing at her eyes and nose, and twisting the Kleenex by turns. She had quite a pile of them on her knee now. Jake finally spied the trash can over by Golding's desk, so he got it and put it by her feet, and with a little flush Maggie Ivey threw the tissues away. Jake decided to leave the wastebasket close by, then sat down again himself and continued waiting. He wasn't sure exactly what he was waiting for, but somehow in the wake of all that emotion he felt Maggie Ivey should be the first one to speak.

She finally did, hesitantly at first, but seeming to gain speed and strength as she went along. Jake leaned back in his chair, rested his hands on his thighs, and listened. It didn't seem like quite the time to correct Maggie Ivey's obvious mistake in thinking he was Dr. Golding, though as she gathered steam, he began to feel uncomfortable again. A few times she paused and he opened his mouth to tell her, but he was slow getting the words out, and each time before he could bring himself to say them Maggie Ivey would begin talking again or shed a fresh batch of tears.

Jake could see she had what his mother would call a sweet face, after she calmed down a little and he finally got a look at it in its virgin state. Which was a figure of speech, since she had a son. No husband, just a son. She told him that, along with a lot of other things, facts and disclosures coming one after another, too fast for him to catalog or question.

Jake tried to get his bearings a time or two, but it was hard to do that and give Maggie Ivey the attention she so obviously needed. Every now and then there would be a slight pause and he would begin to frame his speech, but each time Maggie Ivey would begin talking again before he could make it. Events seemed to take on a life of their own, like a huge, grand play, and Jake felt like a mute actor, needing only to keep silent in order to carry his part. It seemed as if an entire dance had been choreographed around his unrehearsed and unsuspecting movements. A few times he wondered if he even had the power to change the course of events, so powerful was Maggie Ivey's stream of words. He wondered how long it had been since anyone had listened to her. She talked and talked and talked, her words running like water into a sink that had finally been stopped. They ran in and filled it, and then flowed over onto the floor, onto his boots, and up the legs of his Levi's. A whole roomful of words.

She stopped talking once and looked down at his feet, as if she, too, could see the waterline creeping over them. But what she said was "Why do you have on steel-toed boots?" She asked simply, her face wearing that trusting look that Jake would bet was the cause of at least a few of her problems. It occurred to him then that she was trusting *him,* and with a pang he realized now would be as good a time as any to tell her he was Jake Cooper and not Dr. Jason Golding. Instead, he heard himself say something else.

"It's casual day," he replied after a bare moment's hesitation, then realized he had just missed his chance to set things straight. That had been his chance, the mute player's cue to say a line, and with it he could have changed the course of the play. But his time had come and was immediately gone, and Jake realized as soon as the words left his mouth that he had now added his own momentum to the events already set in motion. Like a little rock kicked from a careless boot that loosens a bigger rock and causes a landslide, Jake followed those words right out of his mouth and wondered what sort of avalanche they were going to start.

"I thought casual day was on Friday," Maggie Ivey said, her little brows wrinkled together.

Jake couldn't think of an answer to that so he just shrugged and laid another lie on top of the one he'd just told. "I had to do some work around the office," he finally said, his face heating up.

Maggie Ivey paused a moment, nodded, then gave her head a little shake, as if calling herself to task, and began talking again.

"What in the world was *that* about?" Ethelda demanded once Maggie Ivey was gone. "I've been waiting out here for nearly an hour."

Jake didn't answer her. He just stood there by the secretary's desk for a minute, still a little shell-shocked from what had just happened.

"That girl blew by me like I wasn't even there." Ethelda sounded put out.

"She was upset," Jake defended, already taking the side of Maggie Ivey.

"Well, what took you so long in there?"

"She had a lot on her mind."

"And who are you, Dr. Laura?"

"Hardly." Jake rubbed his forehead.

"What'd you do, listen to the whole story?"

"Pretty much."

Ethelda got up and gathered her things together, then turned and frowned at him when she saw he wasn't following. "What are you doing?" she asked.

Jake opened each one of the drawers of the secretary's desk. He didn't see an appointment book. He flipped on the doctor's computer, watched it boot up and run the antivirus program.

"What are you doing?" Ethelda repeated.

"Looking for something." He was trying to keep his answers cryptic.

"Looking for what?" she demanded.

"For Maggie Ivey's address or phone number."

"What for?" Ethelda frowned.

"I need to call her."

"Why?"

"To straighten something out." Jake frowned. Golding's computer didn't have the same kind of setup as his, and he wasn't sure how to get to his files. He played around with it for a minute and tried to ignore Ethelda, whose questions were becoming more pointed.

"Straighten what out?" Ethelda's voice was sharp, and when Jake glanced up, her face wore the brewing-storm expression he'd learned to recognize. He didn't answer her, just went back to the computer and double-clicked on the word processing program he'd finally found. Maybe Golding kept his patient files as documents there.

"I asked you a question. Exactly *what* do you need to straighten out?" Ethelda leaned over the desk, her face just inches away from his. Jake gave a sigh of exasperation. If he didn't answer her, she was liable to take his chin in her hand and make him look at her, like she used to do to her boys.

"I think there was a little misunderstanding." He eased around the truth, hoping his sketchy explanation would satisfy her.

"Jake," she said, her tone going up a few keys, "what are you trying to say?"

"She thinks I'm Golding," Jake said, and kept his eyes fixed on the list of documents he was searching through, which were turning out to be letters and not the case files he was looking for.

There was silence for a good thirty seconds or so. When he looked up, he saw that Ethelda's brows were arched instead of bunched in the middle, and her voice was dangerously calm. "You never told her the doctor wasn't in?"

"I will," Jake said. "Where do you suppose he keeps his patient information?"

"Why didn't you just chase her down?" Ethelda's voice was rising. "You could have caught her."

"I don't know what I'm going to say yet."

"What if you can't find her number?" Ethelda gave him a disbelieving look.

Jake shrugged. "Worst case scenario, I'll have to meet her here on Thursday and tell her. But it won't come to that. It's got to be here somewhere." He went back to trying to find Golding's patient files, but he was better with hammers than computers.

He looked up to see Ethelda staring at him, her smooth face completely still. "Move out of the way," she finally said, her words short and clipped, and she took his place at the secretary's desk, adjusted the chair, and began clicking her long plum-colored nails on the keyboard and mouse. "Go see if you can find anything in there," she ordered, and jerked her head toward Golding's office without looking at him. Her lips were pressed together tightly, her penciled eyebrows aimed down toward her nose, and the only sound was the little clicks she made as she skimmed through Dr. Golding's computer files.

Eventually Jake thought of the obvious and went to the phone book. There was no Maggie Ivey or Margaret Ivey in the San Francisco listings. There was one listing for M. Ivey, but it turned out to be a man. Jake realized Maggie had never said exactly where she lived, and he felt a little desperate when he realized how many suburbs there were in the Bay Area. He called information for Oakland, Berkeley, and Richmond and inquired. One Ivey was unlisted, the others dead ends. Golding's office didn't yield anything helpful either. Before they finally gave up and left, he and Ethelda covered every square inch of it and found not one shred of paper or byte of information on Maggie Ivey. It was as if the doctor didn't even know she existed.

As a last thought, Jake took a few more minutes to comb Golding's file cabinet and bookshelves for anything he could find on the *21-Day Overhaul.* Just in case. He took Golding's book called *The 21-Day Life Overhaul,* plus another one called *Tuning Up for Love,* from the shelf behind the desk, and promised himself to either deduct the cost from the bill for the remodel or send the guy a check.

When he came out Ethelda had switched off Golding's computer and was leaning sideways, looking inside the top desk drawer and feeling underneath it and along the sides.

"What are you doing?" he asked her.

"Looking for the password for the voice mail." Ethelda still sounded angry. "Golding's got to have somebody checking his messages, and the last thing we need is for *your friend* to talk to them before you can tell her the truth. We'll probably both end up in jail and lose our license."

Jake felt his palms go damp. He hadn't even thought of the telephone problems, and he certainly hadn't thought about going to jail. He hadn't thought at all, he was beginning to realize.

Ethelda pulled out a piece of paper which had been taped to the inside of the drawer. "Real creative," she said dryly, "it's their phone extension." She picked up the receiver, punched in a series of numbers, then another, then paused, listening.

"You got two choices here," she finally said to him. "I can forward Golding's calls to us, in which case whoever is checking his messages is bound to get suspicious, or leave it the way it is and gamble that she won't call Golding before Thursday, *when you tell her the truth.*"

"Don't change the message," Jake said, wondering what he'd gotten himself into now that the complications were mounting. "We'll take a chance on her not calling," he said, prompting another dark look from Ethelda.

"I guess we can check the messages ourselves now that we have the password," Ethelda admitted, and Jake agreed that that might work. "We can leave everybody's but hers," Ethelda said.

Jake's heart began to thump again as he thought about how many things could go wrong. What was he doing? Messing around with the doctor's computer and phones, not to mention his patient. Ethelda was right. They could lose their license over this.

Ethelda gathered up her purse and clipboard again and

switched out the lights. Jake caught her eye and she cocked one slim eyebrow up and the other down in that look of hers that could chill to the bone.

"Thanks, Ethelda," he said, as she passed by him and went out the door.

"Don't thank me," she grumbled as he locked it with the key the security man had given him. He thought for a second, then put it in his pocket. He would return it on Thursday, he promised himself.

"We've got a problem here," Ethelda went on. "I'm just trying to keep it from getting worse."

"Well, thanks for one thing, at least."

"For what?" she snapped.

"For saying *we*," he said, and he thought her face softened just a little.

"None of this would have happened if I'd gotten a chance at her before you did." Ethelda was as much in his face as she could be from the passenger side of the Ford truck. She was now at the rehashing stage, where blame would be placed where it clearly belonged.

And she was right, Jake realized, able to think a little more clearly now that the traumatic little episode was over and he had put some distance between himself and the scene of the crime. He headed the truck back up Highway 101 to Petaluma and tried to get a grip on himself. He got a little shaky when he thought about the web of lies he'd already spun, and confused when he considered his options. But in spite of all the trouble he was in, he had to admit he was a little bit glad Ethelda hadn't gotten to Maggie Ivey first.

"She thinks you're her doctor," Ethelda said, transitioning smoothly from the practical problems of the situation to the ethical implications.

"I know that." Jake could hear the tension clipping his words.

"Well, you should have told her different."

"I know that, too." Jake pressed his foot a little harder than was necessary on the accelerator, causing the truck to give a sudden lurch. He glanced over at Ethelda. She was working a piece of gum pretty furiously and her arms were crossed. Both bad signs.

"Didn't she wonder about the way you were dressed?" She gave him a bottom-to-top sweep with her eyes.

He didn't answer.

"Well?" Ethelda demanded.

"I told her it was casual day."

There was silence for a second or two and in spite of his determination not to, Jake glanced over at Ethelda. Her arms were still crossed, but now her mouth had dropped open, and her expression was incredulous instead of simply annoyed.

"You told her *what*?"

"I told her it was casual day."

Ethelda leaned against the door, as he had asked her not to do a thousand times, and began laughing that loud, braying laugh she had. "*Lord,* have mercy," she said, then looked at him, shook her head, and laughed again. "*Unh,* unh, unh."

Jake ignored her. Stared steadfastly at the road ahead of him and wondered what he was going to do. Fear, no, more accurately terror, was beginning to creep over him like a damp night's chill.

"Why didn't you just tell her the truth?" Ethelda finally asked him when she had finished laughing and wiping her eyes.

Which, of course, was the obvious question, now that it was all over. It was the question he had asked himself as he had thought about patting Maggie Ivey on the back, but settled for just listening to her ocean of words. He had asked himself that as he watched her turn and look back at him when she left, smiling with the brilliant relief of having someone add his shoulder to her burden, her face lit up, but still red from crying, like a bright Christmas light. He had still had the chance to do it when she waved good-bye to him, like a little kid, and then turned and left Dr. Jason Golding's office. So why hadn't he? It seemed like a question that deserved an answer, even if Ethelda was at her most irritating.

"I just couldn't."

"What kind of answer is that? *I just couldn't,*" she repeated. "You don't seem to have those kinds of problems when I want something."

Jake shrugged, and knew he sounded lame. "I don't know. She was so—pathetic. It was like I was her last hope."

"Well, she's going to find out the truth for sure when Golding gets back."

"She'll be finished by then."

"Oh! That's right," Ethelda said, her voice heavy with sarcasm. "I forgot, she's in for a *21-Day Overhaul.*" Ethelda didn't seem amused anymore, and her tone turned ominous. "You think she's pathetic now, she's going to be even more pathetic when she finds out you're not a psychologist. Life overhaul, my foot," she said. "She *will* jump off the bridge then. *Unh,* unh." She stared out the window, shaking her head for a minute or two, then whipped her face toward him, as if she'd just realized what he had said. "What do you mean," she demanded, "*she'll be finished by then?*"

Jake didn't answer. He looked straight ahead at the highway, not seeing the oaks of Marin County, not paying attention to the black-and-white cows in every pasture he passed or the vineyards that seemed to have strayed south, their rolling rows of vines just beginning to leaf and cover their stakes and trellises. He was busy. Trying to figure out what to do about Maggie Ivey, whose last words to him had been "See you Thursday."

He held back his panic by making methodical plans. This was no different than building a house, he told himself, trying to ignore the noises his partner was making from the seat beside him. He would deposit Ethelda at the office and let her carry on the morning jobs, tell Val to cancel his afternoon estimate, then go somewhere and figure out what to do.

Ethelda wasn't finished, though. "You've never been near a psychologist in your life," she said. "This girl could have serious problems. Tell me you aren't thinking of carrying this on for three weeks."

Jake just kept staring straight ahead. When Ethelda got like this it was best to just ignore her. He pulled into the parking lot of Cooper-Jackson Construction and stopped the truck.

Ethelda sat there, not getting out. "Tell me you aren't."

He turned and faced her. Shook his head. "Of course not," he said. "What do you take me for?"

"*Unh,* unh." Ethelda gave him a dark look and continued to make her noises of doom, which went along nicely with what he was feeling himself. "*Unh,* unh, unh."

* * *

Maggie felt the strangest sensation on leaving Dr. Golding's office. It was in her chest, right under her ribs. She put her hand there, and could almost feel it, warm and glowing. She couldn't really put a name to it, and didn't want to try. She would just treasure it.

Gina was right. Dr. Golding was amazing. She could hardly believe it had been only an hour. Well, a little more. She had finally looked down at her watch after she had talked for what seemed like days, and had asked the doctor if her time was up. It was so odd to be the one talking. She was used to listening to everyone else. To Gina and her grandiose plans for her life. To Tim, with his little stories and rehashes of cartoon plots that took longer than the program. To her mother on the telephone, with her advice that seemed to prick and prod even over thousands of miles of phone line. She wasn't used to hearing her own voice as the only sound in the room, and she felt vaguely selfish for taking up so much of the doctor's time, and more than a little guilty for letting Gina pay for it. Which reminded her that the doctor hadn't asked her for any money. Gina must have sent him a check, but she would have to ask. She'd never visited a psychologist before, and had no idea how such things were handled. The very thought was foreign to her.

"Nothing but a bunch of hooey," her mother would sniff on the rare occasions the subject came up. "Just look at what psychology did for Amy Lynn and Buster," she would add, as if that should quiet any potential murmur of dispute.

Amy Lynn was Maggie's cousin Buster's wife. She had gone to a psychologist for counseling and had left Buster not long afterward.

"Nothing but trouble." Maggie's mother would shake her head and frown, but Maggie thought maybe if Buster had spent a little less time at the Dewdrop Inn, Amy Lynn never would have gone to the psychologist in the first place. But she kept her opinions to herself.

She'd been keeping a lot of things to herself, she realized now, looking around her at the fine spring day she hadn't even noticed on the way into town and at the incredible variety of people around her. Some were obviously tourists, wearing jeans, tennis shoes, and fanny packs, cameras slung around their necks. The businesspeople were easy to pick out from their tailored suits, leather shoes, and smart valises, but Maggie's favorites were the entertaining bunch of locals who thought their mere presence on the planet deserved a handout.

She grinned at the man who had set up shop on the sidewalk in front of the BART station. He had two scruffy-looking apricot toy poodles, ancient whiskers growing out of their trembling chins, dressed as a bride and groom. The bride was wearing a doll's gown, complete with a veil and a bouquet of silk flowers hanging from a string around her neck. The groom, in addition to his tuxedo jacket, had a tiny pair of spectacles on his face. They looked bored rather than mistreated, and Maggie impulsively took a dollar she couldn't afford and put it in the man's upturned hat.

"Thank you kindly," he said smiling, courtly and debonair even in dreadlocks and dirty clothes.

"You're welcome," she said, and smiled back. The little exchange gave her another warm feeling, and she realized with a shock that she'd barely gotten to know a soul since she'd moved to Oakland a year ago. Dr. Golding was the first person she'd really talked to, and she even felt a little guilty about that, as if she had taken advantage of his good nature by doing so. It was all right, she told herself. He got paid to listen. But that thought made her squirm, too. Somehow, Dr. Golding seemed more like a kind, gentle friend that someone who was getting paid one thousand dollars to straighten out her life.

She put the thousand dollars out of her mind, and again savored the warm feeling in her middle. The comfort of Dr. Golding. It was odd, now that she thought about it. Gina had said to expect a fifty-minute hour, and to be sure she didn't get cheated. She hadn't even thought about the time, but she had the impression Dr. Golding would have let her go on as long as she wanted.

She couldn't believe it had just been an hour. It seemed as though her whole life had poured out of her mouth. She had sat on that white couch, white pillows behind her, abstract art on every wall, and told Dr. Golding everything. About coming out here with Jeff to study art, but having to quit school and work full-time when she became pregnant and they parted ways, about her parents' disappointment in her, about her dreary job—which she would probably lose, she remembered now with a pang of anxiety—about her grief at Tim growing up without a dad, about her boss's harassment, and even about the daily irritation of living above Mr. Jacobsen. Dr. Golding wasn't what she'd expected at all, sitting there inches from her knees in his plain clothes, just listening to her cry and talk. But he had the kindest eyes, clear, honest blue, and they crinkled around the edges with concern when he listened to her.

And to think she had almost canceled! Even though she had listened to all of Gina's pep talks about Dr. Golding's *21-Day Overhaul,* and finally had reluctantly allowed her to pay for it, even arranged to change her lunch hour so she could go to the sessions without missing work, she had doubted all along that it would do any good. She had almost canceled! Even as late as last night, as she was scrubbing out the tub with Ajax, Tim hanging on to her back. She didn't need a psychologist, she'd muttered to herself as she scrubbed around the rust stains and turned the knob as hard as she could to make it quit dripping. She needed a fixer. A handyman.

Even this morning, when life, as usual, voiced its objections to whatever she wanted to do, she had almost given up on seeing Dr. Golding. She'd awakened from deep sleep around four A.M. to find Tim standing over her. He was sniffling and had been crying. He had another earache and a sore throat. She gave him some Children's Tylenol and wrapped him up in the afghan, and they'd both fallen asleep in the recliner. Tim's ears felt better when he sat up. The pediatrician at the community clinic had said a month ago that he would probably need another set of ear tubes to equalize the pressure in his ears and keep them from getting infected so often, and he should have his tonsils out, too. Maggie had been silent. She had no health insurance. That was another benefit of the new job that had never materialized. The doctor had waited a moment, and then suggested one last strategy. He'd put Tim on a low dose of antibiotics, prophylactic therapy he'd called it, but apparently that hadn't worked.

From the chair in the living room, Maggie hadn't heard the clock radio by her bed go off at six, and it was nearly seven-thirty by the time she woke up. By then she should have been on the bus and halfway across the Bay Bridge so she could step off in front of the marble colonnades of the Bank of Northern California and be at her tiny desk by eight when Mr. Brinnon would make his rounds. It didn't matter, she realized with a heaviness in her stomach. She'd have to call in sick again and take Tim to the doctor. And Mr. Brinnon would put her on probation, as he had threatened to do the last time she had called in sick because Tim had the stomach flu, offering to let the matter drop only if she would have lunch with him "to discuss it."

Maggie could only imagine what it would be like to have

lunch with Mr. Brinnon, and didn't want to imagine what it would be like to do whatever else Mr. Brinnon had in mind. Just feeling his damp hands on her arms when he leaned over to check her work was enough to make her shudder.

She'd tried to ease out from under Tim to get to the phone, but he woke up the minute she moved. She'd put the call off, gotten Tim situated on the couch, and made him some chicken noodle soup for breakfast. She rummaged around in her cupboard and unearthed a can of 7Up she kept hidden for sick days and a box of blueberry Jell-O she had stashed with it.

She put on some water to boil for the Jell-O and tried not to think about the fact that Mr. Brinnon had promised to fire her if she didn't "get her absentee problem under control." She wouldn't have an "absentee problem," she realized with a familiar burst of anger, if the promised sick leave and vacation that was supposed to be a part of the new job she'd taken had materialized. But instead, she'd been put in some sort of employment limbo that the Bank of Northern California called the "Temp Help Pool," and would be allowed to exit only after she had managed to convince them they hadn't made a mistake to hire her. More and more, though, Maggie thought, as she stirred the gelatin until it dissolved and added the ice cubes, she was beginning to think it was she who had made a mistake. She put the Jell-O in the refrigerator and her employment woes out of her mind. She didn't have to force a smile when she brought Tim his breakfast. He was propped up on pillows on the couch like a little king, covered with the afghan, watching cartoons. His cheeks were round, a little flushed this morning, and his blue eyes bright behind his glasses.

"Here you go, buddy," she said, and put the tray on his lap. "I've got some Jell-O in the fridge."

He gave her one of his smiles. Some people smiled with only their mouths, but Tim's whole face participated in his smiles. His cheeks became even plumper, his dimples appeared, and his eyes almost squinted shut behind his glasses. "I'm feeling better now," he said.

She felt his forehead. It was cooler. The Tylenol had done its work. Still, he would need to see the doctor and get a different antibiotic. And schedule the surgery. She would call her parents after supper and ask for the money. She ignored the wave of dread that swept over her at the thought, smoothed Tim's hair, and sat down beside him while he ate his soup.

Finally she couldn't put it off any longer. Her stomach began to twist and churn, but she'd gone to the phone and called Mr. Brinnon. And if possible, he was even more vindictive than she had feared. It had probably been a mistake to tell him about the possibility of needing a week off to nurse Tim after the tonsillectomy, she realized, only after she'd done it.

Mr. Brinnon had been ominously silent when she had told him about the tonsillectomy, and that she would have to have today off to take Tim to the doctor. When he had finally spoken her worst fears were confirmed.

"You're on probation, Ms. Ivey," he had said in that little growl that passed for a voice, and she could just imagine his pockmarked face and tight little red lips. "If you're absent for *any* length of time in the next three months, for whatever reason, you don't need to bother to come back." And then he'd hung up on her.

Maggie had stood there looking at the telephone in her hand, and felt herself tip right over the edge. That was it. The last twist of an already tight string. Suddenly it had all seemed to be too much. She felt as if she were being pulled between Tim and what he needed, the things she needed to do to provide for him, her parents, who called and harassed her to come home every week, and even Gina, who was supposed to be her friend. It was all too much. She felt as if she couldn't be stretched another inch without breaking. And she couldn't allow herself that luxury either. Just the thought gave her little chills of fear. If she broke down, who would take care of Tim? Her hands had begun to shake at the impossibility of her situation. She had sat there while Tim watched cartoons, feeling the tightness begin twisting her stomach, running scenarios through her head, none of her thoughts slowing down long enough for calm analysis. She was losing it, she realized, and that was when she'd decided to keep her appointment with Dr. Golding.

She had gone downstairs as soon as she heard the sound of the *Today* show coming up her heat vent from Mrs. Weaver's television. Mrs. Weaver said she'd be happy to baby-sit Tim for a few hours, and Tim had been happy to go. He liked Mrs. Weaver, who spoiled him shamelessly. She even kept little toys wrapped and tucked away for him to discover when he visited.

"Tim, go look in my silverware drawer, and see what you find," Mrs. Weaver said when Maggie took him down. Tim came back, face breaking into another smile, waving a plastic bottle of bubbles.

Even so, by the time Mrs. Weaver's door shut, Maggie was already beginning to second-guess her decision to see Dr. Golding. She worried about Tim all the way to the bus stop, and then felt more guilt stir into the mix of her emotions when she arrived at the BART station and counted out $4.70 for a round-trip ticket into San Francisco. She usually rode the bus into town for just that reason. The BART took only eight minutes to travel from Oakland to Union Square, but if she rode it every day it would cost her nearly a hundred dollars a month. Today was an exception, she told herself, even as she thought about the twelve cartons of yogurt she could have bought with the money, the four cans of orange juice, or the gallon and a half of milk. She was running late, she argued back to the accusing voice. There was no time to catch the bus, transfer twice, and still be on time for her appointment at eleven.

Three pounds of hamburger, the voice answered back as she climbed on board the car. She found a seat, out of breath from hurrying, and looked out the window just in time to see her neighborhood flash by, looking even seedier from the air. Then the car descended into the tunnel.

At first a few lights flicked outside the window as they raced past, then nothing but blackness and the drone of the rails. It was all dark outside the train, no way to know if they were under the water already or still just underground. The car was almost empty, only a man and one other woman, and both sitting far away from her. Whether it was that fact, or the darkness outside the window, suddenly Maggie had a terrifying feeling of being completely alone, her problems as crushing as the tons of water or earth above her.

The voice began again, this time changing subjects. Her little boy was sick, and she was leaving him. Never mind that he was happily curled on Mrs. Weaver's lap reading *Curious George* when she left, bubbles in hand and a doctor's appointment scheduled for the afternoon. It was the thought of the thing. The picture of Tim, alone in the world, without a father, and with a mother who was so selfish as to leave him when he was ill, overcame her. She would have gone back, but she was already halfway to the city.

Then another torment shoved to the front of the line. One

more day gone, for any reason, and she would be out of a job. Then what would she do? What would Tim do? She had begun to tremble again. What if she lost her job? What if she couldn't find another? She was already late on a few of her bills. What if she couldn't pay her rent? She would lose her apartment. Then she and Tim would be homeless. She would have to go back home to her parents, and why that thought brought such a bitter, bitter disappointment Maggie didn't quite know. Just that whenever she considered it, she felt as though someone or something very precious to her had died.

Maggie hadn't cried for nearly a year. Not since Bill had died and his wife had sold their house and Maggie's garage apartment with it, taking away her home and the closest thing to family she had on this side of the continent. She'd last cried at Bill's funeral, she realized, and not since. For after that, the world-rocking events had come one after the other, and if she'd taken time to grieve each one she would have had to go to bed and do nothing but cry for a week. And she couldn't do that. She had a child to support. So she'd come home from Bill's funeral and dried her eyes, and had stoically patted Millie on the hand and agreed that of course she must sell the house. She had stayed collected during that process, and afterward as she visited Millie, first in the retirement center and then in the skilled nursing facility. She'd even managed to keep her seams stitched tightly together when she stood at Millie's grave.

There had been no good time to cry, and even if she'd found one, what would have been the use? Tears did no one any good. They just derailed you from what you had to do, Maggie told herself as she felt them surging up into her throat now. She tried her usual methods of distraction. She tried thinking of Tim, but that brought a fresh spate of worries. She tried recalling her favorite fantasy of being in the country and breathing clean, sweet air, but that just brought a sharp reminder of West Oakland, her new home.

For the past year, whenever she'd begun to cry, Maggie had been able to fend off the tears. She was afraid that if she ever once gave in to them she would not be able to turn them off, that the tenuous control she had on her life would be lost. She tried again now, her arms crossed tightly over her chest, as though that would help somehow, her face stiffened into a mask of control, her eyes glazed and pointed out the window, unable to stop watching her inner newsreel of past griefs and future misfortunes. And it happened just as she'd feared.

Crying always started in Maggie's throat. It began to ache now as if she had a horrible cold. She felt something like a hot liquid in her chest rise to meet it. Her nose began to clog, and she could feel the blood throbbing in her face and neck. She knew if she looked at her reflection in the window of the train she would see the red blotches that would soon become raised, welted hives if she didn't calm herself. She tried one more time to soothe or distract herself, but it was too late. The steady load of self-accusations and fears had done their work. Her eyes began to spill tears. A year's struggle was over. Maggie began to cry.

No sound came at first. She just tipped her head forward, almost as if she were praying, and put a hand up to shield her face. She would take a deep, shuddering breath and hold it, her shoulders would shake with a few silent sobs, then she would let it out. But then a noise escaped with one of the exhales, and she made a sort of gasping cry with the next intake of breath, and after that the silent phase was over. She was crying, loud, violent sobs, impossible to disguise as a cough or a sneeze. Impossible for anyone to ignore. She was sitting in her seat on the BART sobbing, and just as she had feared, she couldn't stop. She had cried all the way through the tunnel, finally covering her face with both hands to muffle the sound. Even though she knew the other people must be staring, she cried as the BART came screaming into the Union Square station, and she kept right on crying as she disembarked and walked up the stairs to the sidewalk, and then wept her way up the hill to Dr. Golding's office. No one had spoken to her.

She waited now at the streetlight after her hour with Dr. Golding, and felt the clean warmth those tears had brought, almost as if they had scoured out her sadness to make room for something else. She looked around her for a moment before she went down the stairs to catch the Oakland train, and it was as if she had never seen the clean white marble of the big shops and stores, the carefully pruned trees, or the bright banners advertising the San Francisco Symphony whipping in the wind. When was the last time she had gone to a concert or a play? she asked herself. An advertisement went by on the side of a green and yellow bus for Alfred Schilling, the chocolate-themed restaurant. She smiled, imagining it. A whole restaurant with nothing but chocolate. Right on Market Street, not far from where she worked, in fact. And she had never even been in it. She breathed deeply the new spring smell of cut grass mixed with the exhaust of the buses and the salt sea smell of the Bay, a little shudder when she inhaled the only reminder of the morning's tears.

She took one last look around, took one more lungful of air, then walked down the steps to the BART station, inserted her money, and took the ticket the machine gave back. She had a few minutes to wait before the Oakland train was due so she sat down on the bench and rummaged around in her purse until she found what she was looking for—the small sketch pad and pencil she always carried, but somehow never took the time to use.

She flipped it open, and very quickly, with broad stokes, she tried to capture Dr. Golding's face. She worked for a few minutes, and when she was finished she held it out, squinted her eyes, then smiled. There he was. The short blond hair, cowlick right in the middle of his forehead, the little lines on each side of his mouth, the small scar just below his left eye, the squared-off jaw, and best of all, the expression. The slight bunching of his brows, and the softening around the mouth and eyes. Yes, it was him.

Then, because she had a few minutes more, she turned the page and did the same for Dr. Golding's assistant. She closed her eyes for a moment, saw the woman again, and then brought the picture from her mind to the paper, drawing the short hair combed upward in the back into a smart ducktail, sketched the dark plum, perfectly outlined lips, the fine, high cheekbones and slightly almond eyes, the penciled, arched eyebrows, and finally shaded in the smooth, dark skin of her face. She added the bangly hoop earrings and then inspected it, and smiled again. She had captured perfectly that slightly haughty look the woman had given her, as if Maggie had invaded some private territory simply by keeping her appointment. Maggie could almost hear the woman's voice as she had followed her into the doctor's office. "May I *help* you?"

She smiled again and put the pad and pencil away. The Oakland train was pulling up to the stop. She stood up and slung her bag over her shoulder, but it didn't feel as heavy as it had on the trip out, and even the thought of all her troubles didn't weigh her down as it had before. She took a deep breath and put her hand on her middle again, as if checking to make sure the comforting feelings were still there. She couldn't wait until Thursday.

* * *

Jake drove right to this spot, same as he always did when he needed to think. He'd had the site cleared, and had managed to keep it from Lindsay's vacation cottage ambitions, but that's as far as he'd gotten. He pulled the truck under a grove of oak trees, set the brake, and rolled down the window. It was peaceful here. That was why he liked it. If he listened he could hear the creek gurgling over the rocks and he thought for a minute about getting out, but decided to just sit in the cab and do his thinking. He figured he would think better if his stomach wasn't empty, though, so he opened his metal lunch box and took out one of the tuna sandwiches he had slapped together that morning. It seemed like days ago.

It should have taken only a couple of hours to drive from Petaluma to San Francisco to do the estimate. But what with Maggie Ivey, it was almost one before he'd been able to unload Ethelda and have some quiet time to think. He sat now, finally alone, and tried out possibilities, inspecting them for flaws just like he did the lumber he used for finishing work.

He could call Golding and dump the whole thing on his lap. Maggie Ivey was his patient, after all. He took a bite of his sandwich, not tasting it, and discarded that possibility. The guy was having open-heart surgery. What could he do?

He could call the emergency number on the answering machine and hand the whole mess over to them, let them give Maggie Ivey the same message he had received himself that morning: that Dr. Golding had suffered a heart attack while giving a conference presentation. Minus the part about getting the key from security, faxing him the estimate for the remodel, and Golding's warning that the job had to be finished in the three weeks it would take him to recover from his quadruple bypass. Then Maggie Ivey would figure out for herself that she had made a mistake. No. Jake rejected that option. Something about Maggie Ivey's shaking shoulders made that seem like a bad idea.

He opened his thermos and poured himself a cup of his strong coffee, rolling it over his tongue while it cooled. He could meet her on Thursday and tell her he was referring her to some other doctor. Make up some reason why that was in her best interests. This idea had possibilities, which gave Jake a hopeful and a sinking feeling at the same time. It would be a way out of this mess, but it would also mean he wouldn't see Maggie Ivey again. But the longer he considered that possibility the less sure he was. He didn't know any psychologists, and every time he turned around he was hearing about some quack who preyed on girls like Maggie Ivey, alone and trusting. What if she ended up with one of them?

Maybe he could find a psychologist himself, someone he trusted, to hand Maggie Ivey over to. Or a doctor. He shook his head. All of those possibilities would involve telling Maggie Ivey the truth. That she had just told her secrets to a complete fraud.

He shook his head, feeling a little sick, and wondered if the tuna was bad. How could he have gotten in over his head in so little time? Usually it took him weeks or months to get jammed up like this with a woman. He'd broken all his records this time. He sat up straight and inhaled, trying to get a fresh breath, trying to loosen the tight feeling that had been gripping his gut ever since he'd let Maggie Ivey get away without telling her the truth.

He decided his queasiness was due to his current circumstances rather than to the tuna. He took another bite of sandwich, not even seeing the April sun make thin shadows through the oak branches. Seeing only the obvious conclusion that was there, facing him square in the eye and making him feel a strange mix of excitement and terror at the same time. He could go himself.

She had said she would come back on Thursday. Thursday at eleven o'clock. And Jake, not knowing what else to do, had just nodded and said something stupid, like "Take care." Something like that, making Ethelda raise her eyebrows at him over Maggie Ivey's shoulder.

He could go himself. He knew it was nuts, even as he thought it. Ethelda was right. He didn't know anything about psychology. All he knew about was building things and fixing things. But from what Maggie Ivey had said today, that was part of her problem. In addition to her boss being a freak, being sad about her boy not having a father, and being worried about him getting teased at school because he wore a Superman cape, her apartment was a dump and the locks on her doors were broken. But after taking it all in, Jake, not distracted by too much theory, had come to a simple diagnosis. Maggie Ivey's main problem seemed to be that she had no one to listen to her. She was all alone.

He was pretty good at listening. Bad at talking, maybe, but good at listening, no matter what Lindsay said.

"You're emotionally unavailable, Jake" was exactly what she'd said. And a few other things, too, that he wouldn't take the time to review right now, with Maggie Ivey so pressing on his mind. But he remembered them in spite of his decision not to, and could almost hear Lindsay's silky voice tick them off like a shopping list: "emotionally unavailable," "afraid of intimacy," and "challenged in communication."

It had been nearly a month since Lindsay had delivered that verdict, and he knew he wasn't as upset as he should have been that their relationship was over. He was actually a little relieved, and he wondered again how they had ever ended up together. A more unlikely combination he couldn't imagine, though he supposed coming from a small, conservative family, in a small, conservative town, there was something about Lindsay's sophistication and ease of movement around the elite of San Francisco that had attracted him. Like a moth is attracted to the light that will fry it, he thought, satisfied completely with the analogy. She was an investment counselor, made a good living, and had all the right friends, and when he was with her he had gotten a fleeting sense of what it was like to be, however briefly, one of the inner circle.

He gave a wry smile as he thought about it now, and wondered what he could possibly have had that she had wanted, for she had been the one who approached him. He'd been minding his own business, just doing his job of converting the game room of her condo into a fitness center and spa so the residents wouldn't have to walk across the street and mingle with the public. He noticed her coming in and out of course, who wouldn't have? He'd been surprised—shocked, actually—when she'd asked him to have dinner with her. But he said yes, and then one thing had led to another.

He'd begun to realize he might have a problem when he tried to ease Lindsay into the assortment of people who already made up his life. He knew Lindsay was different than most of them, but considering the motley stew they made themselves it amazed him that Lindsay couldn't have been added in, like one more ingredient in an already simmering soup. And the fact that she couldn't be, he knew, said more about her than them. It certainly wasn't as if they were exclusive or refined. He thought of his mother, simple and plain, his brothers, largely oblivious. The only possible sticking point was his sister with her flair for the dramatic and strong opinions, but he'd never known Shelley to be mean, and he even thought he'd noticed a certain admiration for Lindsay the first few times he brought her around. Ethelda and her boys were always open-minded about his friends. No one was haughty or had a preconceived idea about the kind of woman Jake should be with. You like us and we'll like you, they all seemed to say. You give us a chance and we'll give you a chance was their motto, and Jake realized, taking another bite of sandwich, that that had probably been the problem—the first part of that assumption. The part about Lindsay giving them a chance.

Somehow, she had never taken to them. Any of them. And though they were much too kind to say so, except Shelley, who didn't let anything get in the way of voicing her opinions, he knew none of his family had been very aggrieved when he'd shown up by himself one Sunday for dinner—something he'd taken to forgoing—and announced over his mother's coconut cream pie that Lindsay was history.

"It's about time," Shelley had said. His mother had frowned at her, and his brother Joe's wife, Carol, had looked him over to see if his heart was broken, he supposed. Apparently reassured, she had just nodded. Joe hadn't even looked up from his pie at first.

"Well, she was a looker," Joe finally said, lifting his head to refill his coffee cup and try a piece of the lemon meringue. "I'll say that for her." And that had been the family's benediction for Lindsay Hunt.

Lindsay was beautiful, he supposed, with her thick copper hair, and her perfectly squared jaw, even firmer than his, her brown eyes, and that mouth that movie stars would pay a plastic surgeon plenty to duplicate. Come to think of it, Jake realized with a start, Lindsay's mouth could have been helped along. He certainly wouldn't put it past her.

He thought about Maggie Ivey again, and couldn't imagine her going to a plastic surgeon. Not that she needed to. In his mind everything about her was just about perfect, from her own mouth, which was not big, but tidy, and made a neat bow shape when she wasn't talking, to her proportions, which Jake certainly didn't think needed any improvement. She was tiny, with a delicate little fine-featured face and short, straight light brown hair that she wore tucked behind her ears. He wondered if you'd call her eyes blue or green, and finally decided they were sort of a light aqua with little flecks of gold in them. He'd done a lot of looking into them today as she'd dabbed at her nose and talked. Her skin was very fair, at least from what he could see between the hives. He put the two women side by side in his mind, and feeling as though his head were clearing from a bad dream, wondered what in the world had ever kept that relationship with Lindsay going for as long as it had. He shook his head at Lindsay Hunt, but he could still hear her silky voice, this time mocking him and asking who he thought he was to try to help Maggie Ivey.

He sighed, took another sip of coffee, and faced the possibility that Lindsay was right. Maybe there was something wrong with him. He didn't think so, but then he wouldn't, would he? It was true that he'd always been shy around women. He couldn't think of clever things to say, today's debacle being a perfect case in point. The words that seemed so right in his head somehow couldn't find their way out of his mouth. In fact, before this morning he had decided to forget about women for a while. To just swing a hammer and enjoy the sunshine on his back. He was going to forget about women and take pains to avoid that quaking ground and bottomless crevasse that opened up at his feet whenever he took a step toward one.

But somehow Maggie Ivey had changed all that. She had been different. Even though she thought he was Dr. Jason Golding, Maggie Ivey hadn't made him feel like Lindsay always did. She hadn't demanded anything from him. She had just sat there and cried.

He would go. He finished his sandwich and tossed the last of the coffee out the truck window, then screwed the thermos lid back on. He opened the door and unfolded himself from the seat, stiff-legged from sitting so long, and stretched.

He would go on Thursday, and if he was honest with himself he knew he hadn't made the decision just now, even though he would go to his grave before admitting that to Ethelda. But he knew, in his heart of hearts, that when he had pulled up the chair and sat there, just inches away from Maggie Ivey's little knees and shaking shoulders, and could only think to say, "What's wrong?"—he knew it was then that he had decided to do anything in his power to make Maggie Ivey stop crying, and to make sure that nothing ever made her cry like that again.

He would go. He didn't know what he would say or do, and he didn't even want to think about what Ethelda's reaction would be, but the least he could do was to show up. Even an emotionally unavailable fool could do that much.

* * *

By the time Maggie took the BART back to Oakland and then the bus to her apartment, it was nearly time to take Tim to the doctor. She knocked on Mrs. Weaver's door and was surprised when Tim opened it himself. She had been in such a hurry to make her appointment with Dr. Golding that she'd let him leave the apartment wearing his thermal Superman pajama top. She had found it at Goodwill. Superman's logo had already been wash-worn, but Tim loved it. He wore it to bed every night and during the day whenever she would let him. He was Superman crazy. His favorite half hour of the day was between six and six thirty in the morning when the *Superfriends* cartoon show came on. He would watch Aquaman and Batman and Wonder Woman, but when Superman came on the scene Tim would start jumping from the couch and chairs, the red cape she had made for him flying out behind him, usually causing Mr. Jacobsen to pound on his ceiling.

"Walaa!" he said now, and produced a picture he'd drawn from behind his back.

"Hey, cowboy." She knelt down to give him a hug and inspected the picture, a snowball-type figure wearing the ever-present red cape. "This is nice," Maggie said, then kissed his smooth cheek. "And it looks like you're feeling a little better."

"A little, but my throat still hurts." His voice sounded clogged up and swollen. Now that she was closer to the floor, Maggie noticed the sweats he was wearing had a hole in the knee. She hadn't even seen that this morning and she felt a flush of embarrassment that she'd let him leave the house looking so ragged.

"We've been having fun." Mrs. Weaver came to the door behind him. Her blue-tinted hair was sprayed into its usual cap of tight curls around her face, and she was wearing a pair of hot-pink polyester pants and a wildly flowered Hawaiian shirt. If she had noticed the hole in Tim's sweats it didn't seem to bother her. Mrs. Weaver was from Virginia, and her accent made Maggie the closest to homesick for Georgia that she ever came. "We made some pudding, and read some books, and cut up some magazines," she said, stroking Tim's head with her veined hand.

"Thank you so much for taking care of him," Maggie said, and stood up to leave.

"Just a minute." Mrs. Weaver held up a finger and disappeared, then came back with a Tupperware container. "Take the rest of this pudding on home with you."

"Oh, thank you," Maggie said, and to her dismay, felt herself tearing up again at Mrs. Weaver's kindness. She wondered if she would cry all the time now, become one of those people who couldn't watch a commercial without weeping, or be like that woman on the religious station who spoke in sobs. Fortunately, neither Mrs. Weaver nor Tim seemed to notice.

"Well, you're just as welcome as you can be," Mrs. Weaver said. "And you know I'd be glad to watch Tim any time you want to go out with friends." Mrs. Weaver smiled and patted Maggie's shoulder.

"Thank you again," Maggie said, not wanting to have that conversation with Mrs. Weaver right now. She checked her watch and wasn't making excuses when she said they'd better run.

Mrs. Weaver nodded and waved, hot-pink fingernails bobbing up and down. "You come on back now, Tim."

"I will," said Tim, waving good-bye, and before they were even to the door of their apartment he had launched into another story.

The doctor confirmed what Maggie had already known. Tim did have another ear infection, and strep throat as well.

"I guess we're down to playing our last card," the doctor

said. "Call me when he's well and we'll schedule the surgery for a few weeks after that."

Maggie agreed, but felt a sinking realization that she couldn't put off calling her parents any longer, and if Mr. Brinnon made good on his threats she would have to think about finding another job, too. The glow from Dr. Golding was beginning to fade.

They stopped at the clinic pharmacy and filled Tim's prescription. Maggie decided to give him the first dose right there. She sat down in the chair by the dispensing window and fought with the childproof lid, finally won, drew up a teaspoon of the pink liquid, and poured it into his mouth. "How does it taste?" she asked. "Is it really like bubble gum?"

The pharmacist was smiling and watching.

"Not really," Tim said, though he swallowed it all down without shuddering.

She bought more Children's Tylenol, gave him a few tablets to chew, and got a bag of cherry-flavored throat drops that were mostly candy. Tim crunched them, one after another, as they rode the bus back to the apartment. Maggie wished she had thought to buy him a container of juice. The doctor said he should have lots of fluids and she didn't know what he'd had to drink today. Another pang of guilt pierced her.

The bus stop was a few blocks from home, and Maggie took Tim's hand as they climbed down the steps to the sidewalk. He was walking slower than he had been on the way into town.

"Are you feeling bad again, buddy?"

Tim didn't answer, just nodded.

"Here, climb on." Maggie knelt down and Tim climbed onto her back. She gave him a few hefts until she had a good hold on his legs, then carried him piggyback the rest of the way home.

She realized she wouldn't be able to do this much longer. She was out of breath and barely made it to the door of the Embarcadero Arms, where she eased him down on the step. Someone had left the front door propped open with a brick again.

The apartment building wasn't so bad, she told herself, looking at its peeling pink paint and gap-toothed picket fence. It was actually a huge, old, rambling Victorian house that someone had divided into apartments and whimsically named the Embarcadero Arms. There was an entrance hall with the mailboxes, and stairs going up to the second floor. No elevator. Maggie checked her mail and leaned against the wall, resting for a few moments before climbing the stairs.

After a few minutes she took Tim's hand, readjusted the pharmacy bag, and tried to walk quietly past Mr. Jacobsen's door. He made a hobby of complaining about all his neighbors, pounding on his ceiling, part of Maggie's floor, whenever Tim rode his Big Wheel in the apartment or got too wild and ran around.

Tim kept his finger over his lips until they were past Mr. Jacobsen's door, then began talking again in his swollen-sounding voice about a cartoon he'd watched at Mrs. Weaver's. Maggie made listening noises, but she was thinking about other things, and a sharp pang of sadness passed through her that Tim didn't have a nicer home and a safe place to play. There was a weed-choked backyard, but Maggie had been afraid to let Tim play there since the day she'd looked out to see the neighbor's pit bulls running loose and realized they were small enough to fit through the missing slats in the fence. There were no other children at the Embarcadero Arms, none in the neighborhood except some teenagers a few houses down. She saw them from time to time, leaning against their cars listening to music, and she thought they were part of the group of kids that hung out in the vacant lot across the street. They were probably perfectly nice people, all of them, she argued with herself, but when she remembered the way they sounded all together under her window at night, their shouts and laughter, and the sound of breaking glass, she felt a little afraid. West Oakland was no cottage in the country, she realized, and not for the first time. The poor side of any town was no place to raise a child.

She climbed the stairs now, her feet feeling too heavy to pick up and put down one more time. She remembered the lightness and relief she had savored after leaving Dr. Golding's office. It seemed like a long time ago. She tried to put the other thoughts away and smiled at Tim as they climbed the stairs. His cheeks still had a baby fullness to them and his hair, looking like it was cut with a bowl, bounced up and down when he walked. He was a sweet boy, but he was growing up. He would be five next fall.

He looked up at her and smiled back, his flushed cheeks becoming round like little apples, and his eyes squinting almost shut again under his glasses. He would need new ones soon. Last year the doctor said Tim had a lazy eye, and for six months he had watched *Superfriends* each day with a patch on. That problem had been taken care of, but he still needed glasses to see. Maggie had bought the heavy-framed, industrial-strength kind. They were supposed to spring back into place instead of breaking and costing a hundred dollars to replace. But his last exam had been nearly ten months ago. It was time for another one soon. Maggie felt another pang and wished she could do something for Tim without it always coming down to dollars and cents.

Maybe she should go back to Georgia. She didn't love Bobby Semple, but she knew he was still waiting there for her, determined that someday she would see her error and return, and at least then Tim would have a father and a decent home.

They climbed the last stair and crossed the landing to their second-floor apartment. Maggie looked at the carpet under her feet and wondered if it was the original. It was burgundy roses on a dark blue background, nearly worn through in the middle. The building must have been beautiful at one time. The banisters were polished mahogany, as well as the woodwork around all the doors and windows. The foyer floor was a complicated mosaic, though some of the tiles were missing and the grout had darkened through the years. It could probably be beautiful again, Maggie thought, if the owner would do some upkeep. Assuming there was an owner and not just a group of investors. Maggie had rented from a property management company, and had never seen a real human being connected with the Embarcadero Arms. There was a post office box she mailed her rent payment to and a number she called to report any problems. She had left a message about her broken door lock. It stuck about half the time, so she was afraid to use it. She had never heard back from anyone.

She fumbled with the lock, which was jammed. She took out her Safeway Club card—the only plastic she had been deemed fit to carry—and slid it back and forth until the door popped open. When she took the card out she noticed again the gouges in the doorframe, as if someone had pried it open with a crowbar. She gave a sigh and put down her packages, carefully putting the penicillin in the refrigerator as the pharmacist had recommended, then made Tim another bed on the couch.

She spent the next half hour making dinner for the two of them—more chicken noodle soup and mashed potatoes because Tim's throat was hurting worse. The Jell-O was ready. She brought him a tray and sat holding his feet while he ate it. He was too sick to go to day care tomorrow and she would have to do what she hated to do—ask Mrs. Weaver to watch him again. She brought him some paper and crayons and one of her big art books to use for a table, and left him drawing while she went downstairs to ask.

"Well, of course," Mrs. Weaver said, answering the door. "I'm ashamed I didn't think to offer." Maggie was so grateful she almost gave her a hug. Still, she'd seen how tired Mrs. Weaver became on the rare occasions she watched Tim for an entire day. There was no way she could ask her to do it for a week, and especially with Tim recovering from his surgery. She would have to think of something else.

Tim was still drawing when she got back, a pile of super-heroes on the floor by his makeshift bed.

"Let's read three or four books," he said, so they did. They read his favorites, *Siren in the Night, Postman Pig, Hiram's Red Shirt,* and a few more they had gotten from the library. It was eight o'clock by the time she finished washing the supper dishes and got him into bed.

She took two Tylenol herself then, and lay down on the couch. She should call her parents right now and ask for the money for Tim's tonsils. Eight o'clock here, eleven o'clock in Georgia. They might be in bed already, she rationalized with relief. She would call them tomorrow. Or the next day. Maybe she would wait until Tim was well and she was ready to schedule the surgery. That they would send her the money she had no doubt. It was the demands that would come with it, the strings that would be attached that she dreaded. She would put off that complication for as long as she could. Who knows, she mused, maybe Dr. Golding could help her think of some other option.

Maggie stretched, adjusted the pillow behind her head, and did nothing for a full minute, enjoying the silence, or the closest the Embarcadero Arms ever came to silence. Water was running next door, and she could hear someone tapping as if they were hanging a picture. Outside she could hear the ever-present traffic going by and some hoots from the kids in the vacant lot across the street, loud even through the closed window. The synthesized theme from MacGyver drifted up the heat vent from Mrs. Weaver's television.

Now, there was a handy man, Maggie thought, as she rubbed her forehead. She had a dull pain behind her eyes and she knew it was from crying so hard this morning. She thought about turning on the television herself and escaping with the man who could fix anything, solve any problem, escape from locked rooms, and disarm bombs with equal aplomb, all without lethal force, in just one hour, counting commercials.

She wondered, enjoying the fancy, where MacGyver lived and what kind of miracle he could work on her muddled life. Heck, she thought, pulling the afghan around her shoulders, she'd even give him more than an hour. She'd give him twenty-one days, just like Dr. Golding had.

She was seeing Dr. Golding's face floating in front of hers. His eyes were narrowed with concern, his face wearing that look that made her feel as though she could trust him. She replayed the morning's events and saw him run his hands over his short blond hair every now and then, as if he were frustrated for her. She relaxed and drifted off.

The telephone jarred her out of her drifting dreams and set her heart to pounding. She debated whether or not to just let it ring, but she didn't want to wake Tim. Besides, she'd remembered as soon as it rang that she had promised to call Gina, and she supposed she owed her an explanation. She felt guilty again about letting Gina pay for the Overhaul, especially since it had turned out so well. She picked it up on the fourth ring, just before it would switch to voice mail.

"What took you so long? I've been sitting here waiting all evening!" Gina burst right out, filling up the room, even over the telephone.

"Sorry," Maggie said, stifling a yawn. "I had to make dinner and get Tim to bed."

"Well?"

"Well, what?"

"Well, how did it go?"

"It went fine." Maggie didn't know why she felt so secretive, but she realized she didn't want to tell Gina anything about Dr. Golding. Something about the way she had spilled herself out and the tender way he'd listened seemed too intimate to share with Gina. With anyone.

"So tell me!" Gina demanded.

"There's nothing really to tell," Maggie hedged. "I just sort of told him the things that were bothering me."

"And what'd he say?"

"Um." Now that Maggie thought of it, he hadn't really said anything. But she couldn't tell that to Gina. And even if she tried, she couldn't convey the comfort of having Dr. Golding, so solid and kind, sitting just inches away from her while she cried. No, she couldn't do that. "He said lots of things," she said, and the voice in her head called her a liar.

"Like what? Tell me some."

"I don't know, Gina. Gosh, you should go see him again. I feel bad that you paid for me instead." Gina had made a point of letting Maggie know she was postponing her second stab at a life overhaul so Maggie could have hers first.

"Don't be silly." Gina dismissed her protests. "I want to do this for you. I'll go again next month. I get another bonus then."

Maggie had the fleeting thought that if the *21-Day Overhaul* did what it promised, you shouldn't have to go more than once, but she decided not to share that thought with Gina. She tried, instead, to bring the conversation to a quick end. "Well, anyway, it was good. Really good."

"Great. So you're glad you went." Maggie shook her head, weary. Gina was like that. Whenever she did something nice for you, she wanted to be thanked over and over again.

"I'm really glad, Gina," she said, capitulating in hopes that it would wind up the conversation. Besides, she really meant it. "Thanks again."

"Maybe now you'll get some perspective about moving back to Georgia. I mean, I'd really hate for you to go back to that little town. You could make it here," she said, and Maggie hoped she wouldn't start in again about her art. Gina was always telling Maggie she should paint, go back to school, get serious about her career, and try to place her paintings in local shops or paint enough for an exhibition.

There were a few things Gina didn't understand, not having any kids, and things she didn't understand about art, as well. It wasn't as if you could just sit down every spare five minutes you had and paint. You had to have a space for it. In your home, which Maggie didn't really have, and in your life, which Maggie most definitely did not have. You had to have your mind free of little nagging complications, like where you were going to get the money to pay your utilities that month, and what you were going to do the next time your child was too sick to go to day care. Those kinds of concerns had to be taken care of before scouting out picturesque scenes, or experimenting with a new technique, sounded like fun. And for Maggie at least, being creative had always seemed to involve a certain playfulness that she wasn't sure she would ever recapture. She felt very tired and suddenly old when she thought about trying to explain all that to Gina.

"You could always take the real estate course," Gina started in again.

Maggie had hoped Gina wouldn't bring up selling real estate again. She was always trying to convince her to become an agent, revealing another thing she didn't understand. People wanted to look at houses on weekends and evenings, and once Tim started school, if Maggie were selling real estate she would never get to see him.

"We didn't exactly get to the decision-making part yet. But we will. I know we will." And Maggie realized she was telling the truth about that. She had full confidence that before she was finished she would have told Dr. Golding all about her options, which in Maggie's mind boiled down to two simple ones: stay here and have her life be more of the same, or go home to Georgia and Bobby Semple. Neither one sounded attractive, and Maggie suddenly wished she had let Gina's call go to voice mail.

"Are you in love yet?" Gina pressed. She had a real thing about women falling in love with their therapists. She had read a bunch of books about it after her *21-Day Overhaul,* and had tried to explain it all to Maggie last week, something to do with your father and mother and transferring emotions, but when Maggie's quizzical looks had annoyed her she'd ended the conversation abruptly by saying, in a sort of threatening tone, that Maggie would fall in love with Dr. Golding.

"No, I'm not in love." Maggie said it wearily, but she felt a little surge of heat in her cheeks when she remembered Dr. Golding just listening to her cry.

"Isn't he handsome?" Gina asked. "And some of those questions he asked me were so intense. I thought I would die."

Maggie saw Dr. Golding's face before her and somehow didn't like the turn the conversation was taking. She felt a little annoyed, though she wasn't sure why. Fortunately, Gina went on without waiting for her to answer.

"Did he talk about hypnotic regression?" Gina was into hypnotic regression now, and was convinced she'd been a slave in the court of Cleopatra. Somehow Maggie couldn't imagine someone as sensible-seeming as Dr. Golding really thinking that discovering she was an Egyptian slave girl in a past life would help her decide whether to go back to Georgia and marry Bobby, but she didn't say so. She knew better than to try to change the course of whatever hobbyhorse Gina was riding. "No" was all she said. "Maybe he'll get into that later."

"Did he say anything about celebrating your essential uniqueness? That's what his new book's going to be about."

"No. He didn't." Maggie's head was starting to hurt again.

Gina was warming up for another round of questions when Maggie gently interrupted. "I've got to go, Gina. I'm exhausted. I have to go to bed."

Gina usually grew irate when Maggie wanted to hang up before she had pronounced the conversation finished, but tonight her voice turned solicitous. "Oh, jeez, yes. You must be totally wasted. Therapy does that to you. It's very intense."

Maggie said good-bye, hung up the phone, and went into the kitchen to start packing tomorrow's lunch. She washed her apple, spread peanut butter on her bread, and finally fell into bed, thinking about Gina's last statement, and realizing that for perhaps the first time since they'd met, the two of them were in perfect agreement.

2

Thursday, April 23

The third day of the *21-Day Overhaul* was beginning badly. It was actually misnamed, Jake realized after reading the book—after reading it twice, as a matter of fact. He also realized a few other things. According to Golding, your life was supposed to change in twenty-one days, but you met with him on only six of those. That was a rip-off as far as Jake was concerned. If the guy was going to promise people a *21-Day Overhaul,* he ought to be there for all twenty-one of them, and at the very least Monday through Friday, like a regular working person. But Golding, as he outlined in the appendix, "offered two sessions per week of intense psychotherapy for the three weeks of the Overhaul for a nominal fee." Jake wondered what Dr. Golding might consider a nominal fee. Come to think of it, no money had changed hands between him and Maggie Ivey. That thought made him feel a little better. A little less like a con man. Though if anyone should feel like a con man it was Dr. Jason Golding.

Jake put down the book, rubbed the bridge of his nose, and

tried to remember that he'd gotten at least one break today. They'd been given the job of doing Golding's remodel. He had put the bid as low as he dared, and then shown it to Ethelda yesterday morning. They made all their decisions jointly, had done so ever since Erv had died and Ethelda had taken over his half of the business.

"That's fine," she'd said, approving the price, and exhibiting real graciousness by not even making a smart comment or cocking her eyebrow. But the approval was a gift on her part, and Jake knew it. Ordinarily he would have put the estimate quite a bit higher since that was the whole point of taking jobs in the city. But if they didn't get this job, there would be another contractor and crew to evade if he met with Maggie Ivey. *When* he met with Maggie Ivey, he corrected himself. Since Tuesday he had zoomed in close to the decision and then pulled back and away from it just like a nervous pilot attempting his first landing. *When* he met with Maggie Ivey, he told himself. This morning. At eleven o'clock.

Thank God they had gotten the job. He had held his breath from the moment he faxed off their bid until this morning when he'd unlocked the office, still gray in the predawn gloom, and found the curled papers on the floor beside the fax machine. Apparently his low estimate had appealed to Dr. Jason Golding, or whoever was making those decisions for him during his illness. The contract was signed and Golding had sent three pages of instructions back with it.

Jake picked up the slick paper of the fax in his hand now and thought again about what would have happened, what new set of complications would have arisen, if the job had gone to someone else. He felt himself break out in a sweat.

"You may as well give me those," Ethelda said to him

now. "We both know who's going to be taking the lead on this job."

Jake listened for resentment in her voice but he didn't hear anything except her usual dry humor. He got up and handed her the papers.

Ethelda took her glasses from her purse, put them on, then tilted her head up and down until she found the right angle. Jake smiled. It had annoyed her no end when her optometrist had told her she needed bifocals. He went back to his desk and tried to resume his study of Golding's book. He had barely sat down before he was interrupted.

"Jake—"

"Yes?"

"I've got two plans to draw and that Mather job to finish before I can get started on this."

Jake thought for a minute. The Mather job was substantial and only half finished. A restaurant remodel that would take significant bites out of Ethelda's time.

"Well, how long will it take to do Golding's office, do you suppose? All we have to do is knock down interior walls, plumb and wire for the Jacuzzi, and then paint and lay carpet. It sounds like more than it really is."

Ethelda nodded, considering. "If we get everybody moving and all the materials are on hand we should be able to finish in a week. Ten days at the most."

"And I gave us a week of leeway in the estimate."

"We should be all right, then, even if I can't get to it right away," Ethelda allowed, but grudgingly.

"I can get the electricians and plumbers over there to scope things out right away. In case anybody's checking. Just so we put off taking down walls as long as we can."

Ethelda nodded. Gradually, her eyebrows eased back into a straight line and Jake thought it was safe to go back to his reading. He tried to concentrate on what Golding was explaining about babies seeing themselves in their mothers' faces, but it wasn't making much sense.

"Just out of curiosity—"

"Yes?" He raised his head wearily. Ethelda was looking at him over the top of her glasses.

"What would you have done if the job had gone to someone else?" Ethelda didn't sound as if she were mocking him, and he couldn't see any expression on her face besides simple curiosity.

"I have absolutely no idea," he said, and ran his hand over his hair.

"It's a good thing you're not a professional con man." Ethelda cocked her eyebrow again and gave him an appraising look. "You're not very good at conniving, are you?"

He shook his head without putting the admission into words. He was definitely not good at conniving. Never had been good at any kind of pretense or subterfuge, and this portrayal of Dr. Jason Solomon Golding would probably be just another example of that fact. If possible, he was even less confident now than when he'd awakened, heart pounding and adrenaline already high, at five this morning. He had been reading Golding's drivel for two days now, and even without Ethelda's interruptions he hadn't been able to formulate a plan. Golding's *21-Day Overhaul* was all nonsense as far as he could see, and he certainly didn't think any of the doctor's harebrained strategies could help Maggie Ivey, who had real problems. Jake felt his cloud of anxiety condense into frustration, and he picked up Golding's book and gave it a toss. It sailed across the office and landed on the overstuffed chair in the corner.

"Things not going so well?" Ethelda seemed unmoved by his display. With three teenage boys in the house, something like a book flying across the room was probably not hair-raising drama.

"I've read the whole thing and I still don't know what to do." Jake got up and paced around his desk, then bent over to stretch his back and see if the increased blood flow to his head would help him think.

"I can't believe you're seriously going to try to pull this off." Ethelda was leaning back in her fancy, executive-type chair. "Do you honestly believe that after she pulls herself together she's not going to have some questions about the way you conduct therapy?"

Jake sat back down in his own chair, a rickety wooden affair on wheels he had stolen from his mother's garage and had always meant to take apart and reglue. He laced his fingers behind his neck and aimed what he hoped was a bright smile at Ethelda. "That's where you could really be a big help to me, Ethelda."

She gave him a suspicious look. "What do you mean?"

"Didn't you take a psychology class last summer?"

Ethelda snorted. "Only 101 over at Santa Rosa Junior College. You think that qualifies me to coach you on how to pretend to be a therapist?"

"You could help me. If you wanted." He didn't have to try to sound pathetic.

Ethelda was silent for a full minute, then heaved a great sigh and scratched her head with her pencil, something Jake noticed she tended to do when she was frustrated.

"Well." She paused again.

"What?"

"I've been to a therapist myself."

Jake was shocked into silence. If she had confessed to having a side job as a stripper in between going to school conferences and watching her kids' softball games he couldn't have been more surprised. Ethelda, with her smooth, dark face that gave away nothing, her manicured hair, her smart mouth, who had always treated him like an overgrown version of one of her boys, was the last person on earth he could imagine going to therapy. Other people came to Ethelda for advice.

"It was right after Erv died," she said. "I felt like I needed someone to talk to."

Jake felt a stab of guilt. He had been so preoccupied with his own grief and so busy running the business without his partner that he hadn't been there when Ethelda had needed him. He sat quietly and waited for her to go on.

"I went for about six months. Once a week. Insurance paid for most of it."

Jake wasn't sure if he should ask questions so he kept quiet.

"Anyway. That's all." Ethelda gave another sigh, but smaller this time. "Dr. Henry helped me to get past my grief, and then later on I went back for a few sessions when I was trying to make the decision whether to sell out Erv's half of the business or approach you about joining."

Jake nodded. He'd been surprised when Ethelda had approached him about it, taking him out to Denny's for coffee, but he'd been glad for her to take over Erv's share. No one could ever replace Erv, but he and Ethelda made a pretty good team.

"Anyway," she went on, "I guess if you're determined to go through with this I could tell you what it was like. What he said and all." She gave her head another little shake to show what she thought of the idea. "If you're determined."

Jake nodded slowly and gave Ethelda a half smile. "Thank you. I'd appreciate that," he said.

Even after Ethelda was finished Jake still didn't know what he was supposed to say when he next saw Maggie Ivey. He got up and poured himself another cup of coffee. It was looking pretty thick since he'd made it at six that morning, but he drank it anyway, being careful to put the spoon on the saucer Ethelda left out for him instead of laying it down on the countertop like he had when he and Erv had been the only ones here. He still missed some things about the old ways.

"Doesn't sound like he did much." Jake rubbed his neck. The muscles were in a knot.

Ethelda shrugged. "I know. Every now and then he'd ask a question or two, but mostly he just listened."

"What happened if you asked *him* a question?"

Ethelda laughed. "Then he'd sort of cock his head to one side and say, 'What do *you* think?'"

Jake shook his head, walked back over to his desk, and sat down. Ethelda could think this was funny if she wanted, but by eleven o'clock this morning he was going to have to convince Maggie Ivey that he was a psychologist, and he wasn't feeling very optimistic about his chances.

He took one last try. "Didn't he ask you about your feelings and that sort of thing?"

Ethelda smiled as if he had said something funny. "Sometimes."

Jake leaned his head on his hands and went over his options again. They had shrunk to nothing. He had to go now. It was too late to do anything else.

"Look," Ethelda said, "don't get all worked up. The most important thing Dr. Henry did for me was just to listen and be there when I needed him. It wasn't like he said anything magical. Besides, from the look on her face when she left, whatever you did for this girl worked pretty well on Tuesday. Just do it again today and you'll be fine."

"Thanks," he said. It sounded sarcastic. He tried again. "I really mean it, Ethelda. Thanks for telling me all this."

Ethelda took her purse from the bottom drawer of the file cabinet and stood by the door. Jake had succeeded in convincing her to play secretary one more time. Maybe his sincere panic had touched her sympathy. But she had insisted on driving her own car. She would sit at the reception desk in Golding's office, greet Maggie Ivey, see her to the inner office, and then she would leave. "I've got work to do," she said. "Somebody's got to run this office while you're playing."

Now she stood with one hand on the doorknob, looking anxious to get her part over with. "Listen, Jake, you can't solve all of this girl's problems for her. She probably doesn't even want you to try." She gave him what he was sure was supposed to be an encouraging smile, then walked out the door, calling back over her shoulder, "I'll see you there. Good luck."

Jake sat without moving after she left, except for the pencil he twirled in a figure eight between his fingers, over and over again. He remembered something from *The Catcher in the Rye*. Holden Caulfield had said that "Good luck" was a terrible thing to holler after someone. Right now Jake couldn't agree more.

Finally, eleven o'clock closing in on him, he put all his maneuverings aside and just went as himself. Jake the psychologist.

The irony was rich, and he wondered if this was God's idea of a good joke. Jake, the guy who couldn't relate to women, being this one's last hope. Just the thought made his stomach lurch as he climbed into his truck and headed down 101 to San Francisco. But then he remembered Maggie Ivey, looking so sad and unprotected, and his desire to help her rushed through him again. There was something he had seen in her, even in their brief encounter, that had called something from him in response. He wondered if it was hardwired into his makeup, this wanting to step in front of Maggie Ivey and tuck her safely behind his back until he'd made sure her landscape was safe. He gave a wry smile when he thought of how that kind of thinking would play nowadays, and without being invited, the image of Lindsay popped into his mind. She would definitely not like that sort of attitude. He could almost hear her now, spouting off some line of psychobabble about him needing to stop hiding behind an outmoded male image and to get in touch with his feminine side. He couldn't imagine Maggie Ivey making such a speech, even if it were the truth.

He paid the toll for the bridge and joined the lanes of traffic crossing to the city, passed the lush grounds of the Presidio, and turned toward the Financial District and the skyscraper that housed Golding's office. He would be Dr. Golding. He could do it for a day. Then, somehow, he would find a way to end this. He would get Maggie Ivey on her feet just a little more solidly, then find a way to tell her the truth. He'd work it out.

The underground garage for Golding's building was full, so Jake circled the block twice until he finally found a place to park his truck. He had only seven minutes to spare when he arrived, out of breath from running, at the Camden Professional Building. He joined step with a group of businesswomen wearing London Fogs and sharp haircuts, holding the double paper cups of espresso that seemed to fuel everyone around here.

"Did you take the boat out this weekend?" one of them asked another. The answer was lost in the revolving door. He went through himself, then took the elevator to the twelfth floor, most all of which was devoted to the shrinks of the New Beginnings Clinic, and found Golding's suite.

The door was ajar. Ethelda was very official-looking at the reception desk, and had her *New York Times* crossword puzzle half hidden in the top drawer. "You'll do fine," she encouraged as he passed her. "Just be yourself."

He nodded, his anxiety having moved up the scale into fear. He couldn't have been more terrified, he was sure, if he were marching off to war. Maggie Ivey would see right through him. This would be over quickly, he told himself. Undistracted by her tears, she would see right through him today. He would probably be on his way home or maybe to jail in minutes.

He went into Golding's inner office and sat down awkwardly at the polished teak desk, feeling as if he shouldn't touch anything. At least he looked a little more the part than he had the first time they'd met, he told himself. He wore Dockers and a dress shirt and he'd left the steel-toed boots at home. He checked his watch, and it was exactly eleven when he heard Maggie Ivey's voice, recognizing it with a little shock as she spoke to Ethelda. His stomach churned with the same kind of dread he remembered from childhood when he would cast his eyes to the side and see, just in his peripheral vision, a metal-handled syringe and long needle on the dentist's tray, or hear the doctor say, "You'll feel a little sting." He waited for her with that same sense of doom.

Maggie Ivey came in shyly, tapping on the door in a half knock, even though he had heard Ethelda tell her to go on in.

"Hi, Dr. Golding."

"Hi," he said, and couldn't help smiling. He stood up and wondered if he should come out from behind the desk.

She hadn't been crying today. He could see again how pretty she was. Pink cheeks and milky white skin. Her hair was sort of short, and though Jake didn't usually like short haircuts, he thought this one looked just fine on Maggie Ivey.

* * *

Dr. Golding looked different today. Maggie stood by the door, not sure of herself as she had been on her way here. Even after her discouraging time with Tim's illness, having to dodge Gina, and even after having to go back to work and face Mr. Brinnon, coming here this morning had brought back a little bit of Tuesday's glow.

Today she had seen the city, set so lovely and diamondlike on the edge of the bay, with new eyes, as a visitor might, as she had seen it when she'd first arrived. Leaving the bank, she'd noticed the cable cars on California Street making their screeching pull up the hills, stopping for the tourists already lined up to ride them. She'd stood for a moment before the fountain at City Hall and watched the water split the morning light into a shining fan of colors and felt as if a vague memory of happiness were trying to emerge, like a beautiful dream that floated on the edge of her awareness.

Something was beginning to change, though Maggie couldn't exactly say what. It certainly wasn't her circumstances, but something was definitely happening, all the same. And even though her time with Dr. Golding had been the impetus, the solid ground from which she'd gotten her bearings and looked around, she didn't think the changes were all coming from him. It was as if he had widened a tiny crack that had already begun to form in the hard cover she'd put over herself and Tim, and she thought of the urgent, sharp beak of a baby bird, determined to chip its way out of a shell that had become more prison than protection.

The proof positive of her improved state of mind was that she had gotten out her paints. Last night after Tim was asleep she had finally done it, after toying with the idea all day. She had stopped twice on her way to the closet, though, and had even sat down and debated the pros and cons before she finally followed through. Perhaps she was making a mistake to even hope for possibilities that might be taken away or lead to disappointment. But even as she went over the objections, she knew she'd already made up her mind. Finally she'd opened the closet door and dug around until she found the box, neatly packed and sealed these five years. There were five tubes of paint in a Safeway sack behind it, her sister's annual Christmas hint, which Maggie would hurriedly stow away before old longings could rise up. She'd gone into the kitchen and come back with a steak knife, cut open the tape, and had taken out her brushes and paints. She almost held her breath as she tested the tubes of color to see if they were dried out, and rejoiced when they weren't. She moved a few things and set up a table under the window, positioned a lamp beside it, and lined up her paints, brushes, and palette. Then she stretched some paper onto a board so she could begin a new painting tonight.

Afterward she just stood and looked at what she had done, her pulse quickening with excitement. She felt as if she'd been underwater for years, and was finally breaking the surface and drawing in a lungful of air. She felt as she did when she watched her perennials, so lovingly potted and arranged on the back stoop to look like a real garden, slowly come back to life after the cold, rainy winter. And even though she had promised herself she would never again give a man the power to make her or take her apart, as she worked she could almost see, smiling over all her efforts, the earnest, sympathetic face of Dr. Golding.

She had recalled his face so many times, it floated up whenever she closed her eyes. In fact, she'd called it up as she walked into the office this morning, a little scared. It was funny, though. For all his comfort, Dr. Golding's face wasn't soft-looking at all. She supposed most people would call it rugged, but that seemed too harsh somehow, she thought, remembering the furrows on each side of his mouth that became dimples when he smiled. His brows had knitted together as he had listened to her and she could picture him leaning forward, elbows on his knees, his hands clasped between them, and how every now and then he would unclasp them and run his hands over his hair. It was blond, about the color of Tim's, and just a little longer than a crew cut. Maggie wondered how he had gotten the little scar under his eye.

Now she peeked around the door frame of Dr. Golding's office, and the little vision disappeared. The first shock, now that her sight wasn't clouded by tears, was that it was really a very fancy place, the kind Maggie usually felt uncomfortable in. The furniture was clearly good quality, the view of the city impressive, and even the art on the walls, though not Maggie's style, was original and each piece probably cost more than she made in a year.

His secretary was even better dressed than she'd been on Tuesday, though she'd greeted her warmly today, without the haughty tone. And there was Dr. Golding, clear across the room, behind his huge desk, not looking at all the way she remembered him. For a brief moment Maggie wondered if she would rather close her eyes and seek the comfort of the memory—Dr. Golding in his blue shirt and jeans, leaning forward, his clear blue eyes troubled with her own—or go in and be with the real man. His face was the same, of course, but everything else about him looked stiff and polished, not the image she'd called up in her mind so often since Tuesday. Somehow seeing him look so different made her wonder if the relationship they'd had, even though it had lasted for only a short time, had been her imagination, too. She almost wished she hadn't come back, just tucked away the memory of Tuesday morning as one of those rare gifts of a stranger's kindness and left it at that.

"Good morning." Dr. Golding came from behind the desk now and took a few steps toward her, then paused, hovering in the middle of the room. "Please, sit down."

Maggie stepped inside the doorway. She guessed her legs had decided for her that she would stay.

Dr. Golding gestured toward the love seat she had used on Tuesday, so she sat there again. There was a box of tissues on the table beside it, and the trash can was positioned by the table. Obviously he was prepared for her this time. Maggie flushed, remembering her loss of control.

Dr. Golding pulled the chair from the corner, just as he had before, and sat down across from her. Which made her feel a little better, now that at least part of Tuesday's scene was being replayed. Oddly enough, having him sit so close, their knees only a few inches apart, made Maggie feel more at ease instead of awkward, like she usually felt when men got too close to her. Maybe it would be all right after all. She relaxed a little and looked up at him.

He was fidgeting, his thumbs making little circles around each other on his lap. "What would you like to talk about today?" he finally asked her, then leaned forward again for her answer.

Maggie was at a loss. Somehow she had expected to be led along by his questions. "I'm not sure," she admitted, feeling as if she had been called on in class without having read the assignment.

Dr. Golding just nodded and twiddled his thumbs again. He didn't say anything. There was a stillness in the room for what seemed like twenty minutes, though it was actually closer to four, Maggie guessed, not wanting to offend Dr. Golding by looking at her watch.

Dr. Golding cleared his throat. Maggie suddenly feared he was going to delve into something silly like past life regression or ask her if she hated her parents. She didn't think she could bear it if kind, solid, practical Dr. Golding turned out to be a fool.

"Okay," he said, then sat up in his chair, face brightening as if he'd had an insight. "Okay," he repeated, "how about this? How about you tell me the top three things that are bothering you? I mean, I know you told me a lot of the things that were on your mind the other day. But now, how about we just narrow it down? Take the top three."

Maggie relaxed a little. That was a question she could answer. The challenge would be in narrowing down the field of contenders. She thought for a moment, then answered. "I guess my number one worry would have to do with my son, Tim. It always concerns me that he's growing up without a dad, but the thing that's bothering me most right now is that he has to have his tonsils out. I don't have medical insurance, and I can't take any more time off work or I'll get fired."

Dr. Golding looked more relaxed now, like he had something he could chew on. "Tell me about the tonsils," he said, and leaned back again.

Maggie smiled, then got serious again when she remembered she really did have a problem, and it wasn't just an exercise for Dr. Golding's sake. "On Tuesday, after I left here I took Tim to the doctor," she said. "He had another ear infection and strep throat. He needs to have his tonsils taken out and another set of ear tubes put in."

"Ear tubes?" Dr. Golding looked puzzled. Maggie remembered that everyone wasn't as familiar with the middle ear as she was, having struggled with Tim's from the time she had taken him in for his six-week checkup and found they were infected.

"They're tiny little tubes they put in kids' ears to keep them from getting plugged up and infected," she explained. "But as the child grows, so does the ear, and the tubes fall out. Then if they're still having infections you have to put in another set."

"Oh." Dr. Golding nodded. "Sorry. Go on."

Maggie nodded and tried to remember where she'd left off. "Anyway, Mr. Brinnon said I have an attendance problem."

"Mr. Brinnon is your boss." Dr. Golding retrieved the fact triumphantly, like a prizewinning catch from what must be the sea of all her troubles, poured out before him on Tuesday.

Maggie nodded, and flushed a little thinking about Mr. Brinnon.

"Sorry to interrupt," said Dr. Golding. "Go on."

"That's okay," she said. "Anyway, Mr. Brinnon told me on Tuesday that if I took one more day off in the next three months, for any reason, I'm fired." She could feel the heat rising up from inside and preparing to burst forth again in hives.

"Can't you take sick leave?" Dr. Golding was frowning now.

"I don't have sick leave," she admitted. "I was supposed to have sick leave, medical benefits, and vacation, but after I'd already given my notice at my first job, Mr. Brinnon said I'd have to start out on temporary status. That I wouldn't be permanent, full-time until after my first year."

"They didn't tell you that to begin with?" Dr. Golding asked.

Maggie shook her head. "And now I'm on probation, and Mr. Brinnon says he'll fire me if I miss any more work." Maggie could feel that liquid state in her chest that always preceded tears. She sniffed hard twice and blinked her eyes.

Dr. Golding nodded without saying anything.

After a minute she went on. "Anyway, I guess I'll have to ask my parents for the money, and then look for another job because Tim has to have the surgery, and when he's sick he wants me"—she trailed off—"he wants his mother."

"Well, of course he does." Dr. Golding sounded irritated that anyone could think otherwise.

Maggie wondered what Dr. Golding thought of a woman who would buy therapy when she was in danger of losing her job and couldn't pay for her son's surgery. Suddenly it seemed important to explain.

"Dr. Golding, about the money for this—um—Overhaul."

Dr. Golding started shaking his head. Maggie rushed on before he could interrupt. "My friend Gina, she insisted that I come, and she's paying for it. And I asked her about using the money for something else, but she said there would always be other things, but she wanted me to 'get my head together,' as she put it. Anyway, I just wanted you to know that."

Dr. Golding was still silent. The liquid in Maggie's chest had gained territory and had now moved to her nose, which began to clog. She sniffed again and cleared her throat. She could feel the hot spots on her neck and face.

"I guess the second thing that's bothering me would have to do with work, too," she said, determined to press on. Dr. Golding nodded again.

"It's my boss, Mr. Brinnon. He sort of—" Maggie felt uncomfortable, crossed her legs, and shifted in her seat. "He comes on to me."

Dr. Golding straightened up in his chair.

"I mean, nothing has happened yet," Maggie clarified, "but he gives me a hard time."

"What do you mean—a hard time?" Dr. Golding's voice had an edge.

Maggie shrugged, crossed her legs the other way, and adjusted her skirt. She wished she hadn't brought it up. "Oh, it's hard to explain," she said. "It's like he plays with me."

"Give me an example," Dr. Golding said. "What does he say? Exactly." Dr. Golding's voice was soft, but his face looked hard. The gentle expression was gone.

"Well, like yesterday when I came back to work after taking Tuesday off."

Dr. Golding nodded.

"He was waiting by the time clock when I got there, and he asked to see me in his office, and told me to wait until we were finished talking to punch in."

"Which made it look as if you were late."

Maggie nodded. "Anyway, I went into his office and he sat down. He just looked at me for a minute or two. Then he said, 'You're cute, and what's even cuter is the fact that you don't know it.'" Maggie felt ashamed even repeating it to Dr. Golding, as if she had been the one who had done something wrong.

Dr. Golding's face was getting red. "Then what?"

"Then he came around the desk and put his hand on my shoulder and said he was sorry he'd come down so hard on me the day before and that the two of us should have lunch to discuss what could be done about my spotty attendance."

"What did you do?"

"I got up and stood by the door, and I said that we could discuss it, but that I already had plans for lunch. Then he got sort of snippy and mean and said I should think about the difficulties of finding another job without having a good recommendation from the last one."

"How often does something like this happen?" Dr. Golding asked.

"Nearly every week," Maggie said, then took a minute to get herself under control. She didn't want to lose it like she had on Tuesday. "I think I'm a good worker, Dr. Golding. I guess I have had to miss a day or two every month, but I'm hourly, so I don't get paid when I'm not there."

"How much do they pay you?" Dr. Golding asked bluntly.

Maggie felt herself flush again. "I make seven fifty an hour."

Dr. Golding's mouth tightened, and he started making the circles with his thumbs again.

"But it's only temporary," she rushed to explain. "Eventually, when I'm put on full-time permanent instead of temp help, then I'll get my full salary and benefits." Her voice trailed off when she remembered that now the promised promotion would probably not happen. She'd be lucky just to keep her job.

Dr. Golding leaned forward in his chair, his face just inches away from her. He was frowning. "Anyway," she said, "sometimes I don't even want to go through the door at work because I know Mr. Brinnon will be standing there by my desk, waiting for me."

Maggie reached for a tissue and tried to wipe her nose delicately. It was no good. She knew she must look like a hag, with her nose all red and her neck going blotchy like it had since she was a kid every time she cried or got very angry. She cleared her throat and took a few deep breaths, and would have closed her eyes if she hadn't been concerned about how she looked to Dr. Golding. She settled for looking past his head and imagining her favorite daydream, a cabin with a stone fireplace in the woods somewhere. Which led quite naturally into the third item that was bothering her.

"I guess the third thing would be where I live." The reminder of the Embarcadero Arms and industrial Oakland enveloping it made her yearn to go back to her daydream. She wiped her nose again, she hoped delicately. "It's in a bad part of town, and sometimes I don't feel safe." She thought about the understatement of her words, and what she wasn't saying about staying awake at night and listening to the groups of kids on the corner of the lot across the street, bottles breaking and sirens screaming through at regular intervals, something sounding like caps going off every now and then in the distance, and being afraid to even let Tim ride his Big Wheel on the front sidewalk.

"Where do you live?"

"I live in West Oakland, in an old apartment building down near the factories." Dr. Golding's expression became alarmed.

"I have wonderful neighbors, though." She rushed to add something positive, somehow wanting something from Dr. Golding other than pity. "Well, at least one of them." She trailed off, sounding lame, even to herself.

Dr. Golding looked grim again. "You don't *feel* safe, because you probably *aren't* safe. Tell me again what's wrong with your locks?"

Maggie was startled. Somehow that seemed like a strange question. She shrugged. "Sometimes they work, and sometimes they jam and I have to pick them."

"You have to pick them?" he asked.

She nodded and hoped he wasn't going to tell her she should get a locksmith to come and fix them. *I don't have the money* seemed like the chorus to an old, tired song that she was very sick of singing.

Dr. Golding's expression was a cross between amusement and disbelief. "What do you use to pick them with?" he asked.

"My Safeway Club card."

And to Maggie's surprise, at that Dr. Golding stood up. He pushed the chair back against the wall, looking as though he had suddenly remembered something he had to do. He reached behind the desk and took his corduroy jacket from the back of the chair.

"When are you supposed to be back at work?" he asked her.

Maggie looked at her watch. It had been only twenty minutes since she'd arrived. "Twelvish."

Dr. Golding smiled and extended his hand to her. She didn't know what else to do but take it. It was warm and slightly rough, and closed over hers completely.

"Come with me," he said. "We're going on a little field trip."

They went first to Dr. Golding's car, which was actually a blue truck, with the words COOPER-JACKSON CONSTRUCTION on the side. "My brother-in-law's" was all Dr. Golding said when Maggie lifted her eyebrows. Then, to Maggie's growing alarm, they drove straight up the hill past the big marble columns of the Bank of Northern California, and into the underground parking garage. She began to be truly worried when the doctor asked her to take him to Mr. Brinnon's office.

She obeyed, but could feel her pulse in her ears as they rode the elevator up. Why had she begun this stupid experiment? She couldn't afford to make any changes in her life. What if things turned out wrong? Then she would lose what little she and Tim had. "Dr. Golding, what are you planning to do?" she finally asked him, and she could hear the alarm in her voice.

Dr. Golding held the elevator open while she stepped out. They walked down the short hall and then he paused, his hand on the handle of the door to the operations center and typing pool, the last door that stood between the two of them and Mr. Brinnon. "Maggie," he said, "trust me."

She noticed his eyes, not hard and angry as they had been in his office, but kind and tender, looking at her the way she imagined herself looking at Tim. Still, she couldn't allow herself to be carried away by emotion when she was all Tim had.

"What if I lose my job?" she persisted, remembering even as she said it that she would probably lose it anyway.

"If you do, I promise I'll hire you myself," he said. He didn't move, though, just stood there with his hand on the door handle, waiting for her to answer. She thought for what seemed like an eternity, then finally she gave a little nod, and Dr. Golding pulled open the door and motioned for her to go ahead. She led him down the hall to Mr. Brinnon's office, and Dr. Golding walked right in without knocking, one of the first things Mr. Brinnon's own employees learned not to do. Mr. Brinnon was sitting at his desk, his side to them, alternating his attention between a pile of greenbar computer paper and his computer screen, which flickered in the corner. Dr. Golding glanced down briefly at the brass nameplate on the edge of the desk that said STANLEY BRINNON, DIRECTOR OF OPERATIONS.

"Heads up, Stanley," he said. He didn't sound very professional. In fact, he sounded angry.

Mr. Brinnon's head did snap up and his eyes narrowed into the beady little pig eyes that Maggie had learned to dislike so much. He swiveled around in his chair, and looked back and forth between Maggie and Dr. Golding. Maggie could see little flecks of white in his scalp and eyelashes.

"Ah, it's the star of our very own tragic soap opera," he said to Maggie, his voice sarcastic. Then he looked at Dr. Golding with undisguised antagonism. "And you seem to know me," he said, sneering, "but I don't know you."

Dr. Golding didn't answer him, but pulled out a chair for Maggie instead. "Here, sit down, Maggie, make yourself comfortable. I'm sure Mr. Brinnon was just getting ready to invite you to do that. Would you like a cup of coffee or tea?"

Maggie was flustered. She could see Mr. Brinnon's face getting red. She sat down, but Dr. Golding continued to stand. His hands were balled into fists and he walked over and rested his knuckles on the edge of Mr. Brinnon's desk, then leaned forward.

"I'm sorry." Mr. Brinnon was visibly angry now. "I don't know who you are, but as you can see"—he gestured toward the greenbar, which had begun to slide off his desk like a paper slinky—"I am very busy."

Dr. Golding didn't seem flustered by Mr. Brinnon. "That's okay, Stan," he said. "We won't take up much of your time." He pushed back from the desk, took the other chair from the corner, and positioned it next to Maggie's, then sat down and leaned back, his arms resting easily on the arms of the chair. He looked totally at ease, in vivid contrast to the way Maggie was feeling. "There are just a few things we need to go over before we leave," Dr. Golding said, "and something Ms. Ivey wants to tell you."

Mr. Brinnon started to say something, but Dr. Golding put up his hand for him to stop. "First of all," Dr. Golding said, "what you've been doing to Maggie is called sexual harassment. And in case they didn't tell you about that in banking school, it can mean fines and penalties and even jail."

Mr. Brinnon's face went from its usual florid tones to pasty white.

"Second, Maggie has been working for you for some time for a galley slave's wages. I'm sure that for a woman of her talents, you could find a little more money. And I think Ms. Ivey's lawyer will enjoy talking to the bank's legal department about the preemployment promises you made that haven't materialized. Sounds to me like she had an oral contract, but what do I know? We'll let them sort it out in court."

Maggie put her hand over her eyes and rested her elbow on the armrest of the chair. Her head was starting to hurt again.

"And finally, in addition to holding her hostage to your sexual advances . . ." Dr. Golding paused here, and Maggie looked up. Mr. Brinnon's jaw had gone slack. "And threatening her job every time she takes time off," Dr. Golding continued, "I would bet she's worked plenty of overtime without compensation. Which might merit a little complaint to the Department of Labor. They love to investigate big, bloated corporations like this. All those fines fatten up their budget."

Maggie's ears were ringing. Dr. Golding leaned over her chair and whispered in her ear. "Now it's your turn. Tell him to leave you alone." His breath was warm, and his face brushed hers, adding to her agitation. She turned toward him and he bent his head closer so she could whisper back.

"I don't think I can. I'll lose my job." Her neck was starting to itch.

Dr. Golding turned his mouth to her ear and whispered again, firmly. "You're the one who has to do this, Maggie." He settled back in his own chair and crossed his arms, then gave her a nod.

Maggie took a deep breath. She was in it now, she might as well go ahead. "All right." She paused, then said, "Mr. Brinnon, I want you to leave me alone." That didn't seem like enough, now that she had started. Might as well be hung for a sheep as a lamb, her grandmother used to say. So she went on, and her voice got louder and bolder as she did. "I'm tired of your watching me all the time and asking me to have lunch with you," she said. "I'm tired of your threatening me every time I get up to get a cup of coffee or go to the bathroom." Her hands were shaking a little bit, as well as her voice. Dr. Golding reached across and patted her arm. She took a deep breath and felt a little calmer. "And besides that, I resent your constant implications that I don't do good work. I'm a very good secretary. I get here every day on time, and I rarely take more than twenty minutes for lunch. I never take morning or afternoon breaks. I do the work of two people, as you know, since you fired two and replaced them with me. I'm tired of being criticized and threatened and harassed. And I want the wages and benefits you promised me when I hired on," she blurted out, after only a second of hesitation.

She'd surprised herself. She couldn't actually believe those words had come out of her mouth, but she was glad she had said them. She felt a warm glow again, though whether from her own courage or from Dr. Golding's pat on her arm, she didn't know.

Dr. Golding smiled at her, the corners of his eyes crinkling into the smile lines. "Maggie, would you excuse Mr. Brinnon and me for just a moment?"

"Sure." She collected herself, stood up, and marched with all the dignity she could gather into the hall, grateful that none of her coworkers were around demanding an explanation. Her hands were shaking, and she felt a strange mix of elation and terror.

Dr. Golding was in with Mr. Brinnon for another minute or two, and she could hear his voice murmuring something, though she couldn't make out the words. When he came out he motioned for her to go back in. "It's okay." He smiled at her. "He has something to tell you." Dr. Golding waited in the hall this time.

Mr. Brinnon was quiet. Maggie had never seen him looking so chastened before.

"I'm sorry," he said, and cleared his throat a few times. "I've behaved badly toward you. You won't have that trouble again."

Maggie kept her amazement to herself, squared her shoulders, and nodded.

"You can take all the time you need for your son's surgery. I'll talk to personnel about your benefits today and I'll also request a raise for you." He cleared his throat again. "Would it be all right if I got back to you on the details tomorrow?"

The situation had taken on a surreal quality. Any minute now she would hear the clock radio sound or wake to find Tim standing over her.

"That would be fine" was what she said. "What time tomorrow shall I check back?" she pressed, and couldn't believe it was her own voice she was hearing.

"How about as soon as you come back from lunch? That will give me time to process the paperwork in the morning."

Maggie nodded.

"And, Ms. Ivey?"

"Yes?" Now was when he would take it all back.

Mr. Brinnon's beady eyes were a little glazed, his face still pale and sweaty. "Why don't you take the rest of the day off?" he suggested. "With pay," he hurried to add.

She nodded again, then turned and walked out the door without looking back. Dr. Golding, who must have been listening from his station in the hall, was grinning.

"Now." He smiled down at her as they made their way down the elevator and into the squinting bright light of the spring day. "Don't you feel better?"

Maggie was beyond surprise when they drove across the Bay Bridge and exited at Emeryville. They stopped at the Home Depot store on Hollis Street and there Dr. Golding bought shiny new deadbolt locks for her front and back doors and some kind of little things that went on the windows to keep anyone from breaking in. He also threw two smoke alarms into the cart and a twelve-pack of Pepsi.

"Is there anything else around the house that needs fixing?" he asked her, and Maggie blurted out that the bathtub faucet leak was driving her crazy. She blushed as soon as the words were out of her mouth, but Dr. Golding just seemed pleased as he headed for the plumbing section. He paid for everything while Maggie watched, embarrassed.

"It's okay," he said over his shoulder as he handed the clerk his card, cupping his hand over it as he signed. "Life improvements are covered in the cost of the Overhaul."

They climbed back into the truck, and she was almost used to the idea of riding along beside him by the time they wound their way through Emeryville back to West Oakland. Actually, the two of them had settled into an easy camaraderie during the trip across the bay. They had spent the first part of it reliving Mr. Brinnon's humiliation.

"Did you see his face when you said *sexual harassment?*" Maggie laughed. "That was priceless."

Dr. Golding grinned and shook his head. "What a weasel."

They drove on past the paint factory and the pulp mill and Dr. Golding asked her about her family. She wondered if it was part of her therapy, but when she turned to look at him he didn't look as if he had any agenda at all. Relaxed, she answered him.

"I'm the youngest of four kids. My brothers and sister still all live within shouting distance of my parents in Dawson, Georgia."

"I thought I noticed a little bit of an accent." He smiled.

"It comes and goes. Wait until you hear me talk with them." Then she felt embarrassed, realizing that she had slipped into the belief that this was the beginning of a real friendship. For just a moment she had let herself believe he might actually be around to hear her talk to her relatives someday. Dr. Golding didn't seem to notice, just continued his easy steering of the big truck all the way to West Oakland.

"Where's your boy?"

"He's at a preschool near here."

"Want to go get him?"

Maggie was surprised again. Was this part of the therapy,

too? She looked at Dr. Golding, but his face gave away nothing but a warm smile.

Maggie answered honestly, picturing Tim's eager face when he saw her drive up before snacktime to bring him home. "Yes," she said, "I'd like that."

"Good." Dr. Golding nodded and turned his eyes back to the road. "And, Maggie?"

Now what? she wondered, and looked at him expectantly.

"I don't feel much like Dr. Golding today. Could you just call me Jake?"

"Sure," she said. "But I thought your name was Jason."

"I prefer Jake."

"Okay. Sure. Jake."

They drove past more of the flat factories on the Oakland waterfront, into the residential area with the peeling houses and weedy yards, past the shabby, stunted palm trees and the decaying gray stucco building that was Bayview School, where Tim would be entering kindergarten next year unless she won the lottery or went home to Mama. But somehow today those things didn't seem to bother her. She looked over at Dr. Golding—Jake. He must have felt her eyes, because he turned and met her glance with a smile. Maggie turned back to the window quickly, almost afraid he could read her thoughts. The bag of locks rustled at her feet.

They spent the afternoon installing locks and fixing drips. Dr. Golding produced a drill and toolbox from the bowels of his brother-in-law's truck.

"Look at this, Maggie." He pointed to the gouge marks on the door frame. "That's where somebody's jimmied this thing open with a pry bar." He showed her how the deadbolt made that impossible, and made her promise to keep it locked, even when she was at home. "No more getting in with a credit card," he said, shaking his head again.

Tim trailed along at Dr. Golding's heels all afternoon. The two of them went back and forth to the brother-in-law's truck a few times and once, while Maggie was getting the mail, Mr. Jacobsen poked his head out the door.

"What's all that hammering?" He had a frown on his face and was just getting ready to light into her when Dr. Golding and Tim came through the front door with the twelve-pack of Pepsi.

"Hello, there," Dr. Golding greeted him, and Mr. Jacobsen didn't seem to know how to respond. Dr. Golding went to the door, shifted the Pepsi, and stuck his hand out. Mr. Jacobsen looked awkward, but opened the door another inch and took it.

"I was just installing a new lock for my friend here." Dr. Golding tipped his head toward Maggie. Tim was rhythmically bumping into Dr. Golding's leg with his shoulder and Maggie would have told him to stop, but she was fascinated by the exchange between Dr. Golding and Mr. Jacobsen. Besides, Dr. Golding—Jake—didn't even seem to notice, other than to rest his big hand on Tim's head. "I was wondering," Dr. Golding continued, "if you might be interested in having a deadbolt installed yourself. They're a lot more secure than what you've got on there now."

"What do you charge?" Mr. Jacobsen's voice was suspicious, and a little triumphant, as if he had finally discovered the hidden motive.

"Absolutely no charge," said Dr. Golding, and Maggie

listened openmouthed as Mr. Jacobsen agreed. "I'd be glad to do it for everybody in the building. We'll settle on a time before I go," said Dr. Golding, and Mr. Jacobsen even gave her a nod before he scurried back into his apartment and closed the door.

"That was amazing," Maggie whispered, but she didn't think Dr. Golding heard her. He was examining the lock on the front entry door.

"Do these buzzers work?" he asked, indicating the bank of buttons beside each tenant's name outside on the porch.

"I think so," she answered. "Mine does."

He nodded and used his foot to move aside the brick that was still propping open the door. It clicked shut, and he tried opening it twice, and seemed satisfied when he couldn't.

"That's better," he said.

Maggie just nodded. She hardly noticed the threadbare carpet as the three of them climbed the stairs back to her apartment. She made vegetable soup and grilled cheese sandwiches for dinner while Dr. Golding read to Tim. Then Dr. Golding—Jake—popped open three cans from the twelve-pack of Pepsi. Maggie was embarrassed she didn't have any ice. Her freezer was small and it was full of hamburger and a carton of ice cream she had bought for Tim's throat. Dr. Golding said it didn't matter. They drank their warm Pepsi and had a wonderful time sitting around the little Formica table, laughing and eating together.

True to his word, before he left, Dr. Golding had Maggie take him to each of her other neighbors. He offered to come back the following Friday to install door and window locks and suggested they think about starting a building watch so they could look out for each other. Mr. Jacobsen poked his head out again. He was downright friendly, and pumped Dr. Golding's hand up and down after Dr. Golding agreed to check the washers in his sink when he came back the following week.

"What a nice young man. Where did you meet him?" Mrs. Weaver asked Maggie as Dr. Golding started up the stairs to gather his tools. Maggie was a little embarrassed and didn't want to offer too much of an explanation. "A friend introduced us" seemed sufficient.

"Well, good-bye, then." Dr. Golding stood in Maggie's doorway, brother-in-law's tools back in the belt that was slung over his arm. Tim, once again, was bouncing against Dr. Golding's knees.

"Tim, don't do that, honey."

"It's all right, Maggie." Dr. Golding put down the tool belt. "If it starts bothering me I'll take care of it myself," he said, and instantly Tim was upside down. Dr. Golding was gripping his feet and swinging him back and forth. Tim's hair fanned out in a static halo and he was laughing and trying to grab Dr. Golding's legs when he swung close enough. Maggie began laughing, too. She hadn't played whole-body games with Tim in a long time, and even if it had occurred to her to do it, he was getting too big for her to pick up and throw around.

"Okay, that's enough," Dr. Golding finally said. Tim protested, but Dr. Golding stood him upright and readjusted his glasses, which were hanging askew. Tim grabbed on to his forearm and Dr. Golding lifted him a few inches off the floor.

"We'll do it again, but you tired me out," Dr. Golding said, his breath even and slow, and not even needing both arms to lift Tim.

"Do you promise?"

"Tim!" Maggie protested.

"You bet I do," Dr. Golding said to Tim, and then smiled at Maggie. "It's okay," he said. "I like Tim. He doesn't bother me."

Tim's eyes almost squinted shut behind his glasses in the huge smile that spread over his face, and Maggie felt joy springing up that she hadn't felt in years, and at the same time, a tiny breath of fear, like a draft in a warm room.

Finally Dr. Golding made Maggie promise one more time to use the window locks and to keep the door bolted, disengaged Tim, ruffled his hair, and said good-bye.

Tim was wound up from Dr. Golding—Jake—tossing him around. He chattered nonstop while Maggie gave him his medicine and got him ready for bed. But finally, she had him tucked in and the lights out. Then, feeling as if she were in the middle of a long dream that she didn't want to end, she sat down on the couch.

What a day. She cast her mind back to her first hesitant steps into Dr. Golding's office, then the terrifying trip to the bank, which had yielded such unexpected results. She smiled and thought back to her three problems. Two of them had been vaporized in one day. Well, not quite vaporized, but things were definitely improved. She still lived in Oakland, but at least now she had sturdy locks. And she wouldn't lose her job, though she still didn't know where she would get the money for Tim's tonsils. But somehow, after today, she could almost believe it would all work out.

She felt little stirrings of warmth whenever she thought of Dr. Golding. He was good at everything. Practical things, like what he had done here today, but he was wise, too, and she remembered the approach he had taken with Mr. Brinnon. He had known just the right things to say.

She remembered the stony expression his face had worn in

Mr. Brinnon's office, and his solid bulk beside her when she faced Mr. Brinnon down herself, fortified by his presence and example. She remembered his casual happiness at tossing into the cart the locks that could make her apartment safer, and his easy skill at installing them. She was picturing again his diffidence at approaching her neighbors, head down a little as he waited for each one to come to the door, turning and winking at her as she sat on the step behind him, and the calm, friendly way he talked to them.

It was a perfect approach, this Overhaul. She could see that now. It was just the right mix of encouragement and practical help. That was the kind of therapy that really could change your life, Maggie thought, and she could see now why Gina was so excited about it.

She pictured Dr. Golding swinging Tim around in the hall and smiled again. She liked the way he treated her son. Not talking down, like some adults would to a four-year-old, and not ignoring him and acting put out, like Gina did, whenever he did something childish, but with an easy give and take, like— like a father with a son. She felt a lurch around her middle, and firmly put that thought away from her. Dr. Golding was her psychologist, not a date. Besides, there was something about Tim's immediate and fierce attachment to Dr. Golding that gave her just a little flicker of concern. What would happen if he went away? she wondered. And maybe she should say *when* he went away, instead of *if*. Could they keep on being friends when her three weeks were over? Gina was the only person Maggie could think of who might know, but asking Gina was out of the question. Still, she let the hope linger in her mind and smiled when she thought about Tim, hanging upside down and grabbing for Dr. Golding's sturdy legs.

She shook her head. It would do no good to get too attached, she reminded herself. Dr. Golding was her doctor, an author of self-help books, for heaven's sake. In fact, she recalled with a start of guilt, she was supposed to buy Dr. Golding's books, both of them, according to Gina. She hadn't wanted to before, but now she decided she might get them on payday. He had a third one, too, Gina said, that was coming out sometime soon.

"They're my bibles," Gina told her on the phone, "or I'd lend you mine."

She was supposed to call Gina tonight. The realization dampened her pleasant thoughts and presented her with a problem. Somehow she didn't think Gina would approve of the way she and Dr. Golding had spent their therapy time. Even though they hadn't done anything wrong, Gina would not like it. It didn't sound like what Dr. Golding had done for Gina's Overhaul, and even though Maggie thought Dr. Golding was probably smart enough to tailor his approach to each person, she knew Gina would be angry if she hadn't gotten the same personalized attention. She allowed herself for just a moment to think that maybe Dr. Golding had taken special pains with her, but then took herself in hand. He probably takes a personal interest in all his patients, she told herself. That was probably the reason he was so popular.

She wouldn't have any trouble giving Gina all the sincere thank-you's she wanted, that much was for certain. Maggie got up and went to the phone to call her, trying to decide on the way across the room what she would say, all thoughts of reading Dr. Golding's books for the moment forgotten.

3

Saturday, April 25

Lindsay Hunt leaned a little closer to the mirror, taking care not to tip over her tea, which was sitting on the dresser in front of her. Her clothes from the past week were piled on a chair, ready to be gathered into a bag and taken to the cleaners. Lindsay didn't like to wear things twice. She was always afraid they looked mussed. She looked mussed herself this morning. She felt a slight sense of dread and leaned toward the mirror to take a closer look. It was unmistakable. The skin beneath her eyes, the part that used to stretch so enticingly taut over the wide, smooth arches of her cheeks, was beginning to crumple. Like a balloon two or three days after the party, the delicate skin was relaxing into a tiny, infinitesimally tiny, but unmistakable sag. Of course, standing at a reasonable distance, without the intense magnification of self-doubt that she was feeling today, it would never be noticed. But Lindsay noticed. She felt the sense of despair that crept over her every time she performed this ritual lately. It was going. Slowly, and unnoticed at first. But there could be no doubt about it. She was losing it.

Her neck was the other place she looked. At least once a week, without fail, she would stand herself before this mirror, completely naked, turn slowly, stand close, stand far away, and turn again. She had noticed her neck last week, had drawn closer to the mirror and stroked it back and forth, up and down, to see if it was her imagination. It was not. The lovely skin, so warm and golden, even in the middle of winter, was beginning to sag. She could imagine, underneath the skin, the tiny framework of collagen and elastic filaments collapsing under their burden of years, all twenty-seven of them, finally grown too heavy to bear. She was ravaged.

At least her breasts were still good. "I will not have saggy breasts," she had told Jake on the few occasions she had mentioned marriage and he, as if countering her proposal, had brought up children. She shuddered now, just thinking about the sagging bellies and long, thin breasts of the women in the changing room at her athletic club. Even women who kept themselves in shape had the inevitable evidence of childbearing—tiny white broken lines on their abdomen and breasts. Karla, the closest thing to a friend she had, noticed her staring one day in the shower room.

"What's the matter, Lindsay?" Karla had asked, laughing. "Haven't you ever seen working breasts?"

"Working breasts?"

"Breasts that have been used for their intended purpose?" Karla clarified, making rocking motions with her arms.

That was when Lindsay decided that she would never nurse a baby. Would never, in fact, have a baby, if that was the cost in flesh, though she hadn't told that part to Jake.

"Lindsay, I think you hurt Shelley's feelings," Jake had said on the way home from his sister's house a month ago, the last time they had been together, in fact. His whole family had gathered to inspect his sister's new baby and to eat one of their carbohydrate-loaded family dinners. Lindsay felt annoyance rush through her again now as it had on the way home that night. She remembered Jake's sister, spread comfortably on her mother's couch with her extra twenty pounds of fat, and knew she would say the same thing again.

"Well, she brought it up," she'd told him. "She said she was still wearing her maternity clothes, and so I just said if I ever had a baby I would take my regular clothes with me to the hospital and wear them home."

She felt a little wisp of anger even now, like the smoke of a smoldering fire when she remembered Jake's sister's reply. Shelley had turned her face toward Lindsay, freckles blazing, red hair pulled back in a scrunch, one of her husband's white shirts hanging open as she nursed the baby right there in front of everybody. She had made one of those smug little faces she was so good at and said, "Sure, Lindsay." And just the way she had said it, and the way her eyes swept from the bottom of Lindsay's feet up to her face, missing nothing on the way, made Lindsay angry. That's when she had said it.

"Well, I won't let myself go if I ever have children. I think it's disgusting the way some women let themselves go."

Carol, Jake's brother's wife, got up then and excused herself. Jake had walked over right after that and looked around, aware that he had walked into something, but as usual clueless. He'd only raised his eyebrows, and even though Lindsay preferred to leave things as they were, his sister had rushed to tattle.

"Oh, Lindsay was just giving us her views on women

keeping their figures after childbirth," Shelley had said to Jake, her face still red under the freckles, the last of her cake uneaten on the coffee table.

Jake had said they should go then and his family hadn't protested, just said polite good-bye's.

"I'm sorry," she'd huffed to Jake when they were in the car. "I just have a thing about fat."

"Well, it's just no big deal, Lindsay," he had said, looking at her with a little incredulity. "She'll lose it. She did before."

Lindsay said nothing, wishing that she had brought her own car this time, as she usually did when they visited Jake's family.

"Besides"—Jake wasn't finished—"the important thing is who she is, not that she gained a few pounds." He was staring at her again, the way he did more and more frequently, as if he had suddenly turned around to find a woman riding beside him in his truck, and wasn't sure who she was.

Lindsay thought about the exchange the rest of the way back to Petaluma. She had seen the snapshots of Shelley that Jake's mother had on the mantel, and Shelley didn't look the same as she had before giving birth to her first child. Somehow that thought comforted her, and made her feel vindicated in what she had said.

She hadn't said that to Jake, but maybe she should have. But she did repeat what had almost become a liturgy she echoed every time the subject of having children came up between them, and it did come between them again then, as if it were real, sitting on the bench seat right in front of the gearshift and the radio, looking back and forth as each one spoke.

"I will *not* have saggy breasts," she said. "If I ever have children, I will wear my regular clothes home from the hospital." She shook her head, remembering Shelley, still wearing her maternity pants and eating a piece of her mother's chocolate cake, her only worry seeming to be whether or not it would give the baby colic.

Jake didn't answer her, just drove quietly the rest of the way back to his office, where she had left her car. He didn't suggest going someplace after. She looked over at him, one hand on the steering wheel, the other resting on the door. She wondered again what had attracted her to him. He was good-looking, though she didn't like the short haircut. She'd told him so, but as usual, he'd ignored her. He had a good physique, though he didn't work out, except on those weekends when he insisted on going with that Ethelda woman's sons to the gym and lifting weights and playing basketball. It must be the sawing and hammering and carrying all the lumber that kept him in shape. Even Lindsay could find nothing to complain about in that respect. Yes, he was handsome and well built. Still, she had wondered all the way back to the office what had kept them together for nearly a year. He really was not her type.

And apparently he had been wondering, too, because after he parked the truck in the graveled lot under the oaks by his little cedar office, before Lindsay could give him the chilly good night she had planned and drive off in a spray of gravel he had turned those eyes on her, suddenly more gray than blue and looking as cold as iron, and told her they needed to talk.

Jake never wanted to talk. The turn of the table left her completely unprepared, as if literally, someone had given the playing surface a spin, and now in the middle of the game she was suddenly staring at a hand of cards she had never seen before.

She had just sat there, dumbfounded, as Jake—Jake, who never wanted to deal with his issues—told her he thought they needed some time apart.

She had gotten angry then, maybe said a thing or two. She

couldn't remember. She felt angry about it again now, looking in the mirror. She watched her face harden, as she remembered how he had sounded—flat, and tired, but sure, as if he had reached an inescapable conclusion.

That's when she had let loose on him. She told him everything she thought about him. She remembered his silences every time she tried to involve him in discussions about her therapy. She remembered how his eyes would always fix on some point of the landscape beyond her head when she told him about whatever self-help book she was reading. Those memories had fueled her fury and she had let it all out. She told him—she supposed she did remember after all—that he was emotionally incapable of giving a woman what she needed, that he was selfish and piggish because he wouldn't enter into her emotional life with her, that he was incapable of sharing her pain.

"This evening, that thing with your sister, was a perfect example," she bit out at him.

"How?" He looked at her across the seat of that ridiculous truck he insisted on driving. "How?" he repeated again, totally clueless, as usual.

She shook her head in disbelief at his emotional obtuseness. "You know about my issues with weight."

He had just looked at her, frowning slightly, his face blank. She had gone on, her voice like a razor. "You know I've told you how my brother called me thunder thighs, and made fun of me, and how that caused me to develop a dysmorphic body image. That's what I've been working on in therapy for five years."

She watched his response. His face, which for most of their conversation had just worn the slightly baffled expression it always did when she talked about psychological realities, changed. There before her, as she talked about her therapy and her dysmorphia, she watched his expression move from puzzlement mixed with frustration to pity mixed with disgust. And that's when she had decided to hurt him. He had asked for it. She had already told him what his psychological issues were, that he was afraid of intimacy, and that he was emotionally unavailable, but when she saw the pity in his face, she had wanted to hurt him.

"You're pathetic, Jake. You're a loser," she'd said quietly, carefully forming each word. "You can't give a woman what she needs. You don't have what it takes to make a woman happy."

He hadn't said a word. He hadn't defended himself. He hadn't fallen apart. He'd just looked at her, a little sadly, she thought, but without the desperate clinging that men usually exhibited when she told them their relationship was over. Still, she could tell she had hurt him. She had felt satisfaction then, and had left riding the wave of her victory. She had driven off in a spray of gravel, as she had intended. He had still been sitting there in the truck when she had left.

She had waited at home that night for his call, but there had been none. Nothing for a month. And now her steam had hardened into anger. It would take more than a phone call to reconcile now. It was incredibly ironic that Jake, of all the men she had been with, would have been the one to tell *her* things weren't working.

She shook her head, pulled back her hair again, and looked at her face as a whole. She would have to deal with this negativity toward Jake, or it would begin to come out on her face and in her body. Lindsay would not have the frown lines she saw on some women who were too dim or paralyzed to make the changes they needed to make to be happy. She looked at her wide mouth and round brown eyes and her perfect widow's peak, then let her hair fall down, her face looking different again when it covered her angular jaw. She admired the perfect triangle made by her jaw and chin.

Her musings divided themselves equally between wondering how she would know the time was right to let Jake back into her life, and whether to wear her hair up or down today. Down, she decided. When her hair was down it made her face look thinner. When she was working, she liked to wear her hair up. The square lines of her face made her look and feel powerful. But today was Saturday. The office was closed and most of her clients would be out on their yachts, in celebration of the beginning of boating season. Even yesterday her desk had been amazingly clear.

She got dressed, choosing a casual outfit and some sneakers. She looked out the big window at the South Beach Marina, at the double row of palms that lined her street, at the bay, choppy and gray this morning, and at the Bay Bridge, stretching taut and elegant across it. The Bay Bridge. Looking across to Oakland. Not a choice view, no matter how beautiful it was. Lindsay frowned and thought again about getting a condo in Sausalito. Or Tiburon. Those were the hot properties. She definitely wanted to be out of here before the new stadium opened. Just the thought of all those crowds of people and screaming kids make her yearn for quiet, almost as if they were disturbing her already.

The thought of screaming kids reminded her again of Jake, and she felt something stir. She wondered if she had done the right thing. To tell him what had been so obvious to her every time they were together. He was so slow. Not quick and glib like the men she was used to. But she realized, as if admitting an unhealthy dependency, that there was something comfortable about him when she was in certain moods. Like today.

She completed her outfit, choosing earrings and a bracelet. She picked up the pottery mug of green tea and finished it in one draw. She had given up coffee in an attempt to help her PMS. Jake had made some kind of a joke, which again reminded her of the things she didn't like about him. Lindsay sighed, and looked around for her jacket and keys.

She wondered if this desire to have Jake back in her life should be honored and validated—those were the exact words she had used in her journaling this morning—if it was real, or if it was the pull of her sabotaging self, the side of her that wanted her to settle for less than the best the universe had for her.

It had played out this way before. A man totally unsuitable for her became the object of her longing. It was a self-destructive tendency. She would spend time on it on Tuesday when she saw Sharon. She jotted down "self-sabotage in relationships" on the pad she left on her dresser for topics she needed to discuss in therapy.

She thought again of what she had said to Jake, and how right she had been. He was completely emotionally unavailable. The weight issue was the perfect example. He had just defended his own sister, saying again, "It's just not that big a deal, Lindsay," when she repeated her criticisms.

She shook her head again, and dug her keys out of her purse. She realized, for perhaps the twentieth time in the last month, that the only thing that could save their relationship was Jake seeing his need for some intensive therapy. He needed to do his own work. Deal with his family-of-origin issues. She had told him that during one of their many discussions on the subject. After one of their visits to his hopelessly enmeshed family. It had seemed to her at the time that he was barely suppressing a smile. She shrugged and realized that's how some men hid from their emotions—with humor.

Lindsay took one last walk through the condo, turning off lights as she went, checking to see if her cat had food and water, not knowing where she would go but determined to get away from her apartment. She rode the elevator down to the parking garage and walked the few steps to her car. She toyed with the idea that had been poised at the corner of her mind for some time. Maybe it was time to call him.

She pulled the car out of the garage and stopped at the inter-section, debating whether to go downtown and to her office or across the bridge to Marin County. It was a beautiful day. Maybe she should run back in and pack a bag. Go up to the spa at Bodega Bay for some deep body massage and stress treat-ments. She pictured herself sitting in front of the big windows looking out at the beach, sipping a glass of Russian River chardonnay. They were probably booked up, she realized. She'd end up driving all the way back to the city or staying at that tacky Holiday Inn in Sebastopol.

She could look at boats. She considered. Today was the first day of boating season. She would like to have a boat. She could moor it in Sausalito and go over on weekends to take it out. Not a sailboat. That took too much work. Something big enough to sleep—maybe four—and with a large enough deck to grill and stretch out in the sun. With a galley, of course. She could take it down the coast to Catalina, or maybe up to Oregon. She pulled out from the stoplight in a roar of decision. She would go look at a boat.

And as for Jake, she thought, reaching a conclusion on that matter as well, she knew deep inside what the truth was. No matter how attractive he might be in some traditional, nonnur-turing ways, there was really no hope for their relationship un-less he spent some significant time in the office of a very good therapist. Maybe she would call him next week and point him in that direction. He would never find his way there on his own.

4

Sunday, April 26

All in all, Jake thought, shutting his trailer door and climbing into the truck, the week had gone pretty well. No major screwups. Even though his portrayal of Dr. Jason Solomon Golding was less than stellar, and in his more coherent moments he couldn't imagine how Maggie Ivey could be fooled by it, he was grateful that she seemed to be, nonetheless. She must be as ignorant as he was of how these things worked. At this rate, he'd have her shored up soon. That's how he thought of his assignment. Just shore her up a little, like a leaning fence or the walls of a sagging building with a good foundation. He'd shore her up and then he'd go back to life the way it had been. The way it was comfortable.

He drove down the graveled road away from the little cleared spot where he parked his temporary home. He had twenty acres of meadow and oak, traversed by a swiftly moving, shallow creek that paused to burble over a rocky streambed and then down a few feet to make a small waterfall. It was a beautiful piece of land, part green pasture and part woods, full of oak and pine, a fragrant eucalyptus here and there, and ash and willow by the creek. His land was situated just between Clover Creek and Petaluma, making it a stone's throw in either direction to visit his family or work at the office in town. He'd bought up all the acreage nearby so that no builder could put a subdivision under his nose. He'd gotten all his building permits, and had even had the foundation poured. Jake had lived there alone for the seven years he had been in this business, always intending to build a home the next year, but somehow always waiting. For what, he wasn't sure. He felt he would know when the time was right.

For now, he was content enough with his living arrangements. He had only a ten-minute drive along picturesque roads to his office, and he was comfortable in his trailer. It was a single-wide he'd taken in trade from his first client. Providential, as his mother had said. It was a little tired-looking on the outside, brown and white vinyl instead of the T-111 siding the newer ones came with. But it was snug. Jake had ripped out the carpeting, painted over the dark paneled walls, patched the roof, and refloored the bathroom. It suited him fine. There was a long living room, a kitchen, bedroom, and bath. All he needed. More, really. He kept a television, though he didn't watch much, and a stereo on which he listened to his dad's old LPs of Bill Monroe and Johnny Cash when he was in the mood. But usually he just came home from work, maybe read a little, heated up a frozen dinner or scrambled himself some eggs, and went to sleep.

Once every few weeks he brought Ethelda's boys over. There were three of them, and they were all at that halfway stage between boy and man. They would order pizza and watch whatever game was on, then maybe go into town to the YMCA and shoot some hoops or catch a movie. They were good kids, but they missed their dad. He shook his head at the thought of them. He ought to do more.

This last week he hadn't done anything but rush in and out, jumping into his truck and taking off to the city to meet with Maggie, or to run back to the office and reassure Ethelda that he was still her partner. He had done nothing but drive, and traffic was terrible. Too many people, and all the time he was spending in the city was making him even more glad he didn't live there. Even Petaluma was a little too busy for him.

Today, though, he didn't have to go anywhere. It was Sunday, and he took his time. He stopped the truck at the creek and got out, just for a minute. He walked over to the water, hearing it before he approached. He loved how the little stream twisted its way under the gnarled old oaks and willows. The banks were grown up with ferns and other plants he didn't recognize, probably weeds, but he liked them all the same. The water made burbling noises as it eddied and turned among the smooth rocks that lined its bottom. It was deeper and wider a little farther back, and Jake had left the massive oaks there, thinking one of them would be perfect for a rope swing someday.

He knelt down so he could see the stones on the bottom. They were all shades of gray and tan, and worn smooth by the water. He had brought Lindsay here once. She had made him take off his coat and spread it on the picnic bench before she would sit down, but after soaking up the atmosphere for about thirty seconds had allowed that it might be all right for a weekend getaway.

He smiled a little to himself and walked back to his truck, glancing at his watch as he crossed the tall grass, still damp from the dew. He would have to hurry or Ma would be gone.

She'd been delighted when he called and said he was coming, but if pressed, she would leave without him. She didn't like to be late for church. He started his truck and drove a little faster than he should have.

The town of Clover Creek, California, was a little dot on the map. Actually, it wasn't to be found on most California highway maps. But on the better, more detailed ones that you could buy in San Francisco at Thomas Bros. or the Rand McNally store, it showed up as a tiny dot, to the north and west of Petaluma. The town itself was four streets with shops on each side, set down in the middle of a good spread of northern California pastureland. Jake's parents, like the other few hundred natives, had made their living from exploiting the various uses of cows.

There were a few orchards, of course, Gravensteins and Delicious, a few chicken and produce farms, and it seemed as though everyone had their little roadside stand or shed in the yard for selling butter and eggs, baskets of walnuts, and daylilies and irises when they were in season, but the cash crop around Clover Creek was mostly cows. Black and white, red and white, Hereford, Holstein, beef, or dairy. They were everywhere. They dotted the miles of pastures that gently rolled away from either side of the road, and stood placidly, chewing and watching the occasional car with calm stares.

Jake drove past a few pastures full of them now, turned off the highway, and drove on until he came to the town, shuttered tight on this Sunday morning. Even though the state of California had lifted the blue laws years ago, Clover Creek still observed them, being homogeneously dedicated on Sundays either to the worship of the Lord or ESPN. Nothing but the gas station and the four churches would be open today, except Rose's Inn, where Susan Ames would serve up one menu selection of

fried chicken, mashed potatoes, gravy, and biscuits, until everyone was fed or she ran out of chicken, whichever came first.

"There's no law we have to be open on Sunday, is there?"
was all the clarification needed by town mayor, Harry Gardello,
Catholic himself, when the repeal of the blue laws was ex-
plained to him by the city's only attorney, his brother-in-law,
Jim Finucci. When he was answered in the negative he had nod-
ded, and he, along with the merchants and residents of Clover
Creek, continued to do what they had done for eons: get up
Sunday morning, go to the Catholic, Methodist, Baptist, or
Presbyterian church, or watch the game, and then eat their
wives' pot roast or pile everyone into the car to go to Rose's.

This morning Jake drove through the little town center and
headed toward his parents' place, two or three miles beyond it.
They had a big spread, 210 acres of pasture and woods, over
100 head of milk cows, about 70 young animals being raised as
replacements, a few chickens, dogs, and cats, and the obligatory
orchard and garden. When they were little his mother had kept
a small field planted with cutting flowers, which he and his
brothers and sister sold along with eggs and vegetables at a
roadside stand during tourist season. Clover Creek would have
been popular with tourists if they had been able to find it, but
they seldom wandered that far off 101 or I-5 in their mindless
march to San Francisco or L.A. "Like lemmings to the sea," his
dad had said.

Jake drove along the rutted road toward the house, making a
note to bring in a load of gravel and put it on the driveway. He
missed his dad. John Cooper had died almost ten years before
of a massive heart attack, suffered while he rested in the porch
swing after a full day of work. Actually, Jake thought, pulling
into the yard, he couldn't think of a better way for his dad to go

than sitting on his own front porch, looking over the place he had built. It was understood that Jake's brother Joe would stay on and run the farm, which had been a relief to Jake, since he felt no longings in that direction.

He'd gone to college, not a rarity in Clover Creek, but not exactly the norm, either. He'd wanted to see some different scenery, so he'd gone out of state—Oregon State University in Corvallis, a town not that much different than Clover Creek, though, now that he thought about it. He'd stumbled through the first two years, finally settling on doing what he liked instead of what he felt he ought to like. He took a major in history with a minor in literature, and after graduation he had surprised everyone by joining Erv Jackson's contracting firm out of Petaluma instead of teaching or staying on in graduate school.

He supposed it wasn't what everyone had expected him to do, but he'd worked for Erv during summers and school vacations, and when the choice came down to getting his teaching degree or finding a job the decision hadn't been too hard. There was something sort of deadening to him about being in a classroom, and something he liked about being outside in the cool breeze or even in the rain, smelling the resin of the trees and the rich, musty smell of the dirt. And he liked working with wood; making furniture, sanding, and polishing, and staining, joining, and fitting, or framing and building houses, causing them to rise up from the landscape where nothing had been before. He'd approached Erv about working for him indefinitely, and had been surprised but pleased when Erv had offered to let him work into a partnership. The two of them had gone along happily for quite a long time with Ethelda doing the books and an occasional set of plans, until Erv had finally seen a doctor who found a spot on his lung—the legacy of thirty years of smoking.

After an awful year of treatment, Erv had died, and Ethelda had stepped in, and if things weren't as they had been before, they were still good.

Jake pulled the truck into his parents' yard and could see one of his first building projects—Joe and Carol's house on the other side of the far pasture. Ethelda had designed it, and Erv and Jake had built it. It looked as if it, like the one his mother still lived in, had been standing there since 1902, spared from the 1906 quake by some whim of nature while towns all around them were leveled.

He could see Ma now. She was sitting in a lawn chair, in her favorite blue dress, Bible in her lap, waiting for him. Jake thought his mother was delightfully unfashionable. She had strawberry-blond hair that was mostly gray now. This morning it was swirled up in curls that looked as though it would take a hurricane to shake them out, but by afternoon and a couple of hours in the kitchen it would be frizzing around her face in a little halo. She didn't wear much makeup except a little lipstick, which she ordered from Ardell Hawkins, the nearest neighbor, who had been selling Avon as long as Jake could remember. Ardell always tried to sell his mom her freckle concealer, but Ma always laughed and said if God had made them she would wear them. Even though she carried a few extra pounds, Jake thought she looked soft and comfortable. No sharp corners on Ma, though she did pointedly look at her watch as he parked and hopped down from the truck.

"I was getting ready to leave without you."

"You knew I'd be here." He leaned over and planted a kiss on her cheek.

"Eventually," she said, patting his face, and Jake knew that was the closest she would come to a reproach.

They drove to the church, Presbyterian in their case, where they joined most of the rest of the family—Jake's brother Joe with his wife and kids, and his sister, Shelley, her husband, Toby, and their kids. His youngest brother, Danny, was off at school. Danny was the only one technically left at home, and along with Jake, made up his mother's burden. When Jake was safely married off and Danny at least had a job he could stick with for more than a month, then Ma would be able to settle down and enjoy her bingo nights and quilting clubs the way she ought to.

Jake readjusted himself on the pew. The sermon seemed longer than normal today. The room was hot, and Joe fell asleep after the first few minutes, as usual. Jake's thoughts were miles away in Oakland, wondering what Maggie Ivey and Tim did on Sunday mornings. He wondered if they went to church or just stayed at home, making pancakes and reading books together on the couch, as he had done with Tim while Maggie made supper the other day. She had insisted that the best way he could help was by entertaining Tim, so he had done it. Tim had said, "Let's read two or three books," and then came back with an armload of a dozen or more. Jake had sat there turning the pages, feeling the warm squirms along his side, and the sharp elbows in his ribs. He had put his arm around the little boy and Tim had leaned back against him. They read *Curious George, Hiram's Red Shirt, Goodnight Moon,* and finally *Siren in the Night,* Tim's favorite, about a family that takes a walk with their dog and gets frightened by a fire engine. They'd read that one three times.

"That's a scary book." Jake smiled as he remembered Tim's face when he spoke, cheeks round, and eyes—soft greenish blue like his mother's—wide behind those glasses that were almost as big as his face.

The sermon was over. Jake shook himself clear of the thoughts, said the Amen, and bowed his head for the benediction.

"The Lord watch over your coming in and your going out, the Lord make his face to shine upon you, and give you peace."

Jake said Amen, but he wasn't sure about the first part of that. He'd take the Lord's face shining on him and giving him peace, but he wasn't sure he wanted much scrutiny on his goings and comings for the next few weeks. He pushed back his worries, though, shook the minister's hand at the door, and negotiated the crowd out of the church.

"You're awfully quiet," his mother said on the way back to his parents' house—it would always be his parents' house—for Sunday dinner.

"Just thinking."

She just nodded and left him alone. That was one thing he appreciated about his mother. She let him be. Even when he'd come home with Lindsay, she hadn't lectured him, just welcomed her with the same easy warmth she gave everyone. His sister, though, hadn't been so tactful.

"What do you see in her, Jake?" Shelley had asked one night after Lindsay had left.

Jake had just shrugged, not wanting to get into the discussion with his sister, but now, as he put the truck in Park, set the brake, and helped his mother out, he wondered what he *had* seen in her. Her attractiveness, he supposed. But really, standing here, looking over the acres of his parents' farm, built together over the forty-five years of their marriage, he couldn't remember. He looked at the house where they had raised their family, and remembered the outings to Santa Rosa to the movies, and the vacations in the Winnebago to L.A. and up to

Washington to see his aunts and uncles in Port Angeles. Suddenly he couldn't imagine Lindsay being Lindsay Cooper, riding in the front seat of a van with three or four little Coopers strapped in behind them, on their way to Disneyland or even driving into creaky old backward Clover Creek to have Sunday dinner with Grandma.

He followed his mother up the slightly sagging porch stairs, and noticed the paint on the front door was peeling. As soon as he was finished playing doctor and Maggie Ivey was safely on her way, wherever that might be, he needed to do a little work, he thought, and it took him a few minutes to realize which part of that scenario, run by so quickly in his mind, had made him feel a little sad. It was the part about Maggie Ivey going her own way, he realized.

He went in and sat down in the living room, rested his hand on the doily-covered arm of his mother's worn armchair and grunted to his brother Joe. He pointed his face in the direction of the baseball game on the television and asked the score.

"Three to one, Giants," Joe said, and slumped a little lower on the couch. From the kitchen Jake could hear the hiss of his mother's pressure cooker and the murmur of the women's voices. He leaned his head on the back of the chair and let his mind wander back to his daydream, but it had changed. When he returned to it he was still driving the van to Disneyland with the kids in the back. But in the front seat next to him was Maggie Ivey.

"You're doing what?" His sister, Shelley, of course, was the first to have a comment.

"It's only for a little while," he said. "But that's not the point."

His mother spoke now, turning toward him from the sink, where she stood rinsing the last of the dinner dishes. "Jake, this isn't like you. I know you mean well, but have you really thought about what will happen if she finds out?"

Jake's mood, which had been buoyed by his time with Maggie Ivey last Thursday, and his mother's pot roast, began to sag. He never should have told them. But he had wanted to bring her here. It would do her good. He could almost see Maggie Ivey sitting at the long trestle table in the dining room, hear her joining in the easy chatter of his sister and sister-in-law, and could easily envision little Tim running wild with his nieces and nephews. He had wanted to bring her here. Next Sunday. Which had led to the trouble now.

"She's not going to find out," he protested. "Right after the three weeks, she'll go on with her life and that will be that. And I'm not asking you to lie. Just don't say anything about my work one way or the other."

"But, honey," his mother protested, trying to scratch her nose with a soapy hand, and finally being helped out by Shelley, who was drying after losing the coin toss. "The house is full of things that would give you away."

Jake thought a minute of the track and field trophies, and the college diploma from Oregon State, along with the endless pictures of him and his siblings that lined the den, living room, and hall.

"Not necessarily," he said. "It's not like she thinks I sprang from Zeus's head or something."

Shelley looked at him and frowned. His mother looked puzzled.

"I mean, she knows I must have a family. The only thing you'd have to take down is my college diploma. And then just don't volunteer any information. That's all I'm asking you to do. If she asks any questions," he finished, "leave them to me."

His mother turned back to the sink, shaking her head. "Well, honey, you know anyone you bring is welcome. All I can say is we'll do our best."

Joe leaned against the refrigerator, arms crossed, grinning. "You've busted it this time" was all he said. His wife, Carol, took another sip of her coffee and said nothing, but wouldn't meet Jake's eyes.

Shelley went right to the heart of the issue.

"I just have one question, Jake."

"Okay," he said, weary already.

"What are you going to do when the three weeks are over? I mean, are you just going to leave then, and have the two of you go your own ways, like, oh, I don't know, two ships that sort of bumped in the night?"

Jake thought she was mixing her metaphors, but as usual she had hit upon the point with piercing accuracy.

She didn't let up. "I mean, you take this poor girl on as a project, in this sort of patronizing way, you get her all warm and fuzzy at having somebody to finally be there for her, then after three weeks you just, boom, tell her, 'Sorry, the whole thing was a lie. But don't feel bad, I did it for your own good.' Or else you just say good-bye, and leave her to find out herself if she ever looks up this doctor in the future. You just end it? Or if you want to keep on being friends, what, you just expect her to forgive all the lies?"

"She expects it to be over in three weeks." Jake's warm mood was definitely gone. Shelley had a way of doing that. He had a fleeting moment of regret that her husband had had to leave for work right after church. Somehow Toby's presence had a mellowing effect on her. But he had to admit she had just said the things he had known all along, but hadn't wanted to face, because of his warm feelings for Maggie Ivey, and his blind, and probably mistaken, idea that things would all work out in the end. It had been a mistake to bring it up. He could see that now. He felt a lump—part of it, he was sure, was the pot roast and mashed potatoes, sitting undigested right behind his rib cage. But along with it, he felt rising in him that familiar stubbornness that refused to admit Shelley was right, even if she was.

"I mean, what are you going to do then, Jake?" Shelley persisted.

His mother turned around from the sink and gave Shelley the eye, the only thing that could stifle her. She took off her apron and hung it on a hook, then squirted Jergens lotion from the dispenser by the sink and rubbed it onto her hands as she sat down at the table.

"Jacob," she said.

Joe was still shaking his head and grinning. They both knew what it meant when their mother called them by their full names.

"I'll just say this one thing."

Jake's brother's grin became even broader.

"Okay, Ma," Jake said.

" 'Oh, what a tangled web we weave . . .' "

Jake kept waiting for her to finish, but she didn't, just sat there looking at him with a meaningful stare. Jake's sister-in-law smiled into her coffee cup. Shelley looked at him darkly. He said his good-bye's then and left, his dismal mood creeping up on him like black swamp water, already to his ankles and rising. It rose all the way home and through the dull evening and even into the night, when he should have been sleeping.

Finally, about four A.M. on Monday morning, when the sky was just beginning to lighten, going to metal gray instead of thick black, he got up and drove to the office—his office, not Jason Golding's. He pulled out the old plans he had been thinking about, and spread them over his desk. He made a pot of coffee and was still working when Ethelda came in at seven. And through it all, the lines to the little poem that his mother hadn't finished kept echoing through his head.

5

Monday, April 27

Gina Tucci's hair was driving her nuts. She wrenched the rearview mirror toward her so she could take a look at it, nearly hit a parked Volvo, and veered just in time.

"Idiot," she snapped, berating the owner of the car for having had the sheer audacity to park it in front of his house, then went back to her deliberations.

She could cut it short again, and her boss could like it or not.

"You look like you've joined the army," Jack had said, himself an ex-marine. "You'll scare all the customers away."

"Very funny," she'd answered, "but it didn't seem to hurt my total sales last year." Jack hadn't had anything to say to that. He might be the broker, but she'd outsold him three years in a row. Besides, how she wore her hair was none of his business. He wasn't the one who had to fuss with it every day and have it whipping around his face when he was out showing houses. Or try to figure out how to cover the gray streaks that were becoming all too familiar. She was ready to cut it off again. Back to the crew cut, although with the yellow blazer the real estate company made them wear and the ten pounds she had gained, she was a little afraid it would make her look like a parakeet.

She shifted the car into second, slowed down, and consulted the address stuck on the dash with a Post-it note. It had to be around here somewhere. The little note fell off and she stuck it back on, admiring her nails as she pressed it down. She'd just had the cracks filled and a little decal put on, a daffodil for spring, and the Flowerburst ring she'd ordered from the Home Shopping Network looked cute with it. Pink, yellow, green, and blue stones arranged like a daisy. Cubic zirconia, but who could tell without a magnifying glass?

There was the house. She braked sharply, then looked in the rearview mirror to see if anyone was bearing down on her. She'd almost missed it. She pulled to the curb, looked around, and realized she was only a few streets away from where she'd first found Maggie a little over a year ago. That's how she'd felt about it, too. Like she'd been walking along and found a perfectly good ring or necklace that someone had tossed onto the sidewalk. "Well, look at this," she'd almost been tempted to say. "Look what I found."

Maggie had been left there. The old woman who owned the house had already packed up and moved to one of those old folks homes that pretend not to be one, and Gina had come to set the "For Sale" sign and take a look around, only to find this woman and this little kid in the garage apartment packing stuff into a bunch of ragged boxes, looking about as pathetic as anything Gina had ever seen.

"Where are you going?" she'd finally asked the woman—Maggie, of course.

"I don't know," she'd said in that tight voice that really tells you how close the person is to losing it. Gina had looked around then and seen the want ads with a bunch of circles all over them. She'd taken them out for pizza—another of her impulsive good deeds—and offered to help Maggie find a house. She still felt puzzled at Maggie's answer.

"Thanks, but I don't have money for a house."

"You have relatives, don't you?" had been Gina's reply. "Borrow the money."

"I don't really feel comfortable asking them, and besides, how would I pay them back?" Maggie had asked, and Gina had no answer for that.

She picked up the cell phone and punched in the number of the Bank of Northern California. Again. She was a little annoyed with Maggie. Here she had sacrificed this month's bonus—well maybe it wasn't such a sacrifice—but she had given it just the same, postponing her own second Overhaul, and Maggie couldn't even spare a half hour on the phone to fill her in. Okay, so maybe she had talked to her every day, but there was something about Maggie's attitude that was downright ungrateful. Tight-lipped and stubborn, all of a sudden not confused at all about what was Gina's business and what wasn't. She listened to Maggie answer and clicked her tongue in frustration. Voice mail again. She pushed the End button before Maggie's soft voice was finished with the greeting. Leave a message, yeah, yeah, yeah.

She turned her attention to the house. A dump, but the location would help. Anything in this development would sell eventually. At least the guys had come and sunk the signpost. She turned off the car engine and thought for a minute before she got out.

It was really odd how Dr. Golding was going about this

therapy. Not anything like Gina's was or even like the book, which described some other methods. Gina thought about calling him. It was that weird. And besides, it wasn't like they were strangers. They had a personal relationship. She looked off down the street and remembered Dr. Golding's reaction the one time she had called him to clarify something during her own Overhaul.

"This is Gina Tucci," she'd said, and had been greeted by silence.

"Are you there?" she'd finally asked.

"I'm here," he'd snapped, "what do you want?"

He'd probably just been having a bad day, she told herself. Or it could just be his way of making her ask for what she wanted. She nodded, satisfied. Still, she wasn't too excited to call him again. She'd wait a few more days and see how things went. Whether Maggie started talking or not. What little she'd said hadn't been what Gina had expected to hear.

She remembered her sessions with Dr. Golding from a year ago. She'd always come to the therapy sessions ready to work. That's what Dr. Golding had said on the phone, in the taped preconference she'd listened to before the first session. She'd thought it was him at first when the smooth voice said, "Hello, Gina, this is Dr. Jason Golding," in a much warmer tone than their live telephone conversation, she had to admit. She'd just drawn in a breath to answer him when the voice had gone on, and she'd realized with surprise that it was a recording. She'd gotten over her surprise quickly, though, grabbed a pencil, and made a note of what he'd said—just a few general things, about what she could expect, about how the responsibility for growth was her own, and how during most of the *21-Day Overhaul* she would be on her own, with the sessions with Dr. Golding used "for direction and support." It gave her a menu of responses to make to the question about whether she'd purchased her copy of the *21-Day Overhaul* book (press *1* if yes, *2* if no) and gave her the option to order it if she had not. It finished with Dr. Golding's voice, bracing this time, reminding her to "come ready to work." Not at all like what Maggie was talking about.

She leaned over and found the lever to flip open the trunk of her car, groaning slightly at the effort. She needed to go back on a diet. At five one she couldn't afford to gain ten pounds. She climbed out of the car, pulled her jacket down carefully over her behind, took out the "For Sale" sign, and hung it on the newly sunk post, then took note of what more would need to be done before this barking dog would sell.

Actually it wasn't so bad. Not as bad as some. The yard was a mess. Someone would have to take care of that. She pulled her pad from her pocket and made a note to have the shrubbery trimmed and some color spots planted in the window box. The inside was as good as it was going to get.

She walked back to her car, still thinking about Maggie, and gave a slight shudder. What must it be like to be poor and naive, and saddled with a child at twenty-five? What a pathetic mess. And what potential she'd had. Gina had seen some of the watercolors Maggie had produced when she had first come out from Alabama, or Tennessee, or wherever she was from. Georgia, that was it. Her paintings were good, and she'd been only a few credits short of graduating. Gina shook her head. Maggie should have had an abortion and stayed in school, but some people didn't know what was good for them. She breathed in a lungful of air and was grateful she wasn't one of those people. But Maggie was. She definitely was, and this thing between her and Dr. Golding was troublesome.

Gina got into her car, scratched her nose carefully to avoid smearing her foundation, and pulled over the rearview mirror again to check her teeth for lipstick. Nothing more pathetic than walking around all day showing houses and talking to people and then find you've got a big glob of "Heather Mauve" stuck on your front tooth. She bared hers before the mirror, sucked on them for a minute. The hair would have to be another day's project. She would call Charles. Tell him she had a fashion emergency. She smiled. He'd like that. She'd used that line on him a few months ago and he'd laughed and worked her in after he'd first said he didn't have any openings. Maybe it would work again.

She readjusted the mirror, reached for the car key, hesitated, and decided to try Maggie one more time. She got voice mail again. Gina snapped off the phone and tossed it aside this time, again not bothering to leave a message. Maggie never called her back from work. In fact, she had asked Gina not to call her there. But this was important. Gina wanted to grill her again about exactly what Dr. Golding had said at the first two sessions. Maggie had been vague about the first and absolutely evasive about the second. She would only say they'd worked on some projects.

"What kind of projects?" Gina had asked, a little peevishly. Dr. Golding hadn't given *her* any projects at all. In fact, now that she remembered, he had gone through a sort of lecture format, given her a few minutes to report any glitches in the program, and then had gone on to the actual business of the second session—age regression hypnosis.

Gina reached into her leather attaché, pulled out the worn copy of *The 21-Day Life Overhaul* book, and flipped to Chapter Two, titled, "The Second Session." Yes, right, here it was—

"During the second session the patient will regress, with the help of the therapist, to the last age at which he or she felt absolutely safe. The therapist will then, through guided imagery, reparent the patient until he or she reenters the present."

She closed the book and tapped the steering wheel with her acrylic fingernails. Something wasn't quite right about Dr. Golding and Maggie. She shook her head. Maggie was such a babe in the woods. It would be just like her to be seduced, although Gina couldn't imagine someone with the insight of Dr. Golding turning out to be a predator. But you never knew. Gina wondered for a minute why Dr. Golding hadn't made any moves toward her, and decided it must be because she was unusually assertive around men. He probably had known he couldn't get away with it, so he hadn't even tried. But Maggie, she thought with a little shake of her head, now that was a different story entirely.

Maggie could be so aggravating. And slow on the uptake, especially when it came to watching out for herself. She'd realized that for certain about six months ago. She'd dropped in at Maggie's on a Saturday morning. The boy—Tim—had been flying around with that cape. Which was another thing. Gina frowned just thinking about his obsession. Maggie should really have him seen by someone. Anyway, she'd come in and found Maggie counting money. Counting her pay—literally. All these little piles of money all over the table. Did anybody do that anymore?

"Don't you believe in banks?" Gina had asked her.

"It's easier for me to keep track of it this way." Maggie had seemed a little embarrassed.

Gina had reached across the table and flipped through the pile of envelopes labeled FOOD, RENT, MEDICAL, and finally found one near the bottom, the glue still sticking the flap to the back, labeled ENTERTAINMENT. She'd picked it up, pried it open with a fingernail. It was empty, of course. That's when she'd realized it. It had come crystal clear to her then. Maggie would never be able to get out of this rut by herself. She'd taken the two of them out again—for burgers this time—even given the kid a handful of quarters for the video games to keep him out of their hair, and tried to talk some sense into her. Go to real estate school, go to art school, borrow some money from your parents. Do something. Do anything, she'd practically begged.

But Maggie had just sat there looking sort of sad, shaking her head as if she, Gina, was the one who wasn't getting it. Gina had gone home still frustrated, and in the middle of the night when she'd gotten up to go to the bathroom—no more of those damned water pills—she'd known exactly what Maggie needed. She needed the Overhaul. Of course! She'd been so excited she could hardly get back to sleep. She'd realized then that she'd been going at Maggie all wrong. Trying to change the externals in her life when it was the *internal attitude* that needed adjusting. No amount of success or prosperity could make a difference in Maggie's life if she wasn't calling it to come home.

"Calling it to come home." She repeated the phrase to herself. She liked that. It was from a book she'd been reading, *Talk Your Way to Riches,* by Andrew Cashman. She liked that name, too. Clever.

Anyway, it had become obvious to her then that Maggie needed her help. But stubborn as Maggie was, it had taken Gina nearly six months to convince her to go. She'd trotted out that same tired line whenever Gina offered to loan her the money for the Overhaul.

"Gina, I'm barely getting by as it is," she'd repeat. "I won't borrow money I can't pay back."

"Well, figure something out," Gina had snapped. "Make a little envelope and label it Overhaul."

But Maggie had given her an angry look—the first time that had ever happened—and Gina knew she'd gone too far. She had let it rest for a day or two, then just offered to make a gift of it. No, no, no, no, every day for nearly a month and finally just last week, Maggie had said yes. Gina supposed she'd finally worn her down.

But this new development with Golding was a problem, and Gina felt a certain responsibility. After all, this had all been her idea. She started up the engine, looked around to see if anything was coming, and pulled out. Something strange was going on, and she was going to find out what. She sighed, feeling burdened, and wished Maggie would just get it together.

Gina faced the blunt truth. Maggie could *make* her life change if she wanted to. Otherwise, how did you explain her own success? If people's prosperity or poverty was determined by chance, then that would make her only lucky instead of motivated. No, she shook her head, reassured as to the rightness of her views. The world wasn't always fair, but it was like a rigged game. If you watched long enough you could figure out how to play it and win.

Gina drove away from El Cerrito, cracked her window a little bit, and was rewarded by a strand of hair blowing onto her face and sticking to her lipstick. She brushed it away, and felt the familiar chafing irritation with Maggie's stubbornness. People who'd proved themselves inept in managing their own lives should at least have the sense to take direction from those who'd succeeded. Maggie could be so annoying, she thought again, and faced the thought that was occurring to her more and more lately. She wondered if her friendship with Maggie was worth the trouble. She supposed so. There *was* something comforting about Maggie. Gina never felt like she had to hold her stomach in around her, and she never had the feeling Maggie was checking out her wardrobe. But then, what would she compare it to? Maggie was pretty, but she cut her own hair, and her clothes did nothing for her. Gina sighed. She really should take Maggie to Charles. Have at it, Gina would say. See what you can do, she'd tell him.

She dug her appointment book out of her purse, and checked the address of her next clients—a young couple who wanted to look at condos. She put the car in gear and turned toward the freeway, all the while wondering how Maggie would look as a redhead.

* * *

It was hard to tell which was worse, the cure or the disease. Really. Jason Golding sat where the nurse had left him, on the edge of the bed, thin legs dangling bare and white from beneath the hospital-issue gown he wore.

He had actually been feeling okay before all this, even if his arteries did look like cottage cheese, as the cardiologist had said. It was only now, after they'd split him clear down the middle, that he felt like hell. What a way for him to spend his vacation, and at the pinnacle of his career, to boot.

"Here's your paper." Monica came in, heels tapping her arrival before she even entered the room, looking annoyingly perky in a new outfit she had managed to find time to sneak out and buy. She tossed *The New York Times* onto the bed.

"For crying out loud, Monica, hand it to me." She could be so annoying sometimes, really. He felt again the weight of responsibility to think for two people as he always did when

Monica was around. He was thinking of making some changes. Something like this—your heart literally being wrenched out of your chest—could really give a man pause. Make him reevaluate his priorities. He remembered, with a noble sigh, the stories he had heard about people changing their whole lives after an experience like this. How they saw everything differently afterward. Besides, lately it was as if she went out of her way to be irritating. Little things, like throwing down the paper, but still annoying as hell.

"There was a message at the hotel from that contractor of yours."

"What. What."

"He wanted to know if you had a brand preference for the spa and Jacuzzi."

"For crying out loud, that should have been ordered a week ago."

Jay watched Monica brush one long bang out of her eye with a tapered fingernail. Why didn't she cut those bangs? Did she think she looked sexy peeking out between the strands? She answered him carefully, her lips barely moving under God knows how many coats of lipstick.

"I don't know about that, hon." There was that tone again.

"Well, what did you tell him?"

"You're getting too excited. I'll just tell him to wait."

"Wait. Like hell you will, and don't talk to me like a child." Jay climbed down from the bed, his left leg still painful from where they had harvested the veins for the bypass. Harvested. Like he was a commodity, just a big hunk of raw materials for them to play with. "Like hell you will," he repeated. "I'll take care of it myself like I do everything. For crying out loud, just once I wish I didn't have to do everything myself. Just once."

The nurse chose that moment to come in with a little paper cup that held his medications. It was the blonde.

"You're out of bed. That's good. The doctor said you could be taking walks up and down the hall today. That's good."

"When can I get out of here?" Jay growled.

The nurse was unperturbed. She had perfected ignoring her patients, Jay thought, to a fine art.

"You'll have to ask Dr. Hammond about that when he makes his rounds this evening."

"That joker always comes when I'm asleep."

"I'll leave a note for him to wake you up today."

"See that you do." The nurse went out with a smile, just as though he hadn't even spoken. Jay thought of his office, probably stripped to the bone by now, carpet up and interior walls knocked down, and that moron of a contractor hadn't even ordered the materials. That's what he got for trying to save a buck. And the guy had come recommended. He was going to get him on the horn today, and he had better have some good explanations. That, or he would just have to get out of here and go home and take care of it himself. Surprise him. Catch him in the act of ripping him off. In fact, the more he thought of it, the more logical the idea seemed. There were hospitals in San Francisco, for crying out loud. Better than this rat hole. And he'd love to see that contractor's face when he showed up, unannounced.

"Call the airlines, Monica," he said. "We're getting out of here."

"Jay, I really think you should lie back down."

"For God's sake, Monica, could you for once do what I say without arguing?" That was what he meant to say, but all that came out was "For God's sake, Monica," and then his heart started jumping and racing like a runaway train. He leaned back on the bed, and the nurse came running in as the spikes on the monitor came closer and closer together.

"He's upset his rhythm," the nurse explained to them a few minutes later, after things had settled down. "It happens sometimes. It's no big deal, but I think he needs to slow down and take things a little easier." It annoyed Jay when the nurse referred to him in the third person, as though he weren't just inches away from her. "We may have to do a cardioversion," she warned.

"Jay never takes anything easy," Monica said wearily.

"What in the hell is a cardioversion?" Jay asked, clutching his chest.

"Just a little electrical adjustment we have to make sometimes. To get your heart back into rhythm." The nurse was looking at the monitor, and at the IV dripping who knows what into his veins.

Monica, inured by now to the drama, was gazing out the window again.

"Make those reservations for next week at the latest," Jay told Monica when the nurse finally was gone. "I have business to take care of. I have a funny feeling things aren't right at the office. And get that guy—what's his name?"

"I don't know. Something Irish—Kelly or something. I left their card at the hotel."

"Well, get him on the phone and tell him he better have some progress made soon or he's fired."

Monica nodded, seemingly absorbed in using her pinky to separate a clump in her mascara. Jay leaned back on the pillow, his heart racing again, and wondered why everything he touched turned to shit. Really. Of all the lousy luck.

6

Tuesday, April 28

Maggie woke up before the alarm went off. She lay curled in her bed for a moment, her little nest safe and warm in the slight chill of the apartment, the weight of the old quilt comforting on her chest. She could hear poor Tim's breathing, loud and snorting from the next bedroom, but even that reminder of the surgery she'd finally scheduled to remove the offending tonsils and adenoids couldn't dampen the buoyancy she was feeling.

Just one week and already her life had changed. It didn't seem possible that it had just been a week. When she thought of Dr. Golding—Jake—she felt as though she had known him for years. Surely longer than just seven days.

She folded back the covers and pulled on her terry-cloth bathrobe, found a pair of socks, and padded into the kitchen to make coffee, still thinking about Dr. Golding, wondering why she felt as though she had known him forever. Maybe because their time together had been so emotional. At least for her. She felt the warmth around her middle again when she remembered their day together on Thursday, with Dr. Golding working on the locks and Tim following him around. He had even taken her number before he left and called on Saturday just to see how she was getting along. It was a brief conversation and he'd seemed a little awkward, but it had been nice. She was able to say they were doing fine. And really, they were so much better.

Maggie had waited to tell him about the changes at work until today when they met again. She wanted to see his face when she told him. She had checked back with Mr. Brinnon last Friday as planned. Right off the bat, he had offered her a chair and a cup of coffee. Maggie grinned, remembering it.

"No, thank you," she'd said to both. She'd already had several onslaughts of panic at the thought of another confrontation, and was half afraid that the promises he'd made would have evaporated overnight.

"Do you mind if *I* sit down?" Mr. Brinnon had asked her.

Maggie had looked at him sharply to see if he was mocking her. His face was as bland as white bread.

"No," she answered. "Please, sit down."

Mr. Brinnon gave her a little nod, his small eyes flickered toward hers briefly, then darted back to the sheaf of papers he held.

"Your status is no longer Temp Help." He cleared his throat a few times. Maggie held herself around the waist and hoped he wouldn't say her status was unemployed.

"You are permanent, full-time, and your job classification will be as Secretary Two instead of Clerk One."

Maggie was doing calculations in her head, but Mr. Brinnon spared her the trouble. "That entails a pay increase of six hundred dollars per month," he said, and Maggie tried not to stare, slack-jawed.

"Full-time status entitles you to sick leave, vacation, medical, dental, and optical benefits, and they, as well as your salary increase, will all be retroactive from the end of your first ninety days. When you see Human Resources they'll have you pick what medical insurance you want, and you'll need to read these papers and choose your retirement plan, too." Mr. Brinnon's eyes had swooped in for a quick glance at Maggie at this point, but darted away before Maggie could acknowledge it. "The retroactive pay will be reflected in your next paycheck, Ms. Ivey," Mr. Brinnon said, "if that's all right."

Maggie was beginning to feel as if she had won the lottery. She managed to nod and thank him, then went straight back to her desk and calculated the retroactive pay. She did the arithmetic twice on her little calculator, then sat back and just stared at the display. It came to nearly five thousand dollars. Not enough to leave Oakland behind, but if she saved, it was a possibility for the future. Maybe she could buy a car. She had just sat there, thinking about having that much money. And even better, there would be no more hassles with sick leave. From now on if Tim was sick she could call in and tell the truth.

The director of Human Resources, Kay something or other, had called Maggie's extension right after that and invited Maggie to her office, offered her coffee or tea, and explained the entire benefit package to her, and had her choose what kind of insurance she wanted.

"You have one week of retroactive vacation from last year, Ms. Ivey," the woman said, indicating a chart in the personnel manual, "and two weeks that you'll be eligible to take as of June first."

Maggie shook her head again, just remembering it. She had three weeks of vacation at her disposal. She could take a day off

had blamed her downward
 the loss of Bill and Millie,
went further back than that.

 her life, she could see that
 of school—no, choosing to
ovide for Tim—was not the
 to take a wrong turn long
em was inside of her. What
o the girl she used to be, and
tself again in her mind she
d.
Maggie," Jeff had said, mak-
park ride. She'd envisioned
ekends roaming wine coun-
sherman's Wharf, while they
ut after a month or two Jeff
ing on her part-time job for
 had changed. It seemed she
mattered to Jeff was school.
nd more often spent his free
nd he criticized her. Because
when he said she was stupid.
ally said it, she realized, sip-
the walls of her tiny kitchen
 the air, floating around her.
Maggie shouldn't touch the
ggie shouldn't ask Jeff ques-
e should keep the television
ool and work full-time. Her

and do nothing if she wanted to! And none of it would have happened without Dr. Golding.

She pulled her stool to the kitchen window and gazed out at industrial Oakland, already awake and spewing smoke into the gray dawn. It no longer depressed her. In fact, she didn't dread going to work at all anymore. Mr. Brinnon had been positively civil since Thursday. He headed the other way when he saw her coming, which suited Maggie fine. She realized, now that his harassment and criticism was over, that it had been like scraping open a wound every day.

Maggie filled the coffeemaker with water and measured the grounds, flipped the switch, and sat back down and waited, enjoying its sounds and the aroma of the fresh coffee that began to fill the room as it dripped. Now that she had a little room to breathe, she was beginning to see that her life hadn't been bogged down with the weight of one big problem as much as ten or twenty small ones, all magnified by what she now knew to be loneliness. Since Bill and Millie had died she had been alone. She had Gina, she reflected, but Gina didn't really count. Gina was more of a career consultant than a friend, Maggie thought, and felt a little sad to realize it. She could see that it was true, though. Now that she had something to compare her to.

She listened to the coffeepot's last gurgle. It made a cheery counterpoint to the muffled moans of the foghorns in the bay that she would have been able to see if it weren't for the wall of factories blocking her view. She poured some coffee into the imitation Fiestaware mug she had bought at the discount store last week after her first visit with Dr. Golding. She'd bought six of them, bright yellow, green, and red—two of each—and hung them on hooks over her sink. She looked at them now, bright

and cheery, a spot of clear color in what she could now see
a somewhat drab apartment. It was really very drab, she adi
ted, looking around her almost as if she were seeing it for
first time.

She didn't have much furniture. All of her belongings had
into one pickup load when she'd arrived at Bill and Millie's a
they'd furnished the apartment she'd rented. The new owners
Bill and Millie's house, the ones Gina had found, had want
the furniture left in the garage apartment. Millie had insisted s
and Tim be able to bring their beds and dressers, but that w
all the furniture they'd brought with them to the Embarcade
Arms. Maggie had bought a reupholstered couch, a recliner, ai
a dinette set at the Salvation Army thrift store.

The kitchen wasn't bad, Maggie thought, looking critically
the scarred wooden table and mismatched chairs. In fact, wit
some furniture polish or paint and some cheery place mats,
would be fine. The walls were good throughout the apartmen
She'd painted them all when she'd moved in. They were white
and though a little stark, at least they were clean.

It was the living room that needed help, she thought, eyein
the drab brown couch and dark green recliner, and wondering
what could be done to spruce it up. The green shag carpet hac
to have been around since the seventies. She rattled around ir
the junk drawer until she found a pair of pliers, and using then
and a steak knife she managed to pull up a corner of it. She
brushed thirty years of dust away and saw hardwood underneath. Oak. She smiled and was tempted to start ripping up carpet now. No matter what shape the floor was in, it was sure to
look better than the matted-down carpet.

She stood and debated, looked at the kitchen clock, and
knew she'd better wait to start her project, but for just a second

wasn't the problem. Although she
spiral on her forced move here an
she could see now that the problem
Even before Tim.

Now that she had Dr. Golding
having Tim, and having to drop ou
drop out of school so she could p
problem, either. Her life had begu
before Tim came along. The prob
had happened, Maggie wondered,
even before the question formed
knew the answer. Jeff had happene

"Come to California with me,
ing it sound like an amusement
walks in the Golden Gate Park, w
try and Sausalito, and outings to F
both went to school and worked.
had quit his job, both of them rel
income. Then, subtly, more thing
couldn't do anything right. All tha
He studied all the time, and more
time with the other law students.
she loved him, she had believed it
Not that he ever came out and ac
ping her coffee and staring now a
without seeing them. It was just i
Maggie is slow, Maggie is dumb
computer or she'll mess it up. M
tions when he is studying. Magg
turned off. Maggie should quit sc

Maggie felt relief, like
dle and break into the a
he didn't say anything, ju
"Sure," she said. "Tha
"What's the joke?" he
tor.
"Nothing," she answe

Dr. Golding held the doc
her. It was on long-tern
working on.
"Maggie," he asked
parking garage, "have yo
Maggie shook her hea
ded as if he were pleasec
toward Fisherman's Wha
gie looked around in th
from now on—as if she
street corners, waiting f
how she'd decided to lo
lived on to her boss at v
alizing, with a kind of c
and move. Just knowin
second and third time, a
day's memory, no matte
Everything seemed to
she had been seeing th
which had been remove
and she was beginning
looked. Even this morni

She'd
that mo
worn-ou
deep, gu
inside—
to happe
His si
all as if
spoke he
that son
made he
thought
"Tell
Handed
more se
"How
And s
her mind
herself,
And
"Good.
And
ridiculo
"Oh,
the poss
begun to
soulful
the subj
smile. Sl
She v
emerge

work's a joke anyway. Not important like law school. She's just
a child, playing with paint.

Jeff's reaction to her pregnancy was the final blow, she realized now. There had been no discussion, and the conclusion
seemed to be foregone, at least in his mind. There had been an
envelope on the table for her a few mornings after she'd told
him the results of the home pregnancy test she'd bought and administered alone. Five one-hundred-dollar bills, the address of a
clinic, and a note: *Sorry I can't go with you. Study group
tonight, exam tomorrow. Here's the money to take care of it.
We'll talk afterward.*

Take care of *it*. Meaning Tim. Maggie had sat there at the
table, reread that note maybe twenty times, fingered the stiff
one-hundred-dollar bills, and then lay her head on the table and
cried.

She could see it now as clearly as the scraggly palms in the
neighbor's yard and the broken glass on the sidewalk beneath
her window. That was what had happened to the old Maggie.
She'd grown up that day. She'd packed her things, and only then
did she realize how truly isolated she had become over the year
that she and Jeff had lived in Berkeley. In any other place she
had lived, not even counting home, she could have called friends
to come and help her. Here she had no one. She had let herself
become totally immersed in Jeff, and isolated from everyone
else.

She'd finally looked through the want ads, taken the bus to
El Cerrito to see the apartment over the retired couple's garage,
then called someone out of the Yellow Pages who advertised
hauling. The man showed up a few hours later in a pickup
truck, and moved Maggie's things for her. After she paid him

and th
justed,
table,
dollar

Ma
tucked
gency.
as cris
that s
retroa
disaste
now li
ferenc
sendin
never
somet
hand
She
on the
waitin
worth
and re
windc
more
"Yc
one fa
"I'
and a
caugh
were
the cr

sessions were over. Th
heaviness, and now su
long was sprouting wi
over? Maybe Dr. Gol
friend. She nodded, ai
If it wasn't a certaint
Besides, she would see
stove—in exactly five
She heard the alarn
ing stopped. She took
and stretched, then pu
she would see Dr. Golc
a little burst of adre
headed for the show
thought about what sl

Dr. Golding looked ni
Maggie liked. He woi
some boots, a little les
He was waiting for h
Maggie arrived, and p
blue work suits measi
tary's desk was empty
"As you can see, th
Maggie nodded, he
for what was coming
her first rule of survi
just be disappointed.
"Anyway," Dr. Gc
easily, "want to go gc

her first indulgence since the raise—when she'd passed by the Oakland waterfront just before the BART descended into the tunnel, as she'd gazed out at the smokestacks peeking through the layer of fog, she'd seen a picture. Even in that.

Now as she and Dr. Golding drove down the hill toward the waterfront she could see San Francisco Bay, gray-green and choppy today, the tall ships docked at the Hyde Street Pier, the Blue and Gold Ferry chugging out to Alcatraz. They passed the hotels on North Point, and swung around a limousine delivering someone to the Sheraton. They passed huge madrona trees and little sidewalk gardens behind black wrought-iron fences. Dr. Golding finally slowed, and parked the truck in a lot.

"It's just over there," he said, pointing. Maggie could see the Ghirardelli sign peeking above the tops of the buildings around it. She nodded and fell in step beside Dr. Golding. They crossed the street and passed the cable car turnaround on Hyde Street, and when Maggie stepped onto the track she could feel it vibrating under her feet. Tourists were standing in line, and a man with a guitar was singing to them.

"Would you like to ride the cable car?" Dr. Golding followed her eyes toward the little red trolleys, lined up and ready to load.

"I'd better not," said Maggie, looking at the long line of tourists. "I don't want to push my luck."

Dr. Golding smiled and nodded, and they continued on toward the square, past the street vendors and the homeless people with their sacks and carts full of things, past the art galleries and fancy restaurants of red brick, wrought iron, and glass, past the people eating outside. Past a panhandler playing a guitar who singled Maggie out.

"Don't turn your head, drop the bread. Hey you in the blue, I'm talking to you. My name is Jimmy, gimme, gimme."

and do nothing if she wanted to! And none of it would have happened without Dr. Golding.

She pulled her stool to the kitchen window and gazed out at industrial Oakland, already awake and spewing smoke into the gray dawn. It no longer depressed her. In fact, she didn't dread going to work at all anymore. Mr. Brinnon had been positively civil since Thursday. He headed the other way when he saw her coming, which suited Maggie fine. She realized, now that his harassment and criticism was over, that it had been like scraping open a wound every day.

Maggie filled the coffeemaker with water and measured the grounds, flipped the switch, and sat back down and waited, enjoying its sounds and the aroma of the fresh coffee that began to fill the room as it dripped. Now that she had a little room to breathe, she was beginning to see that her life hadn't been bogged down with the weight of one big problem as much as ten or twenty small ones, all magnified by what she now knew to be loneliness. Since Bill and Millie had died she had been alone. She had Gina, she reflected, but Gina didn't really count. Gina was more of a career consultant than a friend, Maggie thought, and felt a little sad to realize it. She could see that it was true, though. Now that she had something to compare her to.

She listened to the coffeepot's last gurgle. It made a cheery counterpoint to the muffled moans of the foghorns in the bay that she would have been able to see if it weren't for the wall of factories blocking her view. She poured some coffee into the imitation Fiestaware mug she had bought at the discount store last week after her first visit with Dr. Golding. She'd bought six of them, bright yellow, green, and red—two of each—and hung them on hooks over her sink. She looked at them now, bright and cheery, a spot of clear color in what she could now see was a somewhat drab apartment. It was really very drab, she admitted, looking around her almost as if she were seeing it for the first time.

She didn't have much furniture. All of her belongings had fit into one pickup load when she'd arrived at Bill and Millie's and they'd furnished the apartment she'd rented. The new owners of Bill and Millie's house, the ones Gina had found, had wanted the furniture left in the garage apartment. Millie had insisted she and Tim be able to bring their beds and dressers, but that was all the furniture they'd brought with them to the Embarcadero Arms. Maggie had bought a reupholstered couch, a recliner, and a dinette set at the Salvation Army thrift store.

The kitchen wasn't bad, Maggie thought, looking critically at the scarred wooden table and mismatched chairs. In fact, with some furniture polish or paint and some cheery place mats, it would be fine. The walls were good throughout the apartment. She'd painted them all when she'd moved in. They were white, and though a little stark, at least they were clean.

It was the living room that needed help, she thought, eyeing the drab brown couch and dark green recliner, and wondering what could be done to spruce it up. The green shag carpet had to have been around since the seventies. She rattled around in the junk drawer until she found a pair of pliers, and using them and a steak knife she managed to pull up a corner of it. She brushed thirty years of dust away and saw hardwood underneath. Oak. She smiled and was tempted to start ripping up carpet now. No matter what shape the floor was in, it was sure to look better than the matted-down carpet.

She stood and debated, looked at the kitchen clock, and knew she'd better wait to start her project, but for just a second she had a flash of memory. She remembered the woman she used to be.

She sat back down on her stool and took a sip of coffee. It was fragrant and strong, and the steam warmed her face. She followed the last thought's thread. What had happened to the girl who was never fazed by anything? Just a small thing like the cups and the carpet had brought it all back. No money? Not a problem. Maggie could live anywhere, and in style. She had rented some real dumps during her first years at school, but by the time she was finished with her move-in rituals, no one could tell. She would go through the same routine. Rip up the carpet, wash down the kitchen and bathroom with Lysol and the floor with Murphy Oil Soap, paint, hang her plants—"the jungle," as Jeff used to call it—go furniture shopping at Goodwill, paint all her finds wild colors, and she was set. Maybe not elegant decor, but definitely clean and cheerful.

She used to never be afraid of anything, she thought, with a slight shake of her head. She remembered cruising the city by herself while she was going to art school, going to Utrecht's to buy supplies, to the free concerts in Golden Gate Park, stopping at the sidewalk produce markets in the Mission District, and riding the bus to North Beach to buy pizza. She wasn't stupid. She never wandered around in the Tenderloin or anywhere by herself after dark, but she hadn't been scared all the time then, as she was now. What, exactly, was she so afraid of? She peered out her window at her neighborhood, brightening up with the sunlight that was burning its way through the clouds. It wasn't so bad. All up and down the street were quaint Victorian houses, exactly the same as the ones the tourists gawked at on Lombard Street and in Pacific Heights. Well, maybe not quite that nice, but close—the point being, she realized, that Oakland wasn't the problem. Although she had blamed her downward spiral on her forced move here and the loss of Bill and Millie, she could see now that the problem went further back than that. Even before Tim.

Now that she had Dr. Golding in her life, she could see that having Tim, and having to drop out of school—no, choosing to drop out of school so she could provide for Tim—was not the problem, either. Her life had begun to take a wrong turn long before Tim came along. The problem was inside of her. What had happened, Maggie wondered, to the girl she used to be, and even before the question formed itself again in her mind she knew the answer. Jeff had happened.

"Come to California with me, Maggie," Jeff had said, making it sound like an amusement park ride. She'd envisioned walks in the Golden Gate Park, weekends roaming wine country and Sausalito, and outings to Fisherman's Wharf, while they both went to school and worked. But after a month or two Jeff had quit his job, both of them relying on her part-time job for income. Then, subtly, more things had changed. It seemed she couldn't do anything right. All that mattered to Jeff was school. He studied all the time, and more and more often spent his free time with the other law students. And he criticized her. Because she loved him, she had believed it when he said she was stupid. Not that he ever came out and actually said it, she realized, sipping her coffee and staring now at the walls of her tiny kitchen without seeing them. It was just in the air, floating around her. Maggie is slow, Maggie is dumb. Maggie shouldn't touch the computer or she'll mess it up. Maggie shouldn't ask Jeff questions when he is studying. Maggie should keep the television turned off. Maggie should quit school and work full-time. Her work's a joke anyway. Not important like law school. She's just a child, playing with paint.

Jeff's reaction to her pregnancy was the final blow, she realized now. There had been no discussion, and the conclusion seemed to be foregone, at least in his mind. There had been an envelope on the table for her a few mornings after she'd told him the results of the home pregnancy test she'd bought and administered alone. Five one-hundred-dollar bills, the address of a clinic, and a note: *Sorry I can't go with you. Study group tonight, exam tomorrow. Here's the money to take care of it. We'll talk afterward.*

Take care of *it*. Meaning Tim. Maggie had sat there at the table, reread that note maybe twenty times, fingered the stiff one-hundred-dollar bills, and then lay her head on the table and cried.

She could see it now as clearly as the scraggly palms in the neighbor's yard and the broken glass on the sidewalk beneath her window. That was what had happened to the old Maggie. She'd grown up that day. She'd packed her things, and only then did she realize how truly isolated she had become over the year that she and Jeff had lived in Berkeley. In any other place she had lived, not even counting home, she could have called friends to come and help her. Here she had no one. She had let herself become totally immersed in Jeff, and isolated from everyone else.

She'd finally looked through the want ads, taken the bus to El Cerrito to see the apartment over the retired couple's garage, then called someone out of the Yellow Pages who advertised hauling. The man showed up a few hours later in a pickup truck, and moved Maggie's things for her. After she paid him and the deposit on the apartment, ridiculously low, and adjusted, she was sure, after a tearful cup of tea at Millie's kitchen table, she'd been left with two of the original five hundred-dollar bills.

Maggie went and got them now, after all these years still tucked away in the sugar canister, just in case of a dire emergency. She took out the sandwich bag and held the two bills, still as crisp and rough-feeling as they'd been five years ago. Now that she had benefits and vacations and five thousand in retroactive pay coming, she realized how close to the edge of disaster she'd been standing. She shook her head at the idea, now ludicrous, that two hundred dollars would make much difference in any extremity. But oddly, instead of that realization sending another shiver of fear through her, she felt as if she had never been in danger of falling over that ledge. She felt as if something—someone—had all along been poised to catch her hand and pull her back just in time.

She thought of Dr. Golding and his kindness, of the new locks on the doors. Of the way he looked at her when she talked— waiting and respectful, as if he expected her to say something worth listening to. She fingered the two hundred dollars, smiled, and returned it to its hiding place, then sat back down at the window, promising herself to get up and get busy in just a few more minutes.

"You'll fall in love with him," Gina had pronounced. "Everyone falls in love with their therapist."

"I'm not going to fall in love." Maggie had been sure of that, and a little irritated at Gina for even suggesting it. But he had caught her somehow, with his kindness, and even though they were few, with his words. She saw that now, looking back with the crystal vision that always came after the fact.

She'd been so unaware when she had stumbled into his office that morning, wearing her ugliest brown pants and her old, worn-out shoes, and crying so hard she couldn't talk—those deep, gut-wrenching sobs that seemed to shake her from down inside—her face all red and blotched. She hadn't planned for it to happen, but she'd been caught.

His silences were deep and full of things to consider, not at all as if he had simply run out of things to say, and when he spoke he was wise and full of good advice. But the truth was that somehow his presence, even when he didn't say a word, made her feel a little less crazy and alone. In fact, now that she thought about it, he hadn't said very much at all.

"Tell me" was all he had said, and she had told him, all of it. Handed it over like a burden grown too heavy to carry one more second.

"How do you feel?" he'd asked when she was finished.

And she had said, blurting out the first thing that came into her mind, "I feel like a soldier who's been standing guard all by herself, and finally gets to rest because someone else is here."

And then he'd looked at her with his kind eyes, and said, "Good. You rest."

And even though she hadn't fallen in love—that would be ridiculous—now she could see why Gina would say that.

"Oh, yes, you will," Gina had insisted when Maggie denied the possibility. "With his looks, you'll fall in love." Then she'd begun to describe Dr. Golding, but had gotten only as far as his soulful eyes before Maggie had become annoyed and changed the subject. She remembered Jeff, with his good looks and easy smile. She knew looks had nothing to do with love.

She wondered now as she watched the low, squat factories emerge from the morning fog, what she would do when the sessions were over. They were a third over, she realized with heaviness, and now suddenly the week that had seemed years long was sprouting wings. What would she do when it was all over? Maybe Dr. Golding—Jake—would still want to be her friend. She nodded, and tucked the comforting thought away. If it wasn't a certainty at least it was enough for right now. Besides, she would see him—she checked the clock on the old stove—in exactly five hours.

She heard the alarm go off in the bedroom, and Tim's snoring stopped. She took one long, last gulp of her coffee, got up and stretched, then put the cup in the sink. Only five hours until she would see Dr. Golding again. She felt her pulse speed up and a little burst of adrenaline surge into her bloodstream. She headed for the shower, humming a little as she went, and thought about what she would wear.

Dr. Golding looked nice today. He had on his jeans again, which Maggie liked. He wore a crisp blue and white cotton shirt and some boots, a little less clunky than the others he'd worn before. He was waiting for her in the hallway outside his office when Maggie arrived, and past his shoulder she could see two men in blue work suits measuring and marking on the walls. His secretary's desk was empty.

"As you can see, there's some work going on here."

Maggie nodded, her good mood sinking. She prepared herself for what was coming next, and wondered why she had broken her first rule of survival: *Don't look forward to things. You'll just be disappointed.*

"Anyway," Dr. Golding continued, his eyes resting on her easily, "want to go get some coffee?"

Maggie felt relief, like a clear bubble, travel up from her middle and break into the air as laughter. Dr. Golding smiled, but he didn't say anything, just looked a little puzzled.

"Sure," she said. "That would be fine."

"What's the joke?" he asked her as they walked to the elevator.

"Nothing," she answered him, smiling. "The joke's on me."

Dr. Golding held the door of his brother-in-law's truck open for her. It was on long-term loan, he said, for a project he was working on.

"Maggie," he asked her as he pulled the truck out of the parking garage, "have you ever been to Ghirardelli Square?"

Maggie shook her head and said she hadn't. Dr. Golding nodded as if he were pleased with the answer, and turned the truck toward Fisherman's Wharf, and on the way down the hill Maggie looked around in the way she had decided to view the city from now on—as if she were one of the tourists bunched on the street corners, waiting for the lights to change. In fact, that's how she'd decided to look at everything—from the street she lived on to her boss at work. Things could change, she was realizing, with a kind of openmouthed wonder. They could shift and move. Just knowing that made her look hard at things a second and third time, and with fresh eyes, not trusting yesterday's memory, no matter how clear it seemed to be.

Everything seemed to be in sharper focus. It was almost as if she had been seeing the world through a gray-filtered lens, which had been removed. Colors seemed clearer and brighter, and she was beginning to see pictures again wherever she looked. Even this morning as she'd ridden the BART to work—

her first indulgence since the raise—when she'd passed by the Oakland waterfront just before the BART descended into the tunnel, as she'd gazed out at the smokestacks peeking through the layer of fog, she'd seen a picture. Even in that.

Now as she and Dr. Golding drove down the hill toward the waterfront she could see San Francisco Bay, gray-green and choppy today, the tall ships docked at the Hyde Street Pier, the Blue and Gold Ferry chugging out to Alcatraz. They passed the hotels on North Point, and swung around a limousine delivering someone to the Sheraton. They passed huge madrona trees and little sidewalk gardens behind black wrought-iron fences. Dr. Golding finally slowed, and parked the truck in a lot.

"It's just over there," he said, pointing. Maggie could see the Ghirardelli sign peeking above the tops of the buildings around it. She nodded and fell in step beside Dr. Golding. They crossed the street and passed the cable car turnaround on Hyde Street, and when Maggie stepped onto the track she could feel it vibrating under her feet. Tourists were standing in line, and a man with a guitar was singing to them.

"Would you like to ride the cable car?" Dr. Golding followed her eyes toward the little red trolleys, lined up and ready to load.

"I'd better not," said Maggie, looking at the long line of tourists. "I don't want to push my luck."

Dr. Golding smiled and nodded, and they continued on toward the square, past the street vendors and the homeless people with their sacks and carts full of things, past the art galleries and fancy restaurants of red brick, wrought iron, and glass, past the people eating outside. Past a panhandler playing a guitar who singled Maggie out.

"Don't turn your head, drop the bread. Hey you in the blue, I'm talking to you. My name is Jimmy, gimme, gimme."

Maggie felt herself blushing. Dr. Golding dropped a bill in the man's hat, smiled at her, and touched her lightly on the back as they climbed the three-tiered stairway toward the chocolate factory. On either side were trees and bushes with gardens at their feet, foxgloves growing wild amid the ferns, azaleas, rhododendrons, and camellias, and paths winding through them, as if someone might climb the wrought-iron fence and wander among them.

They climbed the last step and entered the square itself. The fog was completely gone and the bright sunlight made the red brick almost glow. It was bright and airy, a landscape of water and glass, red brick and lush green plants. A band played some kind of pipes, light carefree music that seemed to float on the breeze. Redwood benches lined every side, beside them pots spilled flowers, and in the center of the square was a fountain with two bronze mermaids, water bubbling up between them. Maggie realized she'd been holding her breath. She let it out slowly, then turned toward him.

"It's beautiful, Dr. Golding," she said, but knew she wasn't doing it justice. "I've lived here six years and I've never seen it."

"I've never been here, either," said Dr. Golding, "and could you try to call me Jake?" His face looked a little pained. "I really like it better if you don't call me Dr. Golding."

Maggie nodded in agreement and they continued on toward the chocolate store itself. Dr. Golding's—Jake's—hand brushed hers once or twice as he walked beside her. He let her go before him into the chocolate store, the only way to the coffee shop, a commercially strategic arrangement, Maggie was sure. They passed bins of chocolate bars in every size and shape, dark and milk, walnut and plain, laced with hazelnut, vanilla, almond, raspberry, mint, coffee, and more flavors she didn't take the time to read. By the cash register were two baskets full of irreg-ular chunks of chocolate wrapped in plastic. Jake picked out the biggest piece he could find and placed it on the counter with a little chocolate cable car.

"For Tim," he said, and handed her the bag.

Maggie felt embarrassed. She always felt embarrassed when someone gave her a gift or tried to do something for her. Dr. Golding didn't seem to notice, though. His back was to her and he was scanning the restaurant for an empty table.

"Are you on a tight schedule?" He looked at his watch.

"I'm okay," Maggie said, and then she blurted out her news, not waiting until they were seated at their table as she'd planned. "You'll never guess what happened," she said.

Dr. Golding smiled at her, a big smile that started at the cor-ners of his eyes and involved his whole face by the time he was done. "What happened?" he asked her, seeming pleased already.

She told him about Mr. Brinnon putting her on full-time sta-tus and giving her benefits, and when she got to the part about the retroactive salary, Dr. Golding just threw back his head and laughed, then patted her on the back. "Oh, Maggie, that's fan-tastic," he said, and looked as happy as she felt.

"Mr. Brinnon told me to take whatever time I needed," she finished up, remembering that Dr. Golding had asked her when she needed to be back. "He is giving me a lot of room," she said. "I think he's a little afraid of me now."

Dr. Golding laughed again and so did Maggie. She could still see Mr. Brinnon's pasty, panic-stricken face when Dr. Golding had said the words *sexual harassment*.

It was a second before either of them noticed that the wait-ress was waiting to show them to their table. "This way," she said with a little smile when they finally noticed her. She put them right by the window and Maggie could look out past the ferns and ivy to see the cable cars in the turnaround and could hear the dinging of their little bells when they pulled out. She stopped to save the moment, not closing her eyes, but thinking hard, relishing the feelings and sights. Just as she did on her computer at work, when she stopped and periodically saved what she was working on, she stopped and tried to save what she was feeling right now. Dr. Golding was studying his menu, and she looked at him, too, and felt the warmth again.

He looked up, and Maggie straightened up in her chair.

"Want some lunch?" he asked her.

"I'll just have coffee," she answered.

Dr. Golding had coffee, too, and they must have managed to hit the dull spot between breakfast and lunch. That, or the tourist season hadn't really begun yet. At any rate, they sat there over their coffee for an hour or so, with no one rushing them to leave, and once again, Maggie found the words flowing from her mouth into Dr. Golding's sympathetic ear. Without any embarrassment or effort she told him about Jeff. How she had met him at the University of Georgia, and had come here with him so he could attend law school. How she'd been a year away from graduating when she found out she was pregnant. She told him about her parents' disappointment with her, and the fact that they never let her forget it.

"I guess I've made a big mistake," she said, but still not able to reconcile that conclusion with the image that popped into her mind—Tim, flying from the chair, cape streaming behind him.

Dr. Golding gave a little shrug and raised an eyebrow, as if he didn't quite agree. "It might have been a mistake that got you here," he said, his eyes not leaving hers, "but I don't think it's a mistake for you to be here."

"What do you mean?" she asked, not quite following him, and hoping he kept his explanation simple and didn't wander off into something psychological and over her head.

"I just mean *this Jeff*"—he made a little face of distaste— "may have been a mistake, and your life might be hard right now, but Tim's not a mistake, and I don't think you should let all this old history be so big in your mind anymore."

"What do you mean?" she asked again.

Dr. Golding breathed in and out, seemed to search for the right words, and finally spoke. "You seem to think you deserve whatever happens to you now because you believe you messed up your life." He looked across at her, calm and steady. "I guess I'm saying I don't agree. Whatever your parents think about the decisions you've made, you've done the best you could to be a good mother and a good person, to make a happy home for Tim, and from what I've seen, I think those efforts have turned out pretty well."

Maggie listened to Dr. Golding's words of praise, and felt as if a warm and soothing stream had just overflowed its banks inside her. It felt like water poured on parched ground, quenching some thirst she hadn't even known she'd had.

Dr. Golding wasn't finished, though. "You said before that you believed *this Jeff* would make things right." His face was serious and the dimples were just lines on each side of his mouth. "But I think that was wrong," he said. "I think *you've* made things right."

Maggie could feel her eyes starting to burn, and she looked away. Dr. Golding dipped his head a little lower, moved into her line of vision, and made her meet his eyes. His blue eyes and his voice were soft. "You're the one who's made them right," he repeated.

Neither one of them said anything for a minute or two. Maggie was afraid she would cry again. She couldn't remember the last time someone had praised her, and especially not this kind of praise—deep and genuine, and seeming to approve of who she really was, underneath all the mistakes and shortcomings.

"Thank you," she finally said, and dabbed at her nose with her napkin.

"You're welcome," he said quietly, and there was another minute or two of silence.

"Anyway"—Maggie cleared her throat—"Jeff and I parted company then. My parents wanted me to come home to Georgia, but somehow I felt like that would be giving up, and besides, it was only part of a package," she said, remembering Bobby Semple, "so instead I found an apartment over the garage of an old couple in El Cerrito and took a job at a bank there. Mr. Conroy, Bill, was a retired policeman, and he and his wife were like parents to me."

"What made you move to Oakland, then?"

"Bill died, and Millie sold the house. She cried, and said she felt like she was turning us out of our home, but she had to do it," Maggie said quietly. "She needed the money to live on, and she couldn't keep it up. She was diabetic, and her health was going."

"Do you still see her?" Dr. Golding asked quietly.

"She died last spring."

Neither of them said anything for a minute. "Anyway," she went on, "Tim was three when Bill died and we moved. We both really miss them. Bill was like a daddy to Tim, carried him around all the time. They took care of him when he was sick and I had to work." Maggie stopped and got herself under control again. She tried not to think of Bill and Millie for just this reason.

"I realize now how much I depended on both of them. Now that they're gone," she said.

Dr. Golding reached across the table and covered her hand with his. Maggie held it tight for a minute, then felt embarrassed, and let it go.

"So then you moved to Oakland," he finished for her.

Maggie nodded. "The secretary's job at the Bank of Northern California came open just about the time I had to move anyway. It paid more money than the teller job I had, at least I thought it would, but you know that story. The other thing I didn't realize was how much of a break Bill and Millie were giving me on the rent," she said. "I pay more now than I did then, and Oakland is still the best I can afford. Anyway"—she made a little face—"moving there seemed like a good idea at the time. The apartment is close to the BART and the bus line, and it didn't seem as bad as Richmond, which was my other choice. But I do hate raising Tim there. I guess I didn't make a good decision." Now that the facts were laid out it seemed like the obvious conclusion.

"You made the best decision you could at the time," Dr. Golding reminded her.

"Yes," she said after thinking a moment. "You're right." She felt the guilt slide off her shoulders like a heavy coat. "I did."

She gathered momentum and rolled on to the subject of Bobby Semple. "There's a boy at home who wants to marry me," she said, "and sometimes I get so frightened at the thought of Tim living his whole life in Oakland, smelling exhaust and having nowhere to play, that I think about calling him." She looked at Dr. Golding, surprised she had told him, but glad somehow that it was out, the decision she had struggled with off and on for the past year, whenever she couldn't pay the rent on time, or they ate hot dogs and beans for the third night in a row. Dr. Golding's eyes got a little wider, but he didn't say anything. "By the time I save enough to move," Maggie continued, "Tim's childhood might be over." The bleakness of that thought almost canceled out her optimistic feelings.

Dr. Golding looked at her without saying anything for another minute. "Do you love him?" he finally asked.

"No," said Maggie without hesitation, thinking of the monthly letters they still exchanged, Bobby's full of crude humor and stories about the guys at the peanut plant, tales of hunting and drinking, and always ending with the exhortation that she should come home, "but sometimes I wonder if it matters all that much."

"What do you mean?"

"I mean, there are things in life besides being in love. Good things—like giving your children a father, and building something instead of just—I don't know." She could feel her face heat up again. "Just getting by. And it's so hard to know what to do sometimes. It would help so much if I had someone to talk to. Sometimes I think it would be worth marrying just to have someone there to bounce things off of."

"I'm pretty solid." Dr. Golding smiled at her. "Try bouncing them off me."

Maggie smiled in spite of herself. Solid is just how she thought of Dr. Golding.

"Well, it sounds silly, but little things bother me," she admitted.

"Give me an example."

"Okay." Maggie felt embarrassed, but she said the first thing she could think of. "I wonder if I should let Tim wear that Superman cape all the time. I mean, he never takes it off except to take a bath. I made it for him just for fun, and I thought it was okay, but my friend Gina says it's a sign of maladjustment—that he's trying to escape his life by assuming another personality. That I should have him evaluated."

Dr. Golding was grinning. "I'm sorry." He shook his head. "My dad read to us from this book, *The Adventures of Zorro*, every night after dinner. When I was"—he stopped and looked at the ceiling—"let's see, Joe was in first grade, so I must have been about Tim's age. Anyway, we begged my mom to make us Zorro masks."

Maggie smiled. "Did she?"

"Oh yeah." Dr. Golding nodded. "If you knew my mom, you'd know the answer to that question. Yeah, she sat at her sewing machine for a couple of hours with some old black material she found. Made a mask for Joe, and me, and even for Danny, who was only one. She asked my sister if she wanted one, but Shelley said no, she was going to be Senorita Rodriguez, she wanted a black lace veil. So my mom cut up one of her slips. Anyway"—Dr. Golding played with his spoon—"we wore those things for a year, I swear."

"But you didn't wear them day and night."

"Pretty much."

"But you were playing with your brothers and sister. Gina says Tim wearing it when he's by himself means he's creating a fantasy world."

Dr. Golding laughed loudly and shook his head. "Well, of course he's creating a fantasy world. That's what being a kid is all about. Who is this friend of yours? What are her qualifications, anyway?"

Maggie looked at him, surprised. "You know her," she said. "She saw you last year—Gina Tucci."

Dr. Golding looked surprised himself. "Right," he said. He was quiet for a minute, stirring his coffee. Then he met her eyes again and smiled. "Look, Maggie," he said, "don't worry about Tim. I can tell you he's a great kid. You're doing a good job raising him."

Maggie let her breath out and relaxed against the back of her chair. "Really? You think so?"

"I know so."

She felt relief run over her like water. Dr. Golding ought to know. He was a trained psychologist, after all. Now that she thought about it, she wondered why she had ever worried about Gina's opinions, but when they piled onto the twenty other things that circled around her head at night as she lay in bed, they felt heavy enough to sink her spirit.

"Besides"—Dr. Golding leaned back in his chair, and smiled, laced his fingers behind his neck—"my dad used to say, 'If you can't be a kid when you are a kid, when can you be a kid?'"

Maggie laughed. "That was a mouthful."

"Words to live by."

They were smiling at each other again.

"More coffee?" The waitress appeared with the steaming pot, and refilled their cups without waiting for them to answer.

"Is there more to your life story?" Dr. Golding asked when she left.

"Where did I leave off?"

"You'd just moved to Oakland."

"Right." Maggie looked past Dr. Golding to the street outside Ghirardelli Square. She felt the freshness sweep over her again, the way it had the day after her first session with him, as she walked past the performing arts center and saw the banners for the concerts and art show, and not even a reminder of

Oakland and the Embarcadero Arms could take the feeling away. "I'd like to finish school and paint," she said, suddenly bold. "And sometimes I have this daydream, of a place where I could live, a place for Tim to run around and play. Like we were a real family," she said.

"Yeah?" Dr. Golding's face lit up. "Tell me what it would look like."

"What? The family?"

"No, the place."

Maggie laughed and shook her head at Dr. Golding's odd question. It must be some kind of technique, like—if you were an animal, what would you be? If you could build a house, what would it look like? If you were a car, would you be a Rolls-Royce or a Volkswagen? She never knew which part of their talks were therapy and which were conversation, which was probably his intention, she realized. She took a minute to compose her answer and tried to be complete. "Well, it would be something rustic, a house or a cabin out in the country, with a fireplace and a stone chimney."

Dr. Golding smiled. "No mansion in Pacific Heights? No estate in Sausalito?"

"No mansion." Maggie smiled. "But there would be plenty of room for Tim to run and play, and a tire swing, and maybe a pond or a lake to play in. No, maybe not a lake," she amended, remembering that Tim didn't know how to swim.

Dr. Golding's smile was broader now. "What else?"

Maggie grinned. "Is this part of my therapy?"

"Absolutely."

"Not much else."

"There's something else," Dr. Golding cajoled, smiling. "What do you see when you close your eyes?"

She smiled back and closed them. "A big front porch. With a swing and a rocking chair."

"That's it?"

"That's it."

"Nothing else?"

"A studio with my paints." Maggie felt her face heat up and wondered how complete she needed to be.

"Come on," he said. "Don't leave anything out."

"That's all," she said, her eyes still closed.

"Who's inside?" he asked after a pause.

She opened her eyes to look, but Dr. Golding's were closed as if he were seeing it, too.

"Me and Tim, and a husband, and another baby," she blurted, then wanted to close her eyes again, she was so embarrassed. She felt exposed, like in those dreams she had where she looked down at herself in a crowd and noticed she was naked. The stupid things she thought of when she was falling asleep at night were hardly what he was interested in hearing. But what did she know? Maybe this was what therapy was all about. Dr. Golding, his eyes open now, certainly didn't look embarrassed.

"Anyway . . ." Her voice trailed off. "That's my daydream. Which is why I think of going back to Georgia and marrying Bobby. It might not be a cottage in the country, but at least Tim would have a dad, and a place to run and play."

Dr. Golding sat up and leaned forward as if she had said something incredibly significant. His forearms looked too big for the little table and his face was just a few inches away from hers. The little scar was white against the slight sunburn on his face. "But do you want to go back to Georgia and marry this guy?" he asked, his expression intense. "I mean, is that really what you want to do?"

"No." She said it quickly without having to consider. She looked at Jake Golding for a minute. Neither of them was smiling now. "But I can't see myself living the rest of my life like this." Her voice sounded flat and grim.

Dr. Golding looked troubled, and seemed to be about to say something else, but he didn't. He just looked at her and nodded.

* * *

This was going too far. Jake realized it even as he drove up 101 past Petaluma and Santa Rosa and then into Sebastopol, that cross between small-town America and the New Age. He passed the sign at the end of the shop-lined boulevard that said NU-CLEAR FREE ZONE and chuckled. He could never read it without imagining intercontinental ballistic missiles being rotated a few degrees in the other direction when the Kremlin got news that the Sebastopol City Council had passed their resolution.

He parked his truck in front of Waldo's Masonry. He was going too far, but instead of feeling inhibited, he felt energized. He hopped from the cab of the truck and went inside.

It took his eyes a few minutes to get used to the dim light. Waldo was there. He was behind the counter, leaning back in the tilting desk chair, watching *Sally Jessy Raphaël,* and eating a sub sandwich.

He looked up when Jake entered. "Hey, man, how's it going?"

"Going good," Jake answered, and realized it was true.

Waldo got up and clicked off *Sally Jessy,* then motioned Jake to come behind the counter.

Jake pulled up a chair, straddled it, and waited for Waldo to finish his sandwich.

"What's up, man?" Waldo asked.

Jake looked Waldo over and grinned. Waldo had gotten frozen in the sixties somewhere, and still spoke like he had in the Summer of Love. Today his long gray hair was twisted up in a thin Navajo bun. He had on a Harley-Davidson T-shirt and a pair of dirty Wranglers that didn't quite hang on to his hips. "I've got a job for you," Jake answered him. "You got time?"

Waldo wadded up the sandwich wrapper and aimed it for the trash can in the corner. It missed, and joined a little pile of other paper wads on the floor. "Nothing but time," Waldo grinned.

* * *

Maggie came through the door of Happy Campers Preschool a good twenty minutes later than she usually did. Tim was in the back row of a circle of kids grouped around the television. He wore his coat and backpack.

"*Pokémon*'s almost over," Tim said, using the four-year-old's version of timekeeping to measure her lateness. Mrs. Greavey at the day care let the children watch cartoons during pick-up hour, from five to six, and Maggie usually arrived just as *Pokémon* was beginning.

"I got to watch almost all of it today," he said, and didn't sound as if he'd wasted any energy wondering what had delayed her, so Maggie decided not to feel guilty for the stop she'd made at home, which had put her off schedule. She changed the subject instead.

"Do you want to go to McDonald's and get a Happy Meal for dinner?" she asked him.

"You bet I do," Tim said, squinting another smile, and Maggie recognized an exact quote of Dr. Golding's answer when Tim had asked him if he promised to come back. She wondered how many times Tim had replayed the conversation in his mind.

"Here," she said, holding out her hand for his backpack, "you can watch the rest of *Pokémon,* and I'll watch for the bus." He went back to the braided rug and sat down again, Happy Campers Preschool style.

"Crisscross applesauce," was how Mrs. Greavey reminded them to cross their legs. "And hands on your knees, so you're not bothering your neighbor," she would say. Tim crossed his legs and carefully positioned his hands. His cape was bunched inside the neck of his jacket. Maggie looked over the little crowd of children and wondered which one had teased Tim about wearing it. They all seemed to be getting along fine now. She turned back toward the glass-fronted door and watched for the bus.

It was right on time, and fortunately coincided with the closing credits of *Pokémon.* She and Tim took a seat up front so he could see, rode for five minutes or so, then got off right by the Kmart. At the McDonald's next door, Maggie ordered two Happy Meals and paid with the crisp hundred-dollar bill she had taken from the cookie jar after work, feeling like a daring thief. She held out her hand for what seemed like forever while the cashier counted back her change.

The two of them ate their burgers and chatted, and then Maggie gave Tim the little Hot Wheels race car that came with her meal. He zoomed and crashed the two of them all evening as he rode around Kmart in the shopping cart, making an obstacle course that became more formidable with every new item Maggie piled around him.

She bought three pillows—bright reddish orange, pink, and blue—a cobalt blue area rug, some terra-cotta pots, and four big plants—a Boston fern, a spider plant, a philodendron, and an asparagus fern. She picked out some unfinished frames for

$1.99 apiece and some wildly colored place mats, choosing three of them after a moment's hesitation. She bought a bottle of Murphy Oil Soap, a new book for Tim, and a new game for both of them to play—Hi Ho! Cherry-O. And then, feeling especially reckless, she picked out a box of bath salts. Aromatherapy. Lavender for relaxation.

It was past Tim's bedtime when they got home, but he didn't seem any more tired than she was so they played the new game, the object of which was to get all of your neighbor's little plastic cherries. Tim won. Maggie wondered how many of the little fruits she would find under couch cushions, or never find at all, as they joined missing socks, the television remote control, and little plastic pieces of the Lite-Brite and Mouse Trap games in some household twilight zone. It was all right, she rationalized. When he lost the little plastic cherries they could still play the game using dry beans instead.

"Let's play again," he said, already setting up the pieces.

"We'll play tomorrow," she said as firmly as she could. "It's time for bed."

"Do I have to take a bath?" he countered.

Maggie hesitated and looked at his eyes, hopeful and magnified even larger because of his glasses. Her household routines had been a sort of glue that she used to hold their lives together. Maybe it was time to relax a little, she thought. She inspected Tim's hair, considered for a moment, then smiled. "No," she said. "You can go to school dirty tomorrow."

He expressed his joy by taking a few bounces on the couch, followed by a flying leap onto the floor.

"All right," she warned, "settle down." She waited for Mr. Jacobsen to pound, but he must have credited Dr. Golding's bonus points to her account.

"Come get your medicine," she said to Tim, and she took the bottle from the refrigerator and shook it while he flew over, actually bounced, from couch to recliner to kitchen chair.

"There's hot lava down there," he said, and tucked his feet safely under him while Maggie measured out the pink liquid and poured it into his mouth.

"Now, go get in bed," she said again, and tried to sound severe. "I really mean it," she said. "I'll be in there in a minute."

"I'm going," he said, then followed the same tortured path he'd taken toward her, only this time in reverse.

Finally, hot lava or no, Maggie had him tucked into bed, his glasses on the table beside him along with the Nestlé rabbit mug full of water and a few of the cherry cough drops. She kissed him good night and listened to his prayers, took a few seconds to lean against the living room wall and consider, then went into action.

She moved all the furniture into the kitchen and her bedroom, then ripped up the green shag carpet. Fortunately, it hadn't been professionally laid, so there wasn't any glue, and not many tacks. She pulled out the few there were with a pair of pliers, then rolled up the carpet. She dragged it out the door and down the stairs as quietly as she could, a difficult project since it kept coming unrolled and she had to stop and get it back under control every step or two. At one point the comic aspects of her situation presented themselves and she started to laugh. Sweating and out of breath, she finally succeeded in wrestling it out to the garbage cans. Mr. Jacobsen, who was also the management company's snitch, would probably have a field day, but who cared, she thought with an abandon she hadn't felt in years.

She climbed back up the stairs, feeling as though she'd had a good workout. The floor, she was surprised to find, was actually in fairly good shape. She vacuumed, finally earning a thump on the ceiling from Mr. Jacobsen. She ignored him. She mixed up a bucket of hot water and the wood soap and scrubbed the floorboards, changing the water twice, and almost danced with impatience while she waited for it to dry. Then she unrolled the new area rug. The room already looked a hundred percent better.

She moved the dark furniture back in, stood back and studied the room, then went to the closet and dug through a few more boxes until she found the granny square afghan and patchwork quilt she had stowed away. The afghan was one of a steady supply her mother turned out and pressed on friends and relatives. The quilt was something she had made herself in high school home ec class. Maybe not chic, but with one on the back of the couch and the other on the recliner there were two more splashes of color in the drab little room.

Maggie pulled the price tags off the new pillows along with the little tags that said not to remove under penalty of law, and tossed the pillows onto the couch and chairs, letting them lay as they landed. She took the picture frames from their bags, peeled off the price stickers, then carried them to her tiny studio area, and, humming all the while, painted the cheap, plain wood to match the colors that buzzed in the room—warm yellow, cobalt blue, spice red, and hot pink.

It was ten o'clock when she finished with them, and she knew she ought to go to bed. Instead she drifted to her radio in the kitchen and found some music. The classical station seemed too composed for the way she was feeling so she twirled the knob until she heard a saxophone and piano. Then she went to her little studio, took out her brush and the paper she'd stretched, and began to paint.

She squeezed out some cerulean blue and cadmium red onto the palette, getting back the familiar feel of the brush in her hand, on the palette, on the paper, and wondered why she had given up on her art. Part of the reason was the grimness that had seemed to dog her for the last few years, that much was true. But she knew that wasn't the only reason.

She thought about what Dr. Golding had said yesterday. About how she seemed to feel she deserved anything bad that happened because she'd messed up her life. She wondered now if she hadn't felt the opposite of that as well—that she didn't deserve the good things, and mustn't enjoy them. She thought about her abstinence from her art, the black and white world she'd consigned herself to, and saw it for what it was—a sort of self-punishment. She had disappointed others, so she would deny herself the things she loved—color and beauty and light.

She brushed the paint onto the paper and almost felt the colors refresh her tired eyes. She remembered what Dr. Golding had said—that it might have been a mistake that got her to this point in life, but her life wasn't a mistake now—and she felt the soothing warmth in her chest again. She didn't have to give up the things she loved, she thought, and felt as wealthy as if Dr. Golding had given her a handful of gold instead of just a cup of coffee and a few words.

Maggie worked until nearly midnight, then washed out her brushes. She would finish her painting tomorrow. She drew a hot bath and tossed in a handful of the new bath salts, and decided that the next time she went to the store she would buy a scented candle.

Finally she couldn't think of any more excuses to stay up, no matter how much fun she was having. Besides, she told herself, the alarm would go off at the same time in the morning whether she was having a good time or not. She checked her locks, as she'd promised Dr. Golding she would, then went to bed. She lay there in the dark, though, for a few more minutes, savored her good feelings, and listened. It was one of the few times the building was absolutely quiet. For a few seconds she didn't even hear a car pass by and the kids in the lot across the street must have moved somewhere else for the evening.

Then, like an unexpected ambush, as if some part of her couldn't stand the fact that she was happy, she was suddenly seized with a feeling of panic. The little voice she hadn't heard in days started in on her. What if the bonus fell through? it asked her. She had spent a hundred dollars today. Half of her savings was gone. What if she got sick or had an accident and couldn't work?

She lay there, feeling her heart speed up, but then, just as if she suddenly realized that she didn't have to do an assignment, or woke up and remembered it was Saturday and she didn't have to go to work, she knew she didn't have to worry, either. The voice inside her head went away as abruptly as if she'd pulled a plug, and Maggie rolled over and was asleep before she could even imagine her cottage.

7

Work was a distraction today, a necessary time away from what Maggie would rather be doing. She flew through it, then came home, scrambled some eggs and toast for their dinner, then picked up right where she'd left off the night before. She even got a little accomplished before Tim went to bed. Mrs. Weaver was outside watering her flowers and offered to watch him ride his Big Wheel on the sidewalk.

"I'll keep an eye on him," she said to Maggie. "You go on in and take some time for yourself."

Maggie thanked her and agreed, without even feeling guilty.

The picture frames she'd painted were dry so she took her portfolio from the closet, chose four of her favorite paintings, and put them in the new frames. They looked wonderful. She even found a bright blue vase she had made in a pottery class— definitely not her area of expertise, but sitting on the coffee table it looked jaunty rather than lopsided and thick. After Tim was in bed and it was good and dark she crept downstairs and stole just a few lilacs from Mr. Jacobsen's patch of yard. Just a few, she told herself, and excused it on the grounds that the bush belonged to the landlord.

She painted the terra-cotta pots with crazy designs and flowers in the same colors as the frames, and after she dried them, hurrying them along with the hair dryer, she potted her plants Then she needed to sweep and clean the kitchen, since there was potting soil everywhere. When she was finished she put out two of the new place mats, and made herself some tea.

She picked the red Fiestaware mug this time, and sipped slowly. She finished it, not hurrying, and then, even though it was late, she felt like painting again, so she went to her table, adjusted the angle of the lamp so it shone directly onto the paper and began to add the details to the painting she'd begun the night before.

It fairly vibrated with color. Like her life. She felt as if everything about her had changed, and not just her apartment. Her entire existence had gone from black and white to color in what seemed an instant, just like that moment in the movie when Dorothy stepped out of the storm-ruined house into the land of Oz. It must be she who had changed, she realized, but the universe she was arranging around herself now seemed a galaxy away from the one she had floated through alone before she had met Jake Golding.

She didn't dread work anymore now that Mr. Brinnon wasn't breathing down her neck. She found herself smiling and talking to her coworkers, and today she had even taken a real lunch break and joined them in the employee lunchroom, instead of hiding from Mr. Brinnon in the mailroom, alone with her sandwich and apple.

At the afternoon break she'd asked one of the other secretaries,

Leann, if she'd like to take a short walk. They'd walked and talked for fifteen minutes or so, around the block and back. Leann was a single mom, too, and Maggie had decided to ask her if she wanted to take the kids for a picnic some weekend soon. Maybe to Lake Merritt. Maybe they could even rent a rowboat.

Tim's throat and ears were okay for the moment, his surgery was scheduled, and all without asking her parents for help. Even Gina wasn't so irritating, now that Maggie had come to the realization that she was just like Mr. Brinnon, in a different way. Always holding her hostage to something, in this case the thousand she had insisted was a gift, no strings attached. It had been disappointing at first to realize that Gina wasn't really her friend, but freeing in a way, too. A huge relief had swept over her, and a kind of weight dropped off. She wasn't crazy after all. You were supposed to feel good with your friends. Like she felt with Dr. Golding.

And here she was painting again. She stepped back and took a critical look at the scene on her paper. It was Ghirardelli Square, with the bricks hot red and the sky bright blue and the plants a buzzing green. It was good, she admitted to herself.

In her mind she called up the scene and began humming along to the music as she brushed in the highlights and shading. The only other sounds were the ticking of the Seth Thomas clock her mother had given her when she left home, and the soft sound of her brush on the paper. The room faded away and everything became slightly unfocused except the work she was doing. She had no idea how long she'd been concentrating, when the telephone's ring, shrill and insistent, jarred her back into reality.

Maggie hesitated, brush in the air. She was tempted to let it ring, but even though Mr. Jacobsen had been friendlier since Dr. Golding had visited she didn't want to press her luck. He hated ringing phones. And she thought she knew who it was. No one else besides Gina would call this late. She stood there another few seconds, through two more piercing jangles, then sighed and picked it up.

"Maggie. I'm glad I caught you." It was Gina. She went on without waiting for Maggie to answer. "Listen. We need to talk."

"About what?" Maggie still held her palette, not ready to surrender to the interruption.

"About this whole therapy thing. Look, I have some concerns, and I think you need to hear them."

Maggie sighed. She knew Gina hadn't been happy for the past few days. It was almost as if she had sent Maggie to therapy so she could take some kind of credit for it, and now she was displeased that things were going so well without her input. As if she would rather be needed than have Maggie be happy.

"Okay. But I'm kind of busy right now."

"Doing what?" Gina demanded.

"What's that supposed to mean?" Maggie's voice sounded sharp, even to herself.

"I mean what could you be doing that's so important?"

"I'm painting." Maggie kept an even tone, though it took effort.

"Oh." Gina dismissed the activity with one word. "Look," she said.

Maggie braced herself. Whenever Gina said *Look* like that, it meant a lecture was coming.

"Look," Gina repeated. "I'm concerned about the way your therapy is going."

"You mentioned that." Maggie was surprised at herself, but

it was getting harder to excuse Gina's rudeness in the name of concern. She gave up on making it a quick conversation and set the palette down on the table.

Gina didn't seem to notice her irritation. "This is nothing like my Overhaul, or like what Dr. Golding described in his book," she went on.

"Well, I think it's going fine." Maggie put down the brush, too, and rubbed the back of her neck.

"I'm not sure you're qualified to judge that."

Maggie felt an unexpected heat. "That's right," she answered, "it's only my life."

"Hey," said Gina, her voice heating up as well. "I'm the one with experience here, and I'm the one who found this guy."

And paid for it, Maggie knew she was thinking.

"And I feel a certain responsibility."

"Well, you don't need to." Maggie was surprised at the firmness of her tone.

"Oh, excuse me." Gina was on one of her tears now. "Are you telling me once I've paid, my services will no longer be needed?"

There. It was out. Maggie gave her head a little shake and kept her tone even. She realized the first check she would write from the retroactive pay would be to Gina. "All I'm saying is that I feel better than I have in years. I'm sorry if what Dr. Golding is doing isn't what you expected."

"He's taking advantage of you."

"He is *not*." Maggie was fully irritated now.

"Coming to your house, for God's sake!"

"It was just that once," said Maggie, "and nothing happened. It's not like he seduced me or anything."

"And taking you out for coffee!"

"His office was being remodeled." Maggie was sorry she had ever described her meetings with Dr. Golding to Gina.

"That's what he *told* you."

"Gina, I saw it myself."

"Right. Did you actually see walls torn down? Did you hear hammering?"

Come to think of it she hadn't, just the men in work clothes measuring and marking. She refused to give Gina the satisfaction, though. "He's telling the truth, Gina. Why would he lie?"

"Oh, Maggie." Gina's tone was full of scorn. "You are such a child."

That was it. The words were out before she had a chance to stop them, like they, along with her apartment, had decided to take on a life of their own. "Look," she said. "I don't really care what you think." She didn't give Gina a chance to answer. "And frankly, I resent your implications, both that Dr. Golding is a man of poor character, and that I'm too stupid to know that. He's a fine man, and he's helping me a lot. And as I told you, I'm busy right now. I'm hanging up." She did hang up then, hard. She didn't even say good-bye.

She stood there, looked at the phone resting in its cradle, waiting for it to let loose with another shrill cry, like a demanding baby. Nothing. She stood a moment longer, and realized, unlike in times past, she wasn't feeling a sweeping wave of remorse for having lost her temper. In fact, she felt just fine. Not even a frontal assault by Gina could take away her warm feelings. The clock ticked on, undisturbed.

She picked up her brush and palette and went back to inspect her painting. It was finished, Maggie realized, and resisted the temptation to fuss with it anymore. She tidied up her little studio, then looked around her apartment again and smiled.

It fairly begged to be shown off, she thought, and for the first time in years she wanted to invite people into her life. She wanted to show them how she was feeling. She'd already noticed a difference even in the way she moved around her neighborhood. Instead of just scurrying from the bus stop to her front door like a scared rabbit, today she'd slowed down and looked around her. The houses weren't really all that bad. Even though they needed a new coat of paint, when Maggie squinted her eyes a little they were quite picturesque. Behind the two-story with the car hulks was a beautiful oak tree covered with clematis vines blooming purple, and the house next to it, although the porch was sagging, had a lush vegetable garden. There were a few dark spots, sure, she admitted, like the burned-out building, but even the empty lot had a fine stand of wild daisies.

The woman who lived on the corner was sitting on her front step smoking and reading a book when she and Tim had passed by, and Maggie surprised herself by saying hello. The woman smiled and raised her hand in greeting. At the house with the pit bulls, the dogs were nowhere in sight and the father was mowing the lawn with a push mower. He paused when they walked by and jerked his head in greeting. She didn't even know his name, she realized, and he lived just one house down from the Embarcadero Arms.

Everything had changed, she realized again, still slightly mystified. And here she was, wanting to have company, and without a conscious plan she'd even taken the first little steps in that direction. She'd detoured by the Safeway this evening and brought home as much as she could carry. She'd bought two brownie mixes, on sale for ninety-nine cents each, and the makings for chili. Maybe she would have a dinner this weekend. Invite the neighbors over. Even Mr. Jacobsen, she thought. Why not?

She smiled again as she washed out her brushes and laid them on a paper towel on the kitchen counter. She could do it Friday and invite Dr. Golding. She shook her head at that thought. Even though it filled her with pleasant anticipation, maybe that was going too far. Besides, Gina would really go ballistic about that.

She gave a little frown and wondered if Gina was right. Maybe this whole friendship with Dr. Golding was illicit somehow. But she didn't feel illicit. She gave the counter a swipe with the dishrag and hummed to herself as she dried her hands and gave them a squirt of lotion. She felt happy. For the first time in years. She thought again of Jake driving the truck across the Bay Bridge and swinging it into the parking lot of the Happy Campers Preschool, his easy patter with Tim, and the way he spoke to her neighbors. Even Mr. Jacobsen. She smiled, remembering.

There was nothing wrong with her friendship with Dr. Golding, no matter what Gina said. She felt certain about that. But asking him to dinner? Maggie shook her head and turned off the lights, taking one more look at the apartment before she did. Maybe that would be going too far.

* * *

Gina sat staring at the phone for a full minute after Maggie hung up on her, her breath coming in hard little pants.

Maggie had hung up on her. She shook her head, hardly believing it. She thought of all the things she had done for Maggie over the last year, each outraged thought joining the next until, like a rapidly expanding funnel cloud, she had worked herself into a swirling fury.

She sat in the chair by the telephone, almost trembling as she reviewed the conversation, the twisting rage all the while gaining strength and about to touch down.

"That little bitch," she said, and the words erased a year of fumbling friendship. She got up and found her purse, dug through it for her address book. She found the number for the investigator she had used for her divorce, punched it in, listened for a few moments, then clicked her tongue in irritation when she got a machine. Somehow she'd expected him to answer, even at eleven thirty in the evening.

"This is Gina Tucci," she said in a hard little voice after the tone. "I have something I want you to investigate. Call me as soon as possible." She gave her home, office, and cell phone numbers, then hung up and sat down again, still steaming from Maggie's insurrection.

She was Caesar and Maggie was Brutus. She could almost feel the knife sliding between her ribs. She was Dr. Frankenstein, watching in horror as his well-intended project turned on him. She tried to follow the train of thought, but it was becoming too much of an effort to think of parallels. The point, she assured herself, was that Maggie had turned on her. Maggie had greedily taken her generous help and then, showing all the loyalty of a—a cat—no, that wasn't good enough, showing all the loyalty of a—a snake, that was more accurate—showing all the loyalty of a snake, she had coiled up and bitten her. Gina looked at her hand, almost as if she expected to see twin fang marks and red streaks.

She thought of the meals she had bought, preferring not to dwell on Maggie's initial refusals and offers to cook for them at home. She thought of the toys she had bought for Tim, not thinking of them as the buy-off price of a few minutes of quiet conversation with his mother. That wasn't the point, she thought. The point was that she had tried to help Maggie, *at great personal cost*. And this was the thanks she got.

"I can't believe she's acting like this," she repeated to herself once again, the memory of Maggie's words stinging. She cast back to rehear them. She frowned. Now that she tried to remember specifics, the worst thing she could remember Maggie saying was that she didn't care what Gina thought. But there was more, she was sure. There must be. She would remember later, when she had calmed down. She was beginning to calm down even now, she realized. Her breath was coming slower, and her pulse was almost back to normal.

She felt her initial fury settle neatly into the shape her action had given it. She would find out what was going on. She would end this friendship, or whatever it was Maggie had wormed out of Dr. Golding. Not that she really thought Maggie had initiated it. Now that she had cooled a little, even Gina realized how ludicrous that thought was. Maggie was so innocent and naive Gina knew that would never happen. But people like Maggie were dead in the water when it came to sharks like Golding. They might as well walk into his office wearing a sandwich board that said WILLING VICTIM. No, she realized, her venom and blame congealing and finding a new target, Maggie was too lame to have initiated this affair or whatever was going on. Dr. Jason Solomon Golding was behind this.

She would bring him down. She had paid one thousand dollars and for what, for him to move in on her friend? Inside her, a thought floated without ever coming into full focus. That Dr. Golding hadn't displayed any romantic interest in her. Barely any interest at all. She recalled what Maggie had told her. Visits to the apartment. Ghirardelli Square. What did that slimy creep think he was doing? She shook her head, snatched the phone off the receiver, and regardless of the fact that she'd just left a message, punched in the number again. She imagined Carson Fuller, like the rest of the world, to exist in some kind of suspended animation until she called him into life by needing his services. She left another message and replaced the phone in its cradle with an impatient toss.

She leaned back in the chair, her initial rage at Maggie homing in for a direct hit on the new target she'd selected. She would bring Golding down, she thought, with the intensity of a vow. She would show him. Nobody messed with Gina Tucci.

8

Thursday, April 30

Lindsay ducked into the executive washroom on her way to Starbucks for her midmorning latte. She checked her makeup, fluffed her hair with her fingers, and nodded wisely at her own reflection, glad again that she had waited for the universe to validate her decision. She had first come to it last Saturday, when she was so upset, but she knew better than to make serious, life-affecting choices when she was feeling that way, so she had faithfully practiced her tai chi and meditated on the problem every day to let the universe know she was ready for a solution. *When the student is ready the teacher will come,* she repeated to herself, admiring the fullness of her lips as she shaped the words. She applied one more touch of lipstick and blotted them, then refocused her attention. She was ready.

She waited, though, until she had finished her coffee and was back in her office to make the call. She hung up her coat, shut her door, flicking the lock so that new secretary wouldn't disturb her, then sat down and punched in the number. She twirled the cord between her fingers as she waited.

"Cooper-Jackson Construction." It was Val, the secretary.

"Lindsay Hunt. I'm looking for Jake."

"Oh, hi, Lindsay."

Lindsay ignored the greeting, and waited for the information she wanted.

Val apparently realized Lindsay wasn't in the mood for small talk after nothing but silence for a minute. Then Lindsay heard her say, "Is Jake at that psychologist's office?" The sound was muffled, as if Val had her palm over the receiver, and though usually that would have irritated Lindsay, today she strained to hear.

"Psychologist's office?" Lindsay said sharply. "What psychologist?"

The girl wasn't listening. Lindsay could hear her talking again to someone else, probably that black woman.

"What psychologist are you talking about?" she repeated, louder this time.

Val came back. "Did you say something?"

"What psychologist are you talking about?" Lindsay tried to keep her voice calm.

"I think his name is Golding or Guldin, or something like that," Val said. "I can give you the number if you want."

More background noise now, the hand over the receiver again. "Lindsay Hunt," she heard Val say to someone. She assumed the other person was asking who wanted to know. Val came back. "I'm sorry, Ms. Hunt, I guess maybe I was wrong."

"Give me that number you mentioned." Lindsay used her authoritative tone, which usually worked with secretaries and other subordinates. It didn't this time.

"I'll leave him a message and have him call you," Val said. "Bye." She hung up.

Lindsay hung up herself, then sat just thinking for a minute. So this was the universe's answer. Jake was in therapy. She couldn't believe it. And he hadn't wanted anyone to know. Why else all the secrecy? She smiled. How like him to be embarrassed about doing his personal work. She shook her head, though, hardly able to believe he had finally taken her advice. Maybe losing her had been the push he needed. And besides, she reminded herself, she had known the forces would converge to answer the questions she had put out to the universe.

She pulled open her bottom drawer and took out the fat San Francisco Yellow Pages, then leafed through them until she found the listing. There it was, just under the ad for PSYCH TO GO, HELP WHEN YOU NEED IT, WHERE YOU NEED IT. She read Golding's advertisement carefully. DR. JASON SOLOMON GOLDING, PH.D., and under his name in bold letters, FEEL GOOD NOW! And a list of questions: DO YOU HATE TO GET UP IN THE MORNING? DO YOU FEEL OTHERS ARE BETTER THAN YOU? DO YOU DESERVE HAPPINESS? COME AND GET IT!

She was familiar with Jason Golding, of course. He was one of the best therapists in San Francisco. At the last party she'd gone to one group was buzzing about his new book, and talking about taking his rebirthing seminars. She wanted to see him herself, if she could ever find the time.

She had a flash of insight then, and sat motionless, telephone book still in her lap, her mouth dropping open. Suddenly the picture she'd been laboring to make out snapped into perfect focus. Of course. That was what the universe had intended. It was perfectly clear to her now. She would join Jake in his therapy. They could work through their individual struggles, and then do some joint therapy as a couple.

She looked back down at the ad and punched in Dr. Golding's number, barely able to contain her excitement while it rang. And rang. Finally it switched to voice mail and a woman's voice said Dr. Golding was busy at the moment, left a number to be called in case of emergencies, and invited her to leave a message.

Lindsay dropped the phone into its cradle a little harder than necessary without leaving a message. Even though she knew he was probably seeing Jake, she had the feeling of the active forces being blocked. She would mention it to him when she saw him. Spring for a secretary, she'd tell him, so people in crisis, or riding a crest of life, don't have to leave their names on an answering machine.

Lindsay pushed herself away from the desk and walked over to the picture window. She was twenty-five floors up and on clear days had a panoramic view of San Francisco Bay and Alcatraz. This morning was foggy, and though the mist was beginning to burn off she could still see only as far as the street below her and the nearby buildings. She glanced down again at the address of Dr. Golding's office. It wasn't far, and she had an hour before her next client would arrive. She went to the closet and took her raincoat from the hanger, pocketed the cell phone, and locked her office. It would do her good to take a little walk, she rationalized, even though she'd just gone out for coffee. The work on her desk could wait. Suddenly nothing seemed more important than catching Jake before he left Dr. Golding's office.

She hurried down the hall to the elevator, and felt a little wedge of happiness slice through her at the thought of seeing Jake again. She had missed him, and in spite of his blockish ways there was something about him that she wanted. She tamped down the little stirring of happiness, not quite able to believe he was actually doing it. His personal work. Going to therapy. But hope won. Maybe he did care enough about their relationship to change. She glanced at her watch as the elevator door opened. It was a quarter till eleven, probably the end of Jake's fifty-minute hour. If she hurried she might just catch him leaving his session.

* * *

They had dispensed with the office entirely this time, and Maggie had taken the day off. She could hardly believe it. Dr. Golding had called early that morning and asked her if she could miss work.

"Want to inaugurate a little of that vacation?" he'd asked her.

And feeling as reckless as she had when she'd taken the money from the cookie jar, she'd answered, "Why not?" Mr. Brinnon hadn't even stammered.

Dr. Golding had said to bring some extra clothes for Tim, not to bother with lunch, and to be ready for some walking. She'd stifled the Gina voice in her mind and told herself every new patient was a unique situation.

He picked them up right on time, coming all the way to their apartment in Oakland even though Maggie volunteered to meet him at his office. She had felt a little thrill when she'd opened the door to see him standing there on the worn carpet, waiting for her, his face already creased into a smile.

Tim hung on his elbow all the way down the stairs and every now and then Dr. Golding—Jake—would lift him off the floor by raising his arm. They piled into the truck. Jake opened the door for Maggie, strapped Tim in the seat between them, then reached behind it and brought out a sack.

"Here you go, buddy, this is for you," he said, and handed it to Tim.

It was a book about farms.

"Oh, you didn't have to do that," Maggie protested. Tim had no such modesty. His head was already bent over the book, and he was looking at the pictures.

"I wanted to," Dr. Golding said. His arm was resting on the seat just behind her, and Maggie could almost feel it touching her shoulders.

She tried not to notice it. "What do you say, Tim?" she prompted.

"Thank you!" He gave Dr. Golding one of his beaming smiles, making his full cheeks look even chubbier.

"You're welcome, buddy," Dr. Golding said, rubbed Tim's head, and started up the truck and headed north.

Maggie watched him with quick glances sideways as they passed Richmond's low, flat stucco houses, a liquor store, a storefront church called Miracle Temple. She smiled. At one time she would have made a fervent wish for a miracle of her own as she'd passed it, but now she felt as if one had already been granted.

Tim chattered, alternating his attention between Dr. Golding and the new book. Dr. Golding smiled and nodded down at him from time to time, explaining things seriously in response to his questions, which never seemed to end.

"We're getting ready to cross the bridge, Tim," Dr. Golding said. "Look out there and you can see San Francisco Bay."

Maggie looked herself, and when they emerged into Marin County it was as if they had entered a different world, trading the flat, littered streets for steep hills covered with green velvet grass and dotted with oaks and pines. The morning fog was almost completely gone and the sun was shining brightly. They passed San Quentin, and Dr. Golding pointed it out to Tim. Looking past the prison, Maggie could see huge, expensive houses tucked into the hillside, though the farther north they went, the more the fancy houses were replaced by farms. Cows dotted the hills, still covered in smooth green, and signs by the road announced farms and ranches and offered produce and honey, eggs, apples, and berries for sale. Now and then they passed a vineyard, the rows of grapes climbing the hills like little soldiers. And Maggie felt happiness rising up inside her just being here. She closed her eyes for a moment, listening to Tim's chatter and Dr. Golding's patient answers.

Soon Marin County became Sonoma County, and just south of what the sign said was Petaluma the truck slowed down, and took a turn off the freeway.

"It's just a little west of here," Dr. Golding said, and Maggie smiled and nodded. Dr. Golding had on his jeans and some hiking boots, and a T- Shirt that said WALDO'S MASONRY across the front. He turned toward her and she could see his tanned face and little scar. She smiled again. Every now and then Dr. Golding would run a hand through his short blond hair, and Maggie could see that his hands were square and capable. He was different than what she'd expected, that much was certain. She smiled and realized that she wouldn't change a thing about him, even if she could.

She had done as he had asked, and dressed for walking through tall grass and woods, worn long pants and her running shoes. At first she had been a little nervous, but she was over it now. She supposed it was understandable. This was all so new to her. She had to admit, too, that she was always a little worried that this easy companionship would any minute deteriorate into something stupid, like some of the therapies she'd seen on TV, where people hit each other with foam bats or beat each other with birch rods.

She looked at Dr. Golding again and couldn't imagine him being so silly. He must have felt her eyes on him, because he turned his head toward her and gave her one of his slow smiles. She blushed, wishing again that her skin was a little thicker and didn't show every flux in circulation with blushes or splotches. They were slowing down, and turned off the blacktop highway onto a graveled road.

"Are you ready for a walk?" Dr. Golding asked her.

"Yes." She said it heartily, glad he hadn't asked her what she was thinking.

"How about you, Tim? Are you ready for a day on the farm?"

"You bet I am," he answered, giving Dr. Golding a smile and then looking back down at his book. He was on the tractor page now, his eyes bright behind his glasses. Maggie watched his lips move, talking to himself as he looked at the pictures. He could sound out some simple words already.

Dr. Golding had been eager to bring him along. "My brother has a farm near where we're going and three kids of his own. Tim will have a great time. You can meet Joe and Carol and make sure you're okay with leaving him there, but I think you'll like them."

So she had agreed, and here they were. They were turning off the graveled road onto dirt.

"What do they grow here?" she asked Dr. Golding.

"Oh, mostly hay and grass and clover." He smiled at her. "This is cow country."

"Milk or beef?" she asked.

"Both," he said. "But mostly dairy. My brother runs a dairy farm. In fact, I'm somewhat of an expert on cows myself."

"How's that?" Maggie smiled.

"It's the same farm we grew up on. He took it over after Dad died."

She nodded. That explained Dr. Golding's weathered looks and multiple talents. She didn't have time to comment, though, because they were turning onto another tidy, narrow dirt road, which led to a large, green-lawned farmhouse nestled in a grove of trees in a dish between three hills. There were oaks and willows all around it, and across the pastures she could see another house and between them two barns and a silo. Two black-and-white dogs ran out, barking and chasing the truck in a tail-wagging frenzy until they were called off by a small boy, a little older than Tim, who came around the corner as they drove up.

"Hey, Uncle Jake." The little boy ran to Dr. Golding.

Jake reached down and ruffled the boy's hair. "Dawson, my man."

The boy looked at Tim, who jumped down into Jake's arms, cape under his backpack, farm book clutched against his chest.

"Dawson, this is my friend Tim, the boy I told you would be coming today."

He sat Tim down on the ground and the two little boys looked at each other, neither assessing nor curious, simply accepting the fact of each other's presence.

Maggie's heart lurched at how small Tim was. His glasses took up his whole face, and he had insisted on wearing the Superman cape. She hoped Jake's nephew wouldn't tease him, like the boy at preschool who had said the cape was dumb. Tim had come home upset, and tucked it into his shirt from then on when he went to preschool. But this boy, Dawson, didn't look as if he even noticed the cape or the glasses.

Jake put his hand on his nephew's shoulder. "Could you show Tim around? He wants to see what a real farm is like."

Dawson shrugged his thin shoulders. "Sure. Come on," he said, and Tim, handing his backpack and book to Maggie, followed him without a word. The two of them disappeared into the barn.

Jake turned and smiled at her.

"Boy, that was easy," she said, remembering the first day at the Happy Campers, when Tim had cried and clung to her leg. But that had been a year ago.

"It usually is with kids," said Jake. "Now, why can't the rest of us be like that?"

A man, looking like a slightly older, heavier version of Jake, came out of the barn the boys had entered, wiping his hands on an orange rag as he walked toward them.

"Well, it's *Dr. Golding*." He grinned, and called toward the house. "Hey, Carol, come on out here. *Dr. Golding* is here."

Maggie looked at Dr. Golding and wondered if he had some family issues of his own. Maybe his brother was sensitive to the fact that Dr. Golding had a Ph.D. and he was a farmer. Why else would he make such a point of teasing him about his title? But he didn't seem to be angry. He acted more like something was funny. Jake's face looked resigned. He smiled. His brother grinned, as he looked from Jake over to Maggie, and offered his hand, most of its dirt on the orange rag, which he stuffed in his pocket.

"Maggie, I'd like you to meet my brother Joseph," Dr. Golding said. "Joe, this is Maggie Ivey, a friend of mine."

Maggie shook Joe's hand. It felt rough and warm like Dr. Golding's. She made some friendly small talk, but she was thinking in different directions. Dr. Golding had introduced her as a friend of his, not a patient. She was still wondering what to make of that when Joe's wife came out the side door of the house. She was a friendly-looking woman, slightly plump, with long brown hair that seemed to erupt from her head in waves and curls. Her jeans were torn at the knee, and her T-shirt, which said CLOVER CREEK COOPERATIVE CREAMERY under the picture of a happy-looking cow, was a few sizes too big.

"Hi, Maggie. I'm Carol." The woman looked right into Maggie's eyes and smiled. She had deep dimples in the middle of each cheek. "It's good to meet you. Jake said he'd be bringing you by."

"It's good to meet you, too," Maggie said, feeling the woman's soft hand squeeze her own.

"How about you two come in for a cup of coffee before you take off?" Carol asked.

Jake looked at Maggie and raised his eyebrows in a question. "What do you say, Maggie?"

"Sure," she said. "That sounds great." Actually, it sounded wonderful. For some reason, Maggie instantly took to Carol, and realized that she wanted very much to follow her inside, sit down in her kitchen, and have a cup of coffee.

Carol led the way into the house, taking them past the flower bed planted with calla lilies and irises, past the two dogs, now lolling on the porch, through the screeching screen door, through the hallway, past the grade-school drawings and picture books piled on the dining room table, through a set of swinging doors, and into a huge kitchen. It was bright and cheerful, the warm sunshine streaming in through insulated windows that held a virtual greenhouse of herbs and flowering plants.

"Oh!" Maggie murmured, moving in for a closer look at the indoor garden.

"Carol's got the green thumb," Joe said, coming behind his wife and giving her a hug.

Carol took one of the place mats from the huge oak table, and used it to sweep the crumbs onto the wooden floor. She gave the place mat a good shake and laid it back down again, then turned to the cupboard and took down four cups, Fiestaware, just like Maggie's own.

"Oh, I have some just like this!" Maggie said.

"Kmart? A dollar ninety-nine apiece?" Carol asked her, grinning.

"Yes!" Maggie laughed.

They sat down at the oak table then, Carol made a pot of coffee, and she produced half of a sour cream and cinnamon coffee cake on a chipped china plate. It had no discount ingredients. It was rich and moist and melted on Maggie's tongue. She could taste the butter and every now and then she came across a little lump of brown sugar that hadn't dissolved. It was studded with walnuts that Carol said they'd grown on their own trees, and she said the rich cream Maggie poured into her coffee was from their own cows. The four of them laughed and talked for probably an hour until Jake finally said they'd better be going. By the time they stood up to leave Maggie felt as if she had known Joe and Carol for years.

"Yeah, you'd better go," Dr. Golding's brother agreed as they moved back through the dining room into the front yard. "I've got a farm to run." Then he turned to Maggie. "Some of us have to actually work for a living instead of just sitting behind a desk all day."

"Don't start, Joe." Carol gave him little shove. Maggie looked over at Dr. Golding. His face was a little flushed, but he didn't seem angry.

"Are you sure you don't mind having Tim?" Maggie asked.

"Not a bit," Carol assured her. "He'll have fun with Dawson, and the older kids when they get home from school, and I won't even notice one more."

Maggie was just getting ready to ask about dangerous machinery and to tell them to keep a sharp eye on Tim, when he and Dawson came running from behind the barn, each carrying a kitten.

"Look what they have, Mom." Tim was rubbing the kitten's head so hard the whites of its eyes showed with every stroke. "Dawson said I could keep one."

Maggie smiled. "Gently, Tim," she said, even though the kitten didn't seem to mind. "We'll talk about it later. Now, are you going to be all right if Dr. Golding and I leave for a while?"

"Sure." Tim pushed his glasses back up on his tiny nose, looked at her through the thick lenses, and smiled, and she suddenly felt that she had been given a gift—if only for a day. Tim had fields to run in, and kittens to play with, and a friend near his own age. She hugged him good-bye, without even feeling guilty. By the time they said good-bye to Carol and Joe and began their walk down the dirt road to begin their hike, Maggie didn't care if the visit was therapy or not. In fact, she realized, maybe this was exactly the kind of therapy she needed. Maybe Dr. Golding had realized that from the beginning. Maybe he was smart enough to not do the same thing for every person. She was certainly different than Gina, she thought, as she fell in step beside him. It made sense. She turned and smiled at him, and waved to Joe and Carol and the boys, still standing in the yard.

They followed the dirt road to the end of his brother's farm, then Dr. Golding said they would cut across a pasture. He pulled the fence post right out of the ground, leaned the fence, really just chicken wire, down on the grass, and took Maggie's hand as she stepped over it.

"Watch out for cow piles," he said, then blushed.

They walked across the pasture, which seemed to be empty of cows. The hills weren't very steep, just the rolling variety.

"That's Clover Creek." Dr. Golding pointed to a double line of trees curving across the pasture. "Those willows always follow the creekbank," he said. They walked a little closer and Maggie could hear it before she saw it, a little stream about a foot deep and four feet wide, ferns and wildflowers growing right up to its banks.

"It's beautiful," she said, and tried hard to keep the wistfulness out of her voice. She would enjoy what she had been given today, she vowed, and not spoil it by wishing for more.

They crossed another pasture, Dr. Golding again moving the fence and replacing it. What trees there were, mostly oaks, were twisted into gnarled shapes.

"The wind does it," Dr. Golding said, following her eyes. Even today it was blowing Maggie's hair. The grass under their feet was full of clover. It made sweet milk, Dr. Golding told her, and every now and then when they topped another hill she would see a clump of the cows, chewing on it and watching them with their huge, peaceful eyes.

They passed another farmhouse, another pasture, and then crossed onto the blacktop highway, Clover Creek Road, Dr. Golding told her.

"We're going through town here. It's not much," he apologized.

"I love it!" Maggie said. The entire town was four streets, Main Street, Petaluma Boulevard, Gravenstein Way, and, of course, Clover Creek Road. It reminded her of Mayberry on

The Andy Griffith Show. They walked past a five-and-dime, a ladies' dress shop, Rose's Inn, a flower shop. At the end of the block, huge, and dwarfing all the other stores, was the Clover Creek Feed and Grain. Then they were back on a graveled road and continued their journey, past a small cemetery, through an apple orchard, and on through another pasture, full of Queen Anne's lace, goldenrod, and, of course, the ever present clover.

As they kept walking the woods became thicker and there were fewer pastures and more orchards. "What kinds of apple trees are these?" Maggie asked him when they passed the next one.

"Gravensteins, mostly," he said. "A few Delicious. We have an apple blossom festival here coming up the end of May," he said with a grin. "Surely you've heard of it."

Maggie grinned back.

"There's some more walnuts." Dr. Golding pointed to a grove of trees by the creek which seemed to have appeared again. "Here's where we cut through the woods," he said.

Maggie followed him into the shade, glad to cool off. It was hot for the end of April, and even with the wind blowing she was beginning to sweat from walking over all those hills, rolling or not. The woods were thick and she could smell something spicy and tangy—eucalyptus trees, she realized when she saw the shaggy bark and gray trunks. Dr. Golding stayed at her side, going ahead of her only when the path narrowed. He walked through the woods easily, as if he knew where he was going. They walked for twenty minutes or so, and finally came into a clearing, where Dr. Golding asked if she'd like to rest for a minute. He pulled two bottles of water from his backpack and gave one to Maggie, keeping one for himself. She took a few sips, then watched him tip his head back and drink. They both sat down and leaned back against a huge rock that looked as if it had tumbled there from nowhere. The rock was hot, and it felt good against Maggie's tired muscles. Jake's knees were drawn up, and his elbows rested on them. He took another drink, then put the cap on his water. His shoulder brushed against Maggie's and felt warm and solid against her arm.

"How did you ever find this place?" she asked.

"My brothers and I used to play in these woods all the time." He was close to her, and they leaned against each other a little more than was necessary. She didn't move away. She liked the feel of his shoulder next to hers. It felt as dependable and warm as the sun-baked rock behind her back. Life would be all right, she thought, leaning back and closing her eyes, if she could just stay like this, the rock behind her and Dr. Golding beside her.

"It's beautiful here" was what she actually said, and took a deep breath and opened her eyes.

"You like it?" He turned his face toward her without moving away, his head still resting on the rock. She turned her face toward him to answer. They were very close.

"I like it very much."

His eyes warmed up again—they were always warm like that when he talked to her.

"I'm glad," he said.

They hiked for about another half hour, and finally they were at the place Dr. Golding said was their destination, a clearing in another grove of oaks. The creek they'd followed widened out and became noisy, spilling over a few big rocks to make a little waterfall.

"This is so beautiful." Maggie looked around. It was like a piece of heaven after the noise and grime of Oakland. Beside one of the creek's small cataracts there was a picnic table, and a way off in the distance, under another grove of trees, was an old mobile home and a cleared spot beside it. Someone had poured a foundation.

"The creek gets even wider down there"—he pointed toward the grove of oaks—"but it's still not very deep. My brothers and sister and I used to go wading there."

"Do you think the owner will mind if we stop here?"

"No," Dr. Golding said, "I don't think he'll mind."

He was disconcertingly close to her again, sweeping the pollen and dust off the picnic table. She felt her heart give an extra thump, and sighed. This was not good. This could go nowhere, though she knew what was causing it. It was pheromones. She had read about them. Invisible little particles that flew across the air and drew a man and a woman together, like little magnets. The air must be full of them right now, she thought. They must be dancing, side by side with the dust motes from the picnic table. Jake's shoulders barely brushed hers as she helped him clean off the table.

"There," he said. "That's about as good as it's going to get." He gestured toward the bench and Maggie sat down.

"It's fine," she said.

He unzipped the backpack and brought out some thick sandwiches, a bag of chips, and some sodas, and they ate sitting in the shade under the gnarled oaks. She could see water spiders skittering across the broad, still shallows of the creek, just before it broke on the rocks to make the short, rushing fall. She waved away a bluefly that buzzed around their heads. She wondered again where all this would lead.

———

It had been a wonderful day. Maggie stood by her kitchen window, looking out once again at the Oakland skyline. When she couldn't see the smokestacks belching into the night she could almost pretend the factories were just pretty city lights. Tim had fallen into bed an hour ago, exhausted but happy, the kitten curled beside him on the pillow. He had named him Jake.

Maggie sipped her nightly herb tea from the red fake Fiestaware mug. She smiled, remembering Joe's rough teasing, Carol's broad smile and plain ways, and felt a warmth and a pain at the same time. She sighed. It had been a beautiful day.

She smiled, thinking how angry Gina would be if she knew about today's walk in the woods. But she had no more doubts after today. Dr. Golding knew what he was doing. She was sure of that now. The best therapy was good people, and sitting at old, scarred tables, sipping coffee, eating sweet cake and laughing, hearing the shouts of the children playing outside. She closed her eyes and leaned against the window. The pressure on her shoulder felt like Jake's arm on hers when they were leaning against the boulder in the shade of the oaks, touching but not talking, just feeling the steady in-and-out of each other's breath. She felt a longing rise up from her chest and come up to her throat. She hadn't allowed herself to feel this way in a long time. Maybe Gina was right. This could lead nowhere. Maybe she was making another mistake.

She felt a moment of panic when she recalled the last thing she had done. She had been carried away by all the good feelings of the day, and when Dr. Golding had asked if he could come by the next evening after work and install the locks for the neighbors, Maggie had invited him to stay for dinner.

"I'll make chili," she said. "We'll have a potluck and invite everyone."

"I love potlucks," he said.

She looked out the window again, north this time, toward Clover Creek and Petaluma, and she wondered what Jake Golding was doing tonight. She tried to imagine his house, and couldn't. She didn't even know where he lived, she realized, though he had said it was somewhere close by where they were today. She wanted to know what his couch looked like, what he ate for breakfast, where he bought his groceries. She wondered what he would be doing a week from now when the Overhaul had ended. He had turned out to be nothing like she had thought he would be, and his practical caring was nothing like the silly psychotherapy she had been afraid he would offer.

Impulsively, she reached into the drawer by the telephone and pulled out a lined writing tablet, and searched until she found a pen. She hadn't written her parents in months, but suddenly she felt the urge to tell them how wonderful her life was becoming. She sat down at the kitchen table before she ran out of energy, and wrote about her new friends, about fixing up the apartment, about the hike to the creek, and Tim's day on the farm. She didn't say much about therapy, though she did say that Dr. Golding was a psychologist and this was part of a program a friend had given her. She folded the three pages carefully, sealing and addressing the envelope and placing it on top of her purse, so she'd remember to mail it in the morning. She finished her tea, now cold, and put the cup carefully in the sink. As she walked toward the bedroom, she turned off lights and checked the deadbolt locks. No matter what, she decided with a firmness that surprised her, no matter what happens after next week, I won't regret this. It's been a gift. And she held that thought as she fell asleep.

9

Friday, May 1

Thirty years on the San Francisco police force, two marriages, three kids, a punctured lung from a stabbing, and a plastic kneecap to repair the damage from a .38-caliber slug had left Carson Fuller with the feeling he had taken the worst life had to offer, but he realized now that nothing had prepared him for Gina Tucci.

She sat across from him in a kelly green dress, a little too short and tight around the hips, her hair big and tangled, her sharp-looking burgundy fingernails poking the air like tiny bloody daggers. Car noticed that Gina Tucci's thumbnail had a piece of jewelry glued onto it. He found himself fascinated with trying to get a look at it and had to forcibly turn his attention back to what she was saying.

"That jerk is seducing my friend, and you'd better get something on him" seemed to be the repeated refrain. Her voice sounded like a hoarse little dog barking.

Car gave her his soothing nod and folded his hands peaceably on his desktop, hoping to calm her down by example. "I checked out a few things already," he said. "No complaints with the Board of Psychology for inappropriate contact."

"He probably bought them off."

"Maybe," Car said, not committing himself. It was possible. Just because no one was crying foul didn't mean there wasn't something going on. Golding could have bought them off, as Gina Tucci said. There'd been a couple of gripes about the therapy not doing what Golding promised, but the file said they'd been "amicably settled." If he couldn't find anything else he could always try to get his hands on a current patient list and dredge up a few more dissatisfied customers. From the ripple of Gina Tucci's pit bull jaw, he didn't think she much cared what he got on Golding, as long as he got something.

She confirmed it, as though she could read his mind. "Just nail him," she said, drumming the little daggers on the top of his desk. "With anything."

"How about we wire your friend and send her in?" Car was always in favor of doing things the easy way, and if Golding was seducing this woman, why not catch him in the act?

"Absolutely not!" Ms. Tucci almost came off her chair at that suggestion. "You are not to approach my friend!"

"Okay, fine." Car backed off from that suggestion right away. He thought about wiring the Tucci woman and sending her in. He grinned. He'd like to see that. He looked at Ms. Tucci's pressed lips and jabbing fingernails and shook his head, even feeling sorry for this Dr. Golding.

"Well, I've got a few more avenues to explore." He pushed his chair back from his desk, his subtle signal, at least he hoped it was subtle, that the interview was over. Gina Tucci looked as though it would take a crane to move her out of her chair. Car, not about to be bested by her, stood behind his desk, and with a little tongue click of exasperation, Gina Tucci stood, too.

"What avenues?" she pressed.

"Oh, business associates, former classmates, school records, IRS and local tax records, auditor's office for liens and encumbrances." He reeled off the list, hoping he would impress her and she wouldn't suggest a tail. He hated stakeouts. He was getting too old to hold his bladder for eight hours at a time and he hated peeing into a cup. But who could get through a night without coffee?

He was moving Gina Tucci toward the door now. She stopped a few feet away from Car's goal and turned toward him. Now that she was standing, Car could see she barely topped five feet. Still, she packed a lot of power into that little fireplug physique.

"I want some results soon." She looked up at him, and her black eyes were glinting with either menace or anticipation, Car couldn't tell which.

"I'll have results," he promised her, and guided her out the open door.

"See that you do."

He just nodded, letting her have the last word so she'd leave. Satisfied, at least for the moment, she turned and walked toward the elevator, and Car darted back into his office and closed the door before she could reload and come after him again.

He sighed, worked his shoulders and neck back and forth a few times, and poured himself a cup of coffee. That woman was like a machine. The Terminator. She just kept coming and coming, relentless, like that battery bunny on the commercials. He rewound and erased his answering machine messages. All six of them from her, and all left between their conversation yesterday afternoon and this morning's appointment.

She'd been even worse the last time he'd worked for her. Then she'd really been in a fury. It had been her husband she'd been after that time, and Car had finally gotten pictures of him cheating on her. He'd prepared himself for Ms. Tucci to be suitably grieved when he'd shown them to her, but she'd been jubilant instead. Happy she'd gotten the leverage she needed for the property settlement. Car shook his head, remembering, and sat down at his desk. Took a sip of coffee. It scalded all the way down, just the way he liked it.

He leaned back in the ergonomic chair, his one luxury in the Spartan office—hell, his Spartan life, and allowed himself a moment of self-pity. It was cases like this that made him wish he was still a detective on the force instead of here in his own office. Being a PI wasn't as exciting as watching it on television. Mostly paperwork and boring as hell. He sipped his coffee again and wondered how to proceed with Dr. Jason Golding's investigation. He'd begun nosing around yesterday, but so far, nothing. He'd come up dry. The guy was slimy as pond scum when it came to bilking all those poor stupid slobs out of their money, but hell, that was the American way. Like P. T. Barnum said, there's a sucker born every minute. With his years on the force shaping his life views, Car knew he was jaded, but he'd seen too much. And he couldn't buy the touchy-feely, humanistic crap all this psychobabble was based on—he'd seen enough muggings, stabbings, and just everyday cruelty to know that was bull. He'd heard an old radio preacher say once that a newborn baby was just eight pounds of sin, only he stretched the word out to two syllables. *Seee-uuuun.* Car thought the guy was probably right. But even if the psychobabble was true and everybody just needed an overhaul or tune-up, he'd seen enough con men in his time to recognize one when he saw one in Dr. Jason Golding.

The guy had to be a crook to sell people that line. But the kind who belonged in jail? Car wasn't sure. Not unless you wanted to lock up all the shrinks in the city. Which might not be a bad start, come to think of it.

He leaned forward and picked up the file, went through it again. The criminal history was clean. No record, and if the guy was a cheat, at least no one had reported him. The credit check was interesting. Golding was overextended, but nothing to go to jail for. Payments a little late, but everybody seemed to think he was good for all his loans. Still, owing as much as he did, he had a powerful motivation to keep the house of cards from tumbling down. He'd called Golding's office and gotten a machine. Left a number, but no call back so far. Which was a little odd. Seemed like a guy with that many bills to pay would be a little more eager for clients. Or maybe he just wanted women clients. Car raised an eyebrow. Maybe Tucci was right.

He would give it one more day, he told himself. He would follow the paper trail today, and then if he turned up nothing he'd do the stakeout tomorrow. If you followed anybody long enough they were bound to do something wrong, he knew, and Gina Tucci had said she didn't care what he nailed Golding on. As long as he nailed him.

Car rose wearily from his chair, took the battered sports coat from the hook behind the door, and headed out for the hall of public records. He hoped he turned up something today. He really didn't want to follow this shyster around for a week. Sounded boring as hell.

* * *

Jake leaned back against the oak tree and wondered what was going on with Lindsay all of a sudden. She was leaving phone messages everywhere he went. He hadn't talked to her yet, but he couldn't put her off forever. He'd tried calling her once, but her cell phone hadn't been on. He had no doubt she would eventually catch up with him. He'd have to talk to her sooner or later and find out what she wanted. But clearly she wanted something. He took that as a given. He put down the blueprints he'd been studying and smiled, turning his face up to the sun.

Why was he so happy? he asked himself. This was all going to end. He reminded himself of his goal—to shore Maggie Ivey up and get out while he could, before she found out that he was Jake Cooper, and had no more clue about how to do psychotherapy than the fly that buzzed around his face right now.

And she was shored up. He could see that. She was talking and laughing. She'd talked to him all the way back to Oakland from Clover Creek the other night, Tim and the kitten asleep in the seat between them, the little boy's head leaning against his arm. Their talk had been easy, give and take, not strained and tense, like the first time or two. He felt the warmth again in his chest, as he did every time he thought of her.

He had no choice but to admit it. He didn't want to shore her up and leave. Just this brief time with Maggie, and he'd finally found what he'd been looking for. Someone solid and real, like his mom cooking in her snug kitchen. He had been looking for someone he could build something with, like what Joe had with Carol, or Shelley with Toby. He knew he wanted that for himself, and to think that he'd even considered that Lindsay Hunt might be the one to find it with was laughable to him now. After just a few times sitting across the table from Maggie, those blue eyes looking at him so trustingly, that sweet smile of hers, he knew he'd found it.

He felt the coldness in his stomach then, and the sense of

doom that he'd been trying to ward off for the past few days by finalizing blueprints and calling in favors whenever he wasn't playing doctor.

This job had a lot of details that needed handling, but he hardly minded. Actually, it gave him something to think about besides his problems. He'd given the crews the day off yesterday due to his little jaunt with Maggie Ivey, but the framers were back at work today, and with the number of them hammering, all the walls would be up before the day was over. Waldo would come tomorrow with his guys to do the chimney, one crew would put on the roof while another one plumbed, and the electricians would be about an hour behind them. Then there would be just the Sheetrock and carpet and paint. He even had them working this Sunday, though Ethelda would have to supervise for him, if his plans worked out. This would be the fastest house he had ever built. He had six different crews lined up, ready to dance around each other like chorus girls in a Broadway musical, and all because he had to take his mind off the boulder that was rolling down the mountain full-tilt toward him. And it would hit next Thursday, the end of his "official" participation in the *21-Day Overhaul,* when he had to say good-bye to Maggie Ivey.

For he saw that now. There was no other way. To tell her the truth would be to tear down the shoring he'd so painstakingly put up. No, the truth was, he would end up having played a minor role in Maggie Ivey's life. He would have to realize that and say good-bye to her soon. To do anything else would be selfish, using her just like that no-good creep who had used her to begin with.

He rolled up the blueprints and again leaned his head back against the tree, running the possibilities around his mind one more time, like tired dogs around a track. Maybe he could tell her the therapy would be extended. The thought left a sour feeling in his mind, though. There was no way he could lie to her again. The reason he had found any peace at all was because he had decided to quit pretending to be anything he wasn't and just be himself. He was no good at pretending. He felt that if Maggie Ivey asked him a direct question now, he'd be unable to do anything but give an honest answer. Yet the thought of coming clean terrified him. What if he told her the truth and she never wanted to see him again? He forgot for a moment that that was what was going to happen anyway.

He couldn't see her doing anything else if he told her he was not Dr. Jason Golding. She'd trusted him and he'd let her believe a lie. And to tell her the truth might set her back to the lonely days he'd found her in. The fact that his deception had been a success only increased his misery. After all, he reminded himself, the point from the beginning was to make her happier and get through the twenty-one days without being caught. He was close to doing that. He'd nearly succeeded. Only a few more days to wait.

He rose wearily, stretched, and walked over to the truck to get his tool belt. After this project and Ethelda's current jobs were finished, the two of them would have to huddle and get busy on Golding's office remodel. That deadline, too, loomed ahead. Suddenly Jake felt hemmed in and irritable. He felt like putting up some two-by-fours. Swinging a hammer.

"Come on, guys," he called over his shoulder as he bent into the canopy and pulled out his belt. "This ain't no piano we're building here."

The Potucek brothers, his lead framers, hollered something back he couldn't hear, probably pitching it back to him, like always. He strapped on the belt, and climbed up to the second-floor bedrooms, the last place left to frame. His crew looked up and grinned at him, gave him some guff about finally getting off his butt. He picked up the hammer and gave the nail a satisfying blow. He'd think of something. The fact that his only option might be to say good-bye loomed over him, but he refused to accept it just yet. There had to be another way. He pounded in another nail. He didn't want to lose Maggie Ivey. He reached for a third nail and hammered again. He would think of something. He put the worrying out of his mind and looked around. They could finish the framing this afternoon, and he'd still have time to shower and change before he was due at Maggie's for dinner. He'd think about the rest later. He would figure out something.

* * *

Maggie hurriedly left work, picked up Tim at the preschool, and changed her clothes at home as quickly as she could. The chili had been simmering in the Crock-Pot all day. She gave it a stir and hoped it wasn't sticking to the bottom. No, it was okay. It tasted fine, hot and spicy, and the aroma of cayenne and onions filled the kitchen when she lifted the lid. She gave it another good stir, and went to work mixing up the brownies.

Both batches were nearly done, and the apartment was filling with the smell of baking chocolate when the buzzer sounded. It was Jake Golding. She just stood there a minute, looking at him. His face was smooth-shaven and he had a clean, soapy smell. He handed her a bucket of chicken.

"Am I early?"

"No. Right on time."

Tim, not bothered by any nervousness, hurled himself at Jake. "I'm Superman, ta dumm."

Jake picked him up and turned him upside down.

"Where's Tim? I thought he'd be here. Maggie, have you seen Tim?"

Maggie laughed, and Jake and Tim laughed, and that was the end of the awkwardness.

They decided to put two tables in the backyard, which, amazingly, Mr. Jacobsen had mowed just for the occasion. He seemed a little embarrassed when Maggie complimented him.

"The yard looks lovely," she said, and really meant it. The lilacs were blooming, the grass was lush and had a new-mown smell, and the flowers that Mr. Jacobsen and Mrs. Weaver so lovingly nurtured were beginning to bloom. They all brought chairs from their apartments and sat around the tables. Mrs. Weaver had made coleslaw and corn bread and biscuits. The tenants from the other side of the hall, a young married couple name Ron and Carla Ramirez, brought a cooler full of drinks. The man in 2C didn't come—Carla said he had to work, but he'd given her his key so he could have a lock installed. Mr. Jacobsen surprised everyone by making a delicious eggplant parmegiana and uncorked two bottles of wine that Dr. Golding whispered in her ear must have cost him.

They ate, and laughed, and talked, and then started to clean up. It was eight o'clock before Jake started installing the locks and nearly midnight by the time he finished. When he was done all five apartments had a gleaming, new deadbolt lock and peephole.

Everyone agreed the evening had been a success. Even Mr. Jacobsen, who had new washers on his bathroom faucet as well.

"How did you ever learn how to do all these things?" Maggie asked over Jake's shoulder as he drilled and worked.

"Growing up on the farm, I guess. I had to do all kinds of things."

"Well, if psychology doesn't work out"—she laughed—"you could always find work as a carpenter."

"Is he asleep?" Jake was putting tools away and folding up the carpenter's belt when Maggie came out of Tim's room.

"He's just where you put him down." Jake had carried Tim piggyback up the stairs and then had gone back for his tools. "I didn't move him, just took off his glasses and jeans." Maggie sat down on the couch and leaned back against the pillow. "He wants to wear jeans every day now. Just like you."

Jake looked pleased and sat down beside her on the couch. "He's a great kid."

"Yes." Maggie was quiet for a minute. "He's a wonderful boy."

Dr. Golding hesitated. He seemed about to say something else, but he stopped and gave a sigh. He looked around the apartment. "I still can't believe what you've done in just a week. It doesn't even look like the same place. And the paintings you did are great."

"I guess I feel like I've come back to life." She looked straight at Dr. Golding, and didn't feel the least bit shy. "Thank you."

Dr. Golding kissed her then. She wasn't even surprised. It seemed the right thing to happen. He didn't touch her with anything but his lips, just leaned across and kissed her, sweet and soft, on the mouth. She kissed him back and he pulled her toward him then, his arms folding over her. She could feel them strong and hard under the cotton shirt, and she held on to him, like she had wanted to do since the day she sat beside him on the rock and felt his shoulder next to hers. She didn't know how long they stayed that way. Finally they just sat there together, her head against Jake's chest, nestled in the spot between his jaw and his neck. She could hear his heart, steady and regular under her ear.

"Maggie." She could feel his voice vibrating through his chest. "I need to tell you something."

She pulled back a little and looked up at him, his tone making her suddenly feel uneasy. "What is it?"

He looked at her a minute, and must have seen the dread in her face. His eyes got soft and he settled her head back on his shoulder. "Nothing. It's okay."

"What is it?" she asked. "It must have been something."

"No," he said. "It's nothing."

He left not long after that, holding her for a long minute again at the door and kissing her cheek this time. She locked the door after him. She could see him in the hallway through the new peephole, waiting until he heard the deadbolt slide into place. Then he turned and was gone, though Maggie stood at the door and listened to his feet on the stairs, and to the front door opening and clicking shut after him.

She sat back down on the couch and thought she might know what he'd been about to tell her. It was all going to end, she thought, facing the fact that she'd worked so hard to avoid. But if it was going to end, she wondered, feeling confusion start to fog her mind, why had he kissed her? That kiss didn't seem like it came from someone who meant to walk away. Maggie gave a sigh, got up, and got ready for bed, knowing she could sit there for hours seesawing wildly between thrilling lurches of hope and bottom-dragging despair. Even if the worst happened, she told herself as she turned down her bed, even if the worst happened and after her last appointment she never saw him again, she still had a little time. She had one more week before it would end, and with a fierceness that surprised her she decided that no matter what happened after that she would take it.

10

Saturday, May 2

Lindsay listened to her messages one more time when she came in from her run. She was taking her pulse and it speeded up a few beats when she recognized Jake's voice. She dropped the stopwatch and replayed the message several times, listening for nuances and hidden meanings, but even she couldn't find any. "Lindsay, this is Jake," he said, sounding almost bored, "returning your call." Was it her imagination or was there a little emphasis on the last phrase? She dialed his home and office numbers and got machines at both. She put the phone down hard in irritation. Why hadn't he just called her at her office like she had told him to? He was so hard to manage.

She sighed, and her mind started working as she changed out of her running clothes. Maybe he didn't want to see her yet. Maybe he was planning this to be a surprise. How like him, she thought, shaking her head. Him with his old-fashioned ways. Couldn't he just realize that they had to be partners in their growth and development? She unbuckled her fanny pack and sat down to untie her shoes. Maybe she should just be patient. She'd tried to call Dr. Golding, but had gotten only the same stupid recorded message. Some secretary had called her back and left a message of her own, offering to send her some material on a rebirthing seminar, but Lindsay wanted to speak to Golding himself. The day she'd gone to the office it had been closed up tight as a drum. She must have just missed Jake. The thought that he had been there, though, just on the other side of the door, working on his personal issues, had given Lindsay a warm glow. She sighed now, the glow definitely gone, and headed for the shower, bringing the cell phone into the bathroom with her. She'd give him another day or two and then she would find him, she decided, as she stretched her hamstrings and quads. She'd given the universe plenty of time to act. Maybe it was time to help it along.

* * *

Maggie and Tim had breakfast at Mrs. Weaver's. Biscuits and gravy, scrambled eggs, and grits, just like the breakfasts she'd been used to at home. Mrs. Weaver brought her a plate with a candle in the biscuit, and she blew it out and made a wish.

"Happy birthday!" Mrs. Weaver's wavery voice and Tim's chirpy one called the greeting. They even sang to her. Tim had made her a flower vase from air-hardening clay in preschool, complete with a silk daisy, and Mrs. Weaver gave her a small box tied with grosgrain ribbon. Inside was a gold locket and chain, beautiful and old, the etching on the locket slightly tarnished in its curlicues.

"Oh, it's lovely," Maggie whispered.

"It was my mother's." Mrs. Weaver smiled. "I don't have a daughter of my own, so I'd like you to have it."

She had put it on right then, and fingered it now, as she looked out the window of her own apartment while Tim watched cartoons.

The factories were again belching smoke, not even resting on Saturday morning. Maggie felt the tiniest stirring of grief. She didn't attend to it at first, but when she did, she knew its source. There were only two days left to see Dr. Golding. That had probably been that undelivered message—that their therapy time was coming to an end, and their relationship with it. He had probably regretted kissing her as soon as he had done it, but was too kind to tell her so. That's why there had just been a peck on the cheek at the door.

The telephone rang, making her startle. She hoped it wasn't Gina. She had left Maggie a few messages since their spat, but Maggie was enjoying the silence, and had put off returning them. She didn't move to answer the phone right away, and finally Tim picked it up.

"Mom," he called to her after a few minutes, "it's Grandma."

Maggie felt her stomach sink a little lower. Even though she'd impulsively shared her happiness with her parents through the letter, Maggie's mother was the last person she wanted to talk to right now. Her mother had the uncanny ability to take a whisper of pessimism and amplify it into a shout. She said none of this, though, but went to the telephone.

"Hello, Mama," she said, then turned aside. "Tim, turn down the television, please."

"My land." Her mother's brusque voice filled the room, a lot like Gina's, Maggie realized with a little shock. "I was just fixing to hang up."

"I'm sorry," Maggie said. "I was busy, and Tim was watching cartoons."

"Um-hum." Her mother sounded skeptical. "Well, happy birthday, sweetie."

"Thank you." Maggie slid the words into the slight pause before her mother went on.

"I thought I'd better see how you were. I just got your letter and I'm a little concerned."

"Why?" Maggie was truly astonished, though if anyone could find cause for worry in the first happy letter she'd written in four years, it would be her mother. She tried to remember exactly what she'd said, and just recalled a warm, chatty note, describing Jake, and his brother and family.

"I talked to your sister and she agreed that this *doctor* doesn't seem quite on the up and up." Her mother was the only person she knew who could speak in italics. She paused after this, just long enough to let her words sink in, but started up again the second Maggie drew in a breath to reply.

"Julie and I are *very concerned* that this *doctor* might be taking advantage of you. There was a special on *20/20* just the other day about these doctors, psychiatrists and such, who *use* these young girls to meet their *own needs*." Her mother's voice took on an ominous tone with the last two words, as if Maggie should ponder what they meant.

Maggie didn't want to hear any more about the doctors on *20/20*. "Really, Mom, he's not like that," she said. "He's a very kind man." That didn't begin to describe him. She could almost see him standing in front of her, hands in his pockets, blond cowlicks on his forehead, blue eyes warm and soft. She lost herself for a moment.

"Well, we think you may be getting deceived. *Again*."

Maggie felt her cheeks go hot. Dr. Golding's image disappeared. Her mother would never come out and say how disappointed she was in Maggie for getting pregnant without the benefit of a husband, but neither did she ever miss a chance to refer to it in some way every time they talked.

"In fact, Margaret," her mother continued, "I spoke to Bobby Semple today. He still cares for you. In spite of everything."

"Mother! I can't believe you would do that! I haven't even thought of Bobby Semple in years." Not exactly factual, but essentially true. She certainly hadn't thought of him the way her mother hoped. She would rather die than admit to the monthly letters, an exercise in bridge maintenance that she was a little ashamed of.

"Well, he thinks of you often, and said as much."

"Mama," Maggie said, her voice more pleading than firm. "Please let me make my own decisions."

"Margaret"—her mother paused—"some women just can't tell if a man is sincere or not." Her mother had that decisive tone. As if her last pronouncement was the definitive word on Maggie's ability to judge character.

Maggie felt anger creep up her chest and out her voice. "I don't love Bobby Semple."

"You could grow to love him, once your commitment was made."

"I don't want to have to *grow* to love someone."

"Well, how do you feel about this doctor?" her mother demanded. "Do you love him?"

"I don't know!" Maggie snapped. "Maybe. I don't know."

But she did know. Holding the telephone to her ear, over three thousand miles of fiber-optic arguing, she did know.

After she got off the telephone, Maggie felt too disjointed to paint, or even to read a book. And she was tired of looking out the window. The sun was fighting to come out, but so far was losing. It was a little drizzly. Not exactly the kind of weather for taking a walk, though people weren't made of sugar, like Mrs. Weaver said when she weeded her garden in the rain. They wouldn't melt. Tim had quit watching cartoons and was playing with the kitten, teasing it with the ribbon that had tied Mrs. Weaver's package. Maggie shook her head, annoyed at herself. It was only ten thirty and she was already out of ideas for the day. Finally, she decided to clean. Maybe the activity would clear her mind as well as clean her house, and by the time she was finished maybe the sun would have won its battle with the fog. She took the Ajax and Lysol into the bathroom, and came out a few minutes later when she heard Tim hollering.

"What's the matter?" she asked.

Tim was bouncing up and down, pointing toward the door. "Mom, look who's here."

And there in the doorway stood Jake Golding, holding a potted plant and a paper sack from Utrecht's art supply store.

"You shouldn't open the door until your mom gets here, Tim." Jake sounded more conversational than scolding, though, and reached over and rubbed Tim's head as he spoke. He handed Maggie the paper sack. "I'm sorry. It's not very pretty."

Maggie smiled at him, feeling like she was sixteen again, her heart was racing so. She put down the Ajax and Lysol, dried her hands on her jeans, and lifted out the gift. It was a set of Prismacolor watercolor pencils, a good supply of watercolor paper, and a set of fine sable brushes.

"Oh, Jake, thank you! All my brushes are hard and barely bend on the paper anymore. How did you know? And how did you even know it was my birthday?"

Jake smiled down at Tim, who was convulsed with laughter. "I had a helper," he said.

"I told Jake yesterday. I kept the secret!" Tim laughed and started pulling on Jake's jacket, jumping up and down.

"Tim, let go of Dr. Golding."

"He doesn't care, Mom."

"It's okay, Maggie." And Dr. Golding really did look as though he didn't mind, standing there like a rock while Tim bounced up and down all around him, even landing on his feet from time to time.

Dr. Golding took Tim by the arms and let him walk up his legs, then flipped him over back onto his feet. "I guess I shouldn't have just come by, but the phone was busy, and I wanted to bring your gift."

"My mother called." Maggie said no more, but wondered if Dr. Golding could read the flat desolation behind her voice.

"Ah." Jake carried on the conversation as though a four-year-old boy weren't at that moment climbing up his thighs. "Well, if you have other plans, that's okay, but I wondered if the two of you would like to go on a little trip with me." Tim flipped over and landed on his feet again, his glasses flying. Dr. Golding bent over and picked them up, opened and closed them a few times, and put them back on Tim's head. "I brought us a lunch and I thought we might take the ferry over to Angel Island, rent some bikes, ride around, and have a picnic."

Maggie looked at him, and held his image up against the Dr. Golding her mother had accused him of being. He was standing here in his jeans and hiking boots, barely moving except using his arms to flip Tim, as if he were a dad playing with his own son. He didn't seem like Dr. Golding the Predator, looking for another young girl to rape under hypnosis. He just looked like

Jake, big and solid and warm, standing in her living room, having fun with her boy, asking her to go for a ferry ride with him. Her mother wasn't here. Her mother didn't know. Neither did Gina, no matter what she said. Somewhere there was something wrong—something that didn't line up. But she knew, with a certainty she had never felt with Jeff, that she could trust Jake Golding.

She smiled at him, and watched his face brighten. "I'll get our jackets," she said.

* * *

It was too late to take the ferry from San Francisco, Jake had realized as he prepared to leave his trailer that morning at nine. It left at ten in the morning and didn't return until four in the afternoon, according to the recording at the Blue and Gold fleet he had called. He had listened to the rest of the message, though, and found that he could catch one just about any time from Tiburon, so here they were. He liked Tiburon, a little fishing village just north of Sausalito, in Marin County. He'd been happy to show it to Maggie Ivey.

They followed the same route they'd taken the last time on the way to Clover Creek, taking the Richmond–San Rafael bridge, only turning south this time after they crossed it, and heading back down the coast, passing office buildings, more trees, less pasture, and big hotels along the freeway. These hills weren't covered with cows but with expensive houses that perched on them like uneasy birds. They passed Benz and BMW dealers, golf stores. They climbed up a winding hill, and when they came down the other side there was the bay, a long, flat sandy beach, and the town, old, tiny, and quaint, with lots of redwood and roof tiles. There were flowers everywhere.

Jake watched Maggie Ivey's eyes go wide and warm as she looked around her at the little village. He parked the truck in the public lot and helped Tim out, and then they walked across the wooden bridge over the little man-made lake, fountains in the middle spraying into the air.

"It's so pretty here," Maggie said.

Jake smiled. He loved showing Maggie Ivey pretty things and taking her places she enjoyed.

"All these shops here"—he gestured to the row of little square buildings jammed side by side along the main street—"these are old houseboats they've pulled ashore and put on foundations. They call them arks."

"Oooh" was all Maggie Ivey said, but long and amazed, like a kid opening her favorite present on Christmas morning. She was walking slowly down the sidewalk, a little ahead of him, looking in the windows of the fancy shops that the arks were mostly used for these days. He wished he could take her inside. "Pick out anything," he'd like to say, "anything at all." He'd love to do that for Maggie Ivey, but he couldn't. He couldn't do much of anything as long as he was pretending to be Dr. Jason Solomon Golding, and it was beginning to annoy him.

Just last night he'd made a big mistake, but still, if he had it to do over, he couldn't swear he wouldn't kiss her again. But no more of that, he told himself. No more kisses. Still, the whole charade was beginning to make him chafe with irritation, the persona of Dr. Jason Golding as uncomfortable as an outgrown wool shirt on a hot summer day. He would love to throw it off.

Instead, he continued his tour, showing Maggie Ivey the sights, and finally they wound their way down to the ferry dock. Tim was bouncing with excitement.

"Don't go too close to the edge," Maggie warned him. She looked a little worried.

"You enjoy yourself," Jake told Maggie, taking Tim's hand. "I'll watch old knucklehead here." Tim responded by going limp and hanging on Jake's arm, and Jake lifted him up onto his shoulders so he could see the bay. Angel Island was directly across from them, just a bunch of sharp hills covered in green. The weather had cleared and the sun glittered on the water. The *Bonita,* the little ferry they'd be taking, was docked just in front of them. An older couple wearing matching warm-up suits joined them by the gate, but it looked as though the five of them were the only passengers for this run.

"Are we ready?" The captain appeared from one of the arks behind them. She was a woman, about the same age as Maggie, with tangled red hair, a bright green windbreaker, and hiking boots just like his own.

"We're ready," he answered for all of them.

"You and your little boy can ride up front if you like," the captain told them once she'd collected their fares. "Kids like to see all the gauges and the wheel," she said, and Jake wondered if she noticed his smile or Maggie Ivey's bright red cheeks.

"We'd like that," he said, taking Maggie's arm and helping her on board.

The ferry captain, skipper of the last family-owned ferry system on San Francisco Bay and granddaughter of Sam McDonogh of Sam's Boarding and Chowder House, she informed them, knew everything about Angel Island and filled them in on all kinds of interesting facts on the trip across the bay.

Jake was hardly listening. He heard something about a Mrs. Perles watching the 1906 earthquake from her house on Angel Island and banging the lighthouse bell with a hammer for twenty hours when the ringer broke, or maybe he was getting two stories confused. He was busy watching Maggie. He thought about taking her hand, but he decided to wait. Maybe that should be put on hold, like kissing, until the twenty-one days were over. Just what would happen then, he wasn't sure. The ferry captain finished her tour and the three of them went out and leaned on the rail while she docked. Jake watched the sharp little hills of the island draw nearer while the wind whipped the salt air into his face and the sun shone brilliant on the water, and decided not to think about his troubles any more today.

Still, the more he watched Maggie Ivey, the more he was convinced that there was a little something wrong with her. Something in her eyes when she looked at him, like she wanted to say something but couldn't get it out.

Maybe she was tired of him coming around but didn't know how to tell him. He felt a sinking sensation at that thought but faced the possibility anyway. Maggie might not care for him in the same way he was beginning to care for her. But he didn't think that was it. She had looked happy to see him today. Very happy, in fact. Still, he looked at her now, the wind blowing her light brown hair away from her pretty face, and felt a sadness sweep over him. What had he been thinking? That they could go on? Even if she wasn't tiring of him, if something else was troubling her, how would he explain the lie he had told—no, more correctly, lived? How could she be anything but furious or coldly disappointed when she found out the truth?

He kept his thoughts to himself, though, and didn't speak again until Captain McDonogh had docked the little boat. They climbed off and followed the path to the visitors' center.

Tim was the only one who was really himself. He chattered and pulled the other two along in his wake as they went through the business of renting bikes and made their way down the bike path, out onto the island, and toward the immigration center.

"I haven't ridden a bike in years." Maggie smiled at him, lifting his spirits a little.

"Well, you know what they say." He smiled back at her.

Tim rode in a seat behind his bike, and Jake could feel his hands gripping tight around his waist. They'd had to be firm about leaving the kitten at home. He'd felt a burst of love for the little boy when he heard what he'd named him. Jake.

They pedaled for the next few minutes, no one saying anything, the ride level, the wind soft on their faces. Jake suddenly thought of Lindsay, and how she would not have liked riding bikes and having the wind whip her hair on the ferry. Lindsay got her exercise in measured doses. He couldn't imagine her in walking shorts and tennis shoes, like Maggie Ivey, turning around now on her wobbly bike to smile at him and Tim.

By the time they reached the immigration center it was after noon. They found a grove of gnarled madronas, and leaned their bikes against one.

"Looks like we'll have to sit on the ground." Jake thought about spreading out his jacket for Maggie, but she was already sitting, Indian style.

"Come on, boys," she said, and opened the lunch sack. "Let's see what we have."

Jake did put down his jacket then, and they unloaded the lunch onto it.

"I should have brought a tablecloth."

Maggie smiled at him. "This is fine."

They drank fruit juice from little boxes, ate their sandwiches and grapes, and each had a Hostess cupcake.

"In honor of your birthday," Jake said. He was leaning against a tree, across from Maggie. Tim sat as close to Jake as he could get without being on his lap.

They finished eating, and Maggie gathered up the wrappers. She looked up at Jake. "Does anybody want more? There's another sandwich here."

"I can't think of anything else that I want." Jake pulled Tim onto his lap and he looked hard at Maggie, wishing he had the nerve to just tell her everything right now, right in front of Tim, to ask her forgiveness and tell her she was the woman he wanted, that he wanted nothing more, now or ever, than her and Tim. Instead, he just repeated himself. "I don't need anything more."

Maggie Ivey looked at him for a long minute. She seemed about to say something, but she just crumpled up the lunch bag and got up to throw it away.

It was dark and cool inside the immigration center, and they listened, even Tim—standing quietly, looking serious, and every now and then adjusting the tortoiseshell glasses—while the slight Asian tour guide explained to them that Angel Island was the port of entry for immigrants arriving in the United States on the West Coast.

"Like Ellis Island in New York," Maggie murmured.

Jake nodded. He was thinking of other things all the while the tour guide talked about the physical exams and literacy tests and the Chinese Exclusion Act. Then the speech was over, and Maggie wandered toward the little museum. He followed along behind her, holding Tim's hand. The tour guide's speech seemed to have gone over Tim's head, but he did have a few questions about Captain McDonogh's statement that there were no squirrels or chipmunks on the island.

"Why not, Jake?" Tim asked. "There's trees."

Jake wasn't really sure, and told Tim so, but that took some discussion and in the meantime, Maggie had gone ahead of them. She was standing by herself, looking at a Spartan corner, a re-creation of the "dormitory" the Chinese immigrants had stayed in. The rest of the tour group must have passed on while he and Tim had been discussing wildlife. Tim wandered out the door and began to pick up rocks. Jake thought about calling him back, but he could still see him. Now he was sitting on the steps.

Jake walked toward Maggie and into the corner of the barracks. There were two stacks of beds, and one metal table with a washbasin on it. No sheets. No pillows. No windows. Maggie was close to the wall, inspecting the Chinese characters that the immigrants had carved on it. In the dim, filtered sunlight, Jake could see that there were tears on her face, and he felt a sudden swell of tenderness toward her. "What's wrong?" he asked, and walked toward her.

She gave her head a shake. "I was just reading how they were going to tear this down, when they found these things written on the wall in Chinese. When they translated them, they discovered they were poems, written by the people who were waiting here. Poems about how lonely they felt, and how they had left their families, and now they were prisoners here. After they'd come to be free."

Jake thought about the people at Angel Island, and why they would make Maggie cry. They were people without a home, sort of caught between two worlds, the one they'd left and the one they'd come to find. Only, the new place hadn't lived up to their expectations. By a long mile. He remembered Maggie's apartment on the seedy street in Oakland and the boy back home who wanted to marry her. He could understand why reading something like that would make her sad.

He put his arms around her then, in spite of his resolutions not to do just that kind of thing. She put her head on his chest and he remembered how much he had wanted to comfort her when she cried before, when he had first sat across from her that day in the office. She tipped her head up and looked at him, and then, just as he had promised himself he would not do, he bent his head and kissed her. Her lips were soft, and he could feel her arms around his waist. He tasted salt. He kissed her again, and then again.

"It's all right, Maggie," he said. "Everything's going to be all right."

She didn't say anything at all, just stood quietly, her head again nestled perfectly in the hollow under his chin. He wrapped his arms around her and held her, and this time he said the one thing he'd been holding back from saying ever since that day in Ghirardelli Square, when she had told him about Bobby Semple. "Don't leave, Maggie," he said. "I don't want you to leave. Stay with me."

It was late by the time he got them home. Tim had fallen asleep in the seat between them, but he woke up again when the truck stopped. He and Maggie hadn't touched again since he had kissed her in the barracks. He wondered if she regretted it. Something was still wrong. He could feel it, and wondered if part of it might be emanating from him. His head was suddenly heavy with the weight of all that had happened in the last weeks, and with the confusing fear that he would not be able to keep all these spinning plates in the air until next week. And then what? he wondered, returning to the same tired thoughts. What would he tell her then? He had to believe his own words. It would be all right. He would think of something. But the steady repetition of those words was wearing a little thin.

They were in front of her building. He chatted with Tim all the way up the stairs and went with him to check on the kitten, who was curled into a ball on Tim's bed. Then he went to find Maggie, who was looking out the kitchen window, her back toward him.

He felt a little awkward, and wondered what he should say to her. She turned around, and her eyes were bright again.

"Thank you, Jake, for everything. For the gifts, and the trip to Angel Island."

"It was my pleasure."

She stood, as if gathering courage to speak, then shook her head.

He knew he should go, but he wished somehow he could think of the right words to say. He wanted to tell her the truth, all of it, right now.

"Maggie."

"Yes?"

He started to tell her, or at least to say, *No matter what happens I want you to know I've meant every word I said to you,* but then he couldn't remember having said anything to her at all. Nothing that would really have told her how he felt, that he loved her. Then he thought of saying, *Maggie, do you believe in giving people second chances?* but that would bring up entirely too many questions. Then he finally thought of saying, *You may find out things about me that make you wonder if I care for you, but I want you to know that I do.* But all of these speeches sounded like things a junior high school boy would say. Still, he had to say something, and now was as good a time as any.

He had his mouth open to do it when the telephone rang. Shrill and insistent, it broke into the quiet arc between them.

She moved to answer it, but it stopped. He could hear Tim's voice from the other room.

"I'd better see who that is," Maggie Ivey said without moving.

"Good night, then," he said. "I guess I'll see you Tuesday." Maggie just nodded and followed him to the door. He gathered up his jacket, and waited again until she locked the deadbolt, then headed out, his feet feeling suddenly heavy on the worn stairs of the Embarcadero Arms.

He was going to lose Maggie Ivey. He knew that as he drove up the highway toward home, the lights of houses fewer and farther between the farther north he drove. He thought of her and Tim back at the little apartment, and wished more than anything that he had met them under different circumstances. Why not at a church social, or even at the bank where she worked? Why, for the hundredth time, he wondered, did it have to be as he was measuring the office of some flaked-out shrink, and why had he let this deception go on as long as it had? Until now, when it was too late to correct. Too late to say, "I'm not the doctor, but maybe I could help." Why not that? Why not the simple truth? He could have told her the truth right off the bat. He realized now that's what he should have done. Now she would never be able to get past wondering if he had been using her. Lying to her, kissing her, like that jerk had done before he left her, pregnant and alone.

He shook his head at his own stupidity. If he was going to wait to tell her the truth, he should have waited to hold her and kiss her, too. He should have waited to love her.

She had gotten stiff and quiet after he had asked her not to leave, to stay with him, and had hardly said anything on the way home. He couldn't blame her. She thought he was her psychologist. No wonder she was confused and afraid. She probably thought he was one of those guys who took advantage of their patients. Jake shook his head, a tight knot in his chest at the thought that he might have hurt Maggie. Up until yesterday, when he had been such a fool as to let her know how he felt, he had been sure there would be a way to solve this. There had to be a way to end the charade without losing Maggie. Now he felt sick. He had been so close to the woman and the life he'd wanted.

He drove, almost without thinking, to the building site, following the road as it wound beneath the towering, twisted oak trees, and parked by the little stream. The house was going up smoothly, blending in with the earth and the countryside almost as if it had sprung up from it. Its cedar siding, which would turn a silvery gray over time, glided seamlessly into the stone fireplace made from rocks identical to the ones the creek tumbled over a few yards from the back porch. He parked his truck and walked through the rooms, hearing his footsteps echo against the plywood subflooring, and against the new wallboard. The electricians and drywall installers had come. The painters would come tomorrow, and on Monday the carpets would be laid. The landscaping could wait. Even though he had worked like a madman on this job, he almost wished he hadn't. His original plan in building it now seemed hopelessly naive.

He walked back to his truck and sat there a minute, desperately needing something to occupy his mind. He couldn't face going into the little trailer, so instead he started up the truck, backed up in the turnaround, and drove down the dark roads toward Petaluma.

The office was dark as he'd expected, since Ethelda, at least, kept normal hours. Like clockwork, she was in every morning at seven and gone every afternoon by four, and worked weekends only by special request. He went in and turned on the light. There was a six-pack of Pepsi and a little milk in the small refrigerator. The coffeepot was scrubbed and neatly draining on a paper towel. He filled it with water and measured out the coffee, then went to his desk. Centered on it was the file on Dr. Golding's remodel. In all the fuss of the last week he hadn't even discussed it with Ethelda.

A hot-pink Post-it note on the front of the folder said that Dr. Golding had called from New York and wanted to speak to him. *Not to me,* Ethelda had written in her loopy hand. *I guess he can't imagine dealing with a woman contractor.* Jake tossed the file aside, sick to death of Dr. Jason Golding. He wished he had never heard of the man. But, he realized with a sigh, then he never would have met Maggie Ivey. He sat at his desk for a long time, just making a figure eight with the pencil between his fingers. Suddenly the office felt stifling. He had to talk to someone, but the only person he really wanted to talk to was Maggie, and he couldn't do that. Not now. He picked his brother instead.

* * *

If Maggie had known it was Gina on the phone she might not have been so willing to take the call. Still, she had felt an urgency to get away from Dr. Golding before she spilled her love for him all over the kitchen floor. Gina was like an angry wraith, freed at last from the telephone's bowels of saved messages.

"What the hell do you think you're doing?" Gina had practically screamed.

Maggie had been too stupefied even to answer her at first. "What are you talking about?" she had finally asked.

"I'm talking about this affair you're carrying on with your therapist." And off she had gone, oblivious to Maggie's protests that they were not having an affair.

"Are you saying your relationship is purely professional?" Every word like a thrust with a sharp knife.

"I don't know what professional is," Maggie hedged.

"Well, it's not kissing."

"How did you know about any kissing?" The words were out before she could stop them.

"I asked Tim."

"You've been interrogating my child?"

"Oh, Maggie, you are such a baby." Gina's tone was disgusted. "And he is such a louse. He could lose his license over this."

"What do you mean?"

"I mean it's against every professional code of ethics for a therapist to do this. No romance with the patients. He's violating the code of ethics and he could lose his license." Then Gina had added, with spite, "And I'm going to see that he does."

"What are you going to do, Gina?"

"It's not what I'm going to do, it's what I've already done."

Maggie just sat there, holding the telephone in her hand, dumb as a post, for the life of her not able to imagine what Gina could be talking about.

"I hired an investigator." Gina spat the words out like little bullets. "And I'll tell you something else—there's a bigger scam going on than this little dalliance with you."

"What are you talking about?" Maggie's voice sank like a stone.

"Never mind. Just be ready. I'm going to see that Golding gets what's coming to him."

Maggie hung up the phone then, right in Gina's ear. Without even saying "I'm going to hang up now." She talked to herself as calmly as she could, reminding herself of what she knew. Gina was always threatening to sue somebody, and very rarely followed through with it, but Maggie could feel again the tight little knot that had been in her chest ever since Gina had first called and expressed doubts about the way Dr. Golding was helping her. Maggie didn't really see why it should be a problem. But it was becoming clearer, even to her, that Gina might be right. And Jake—Dr. Golding, she corrected herself—must know it. She would have to get used to calling him Dr. Golding again, she knew. She would have to get ready for it all to end.

It was inescapable, she realized, as she gave Tim his medicine and tucked him into bed. Even Gina couldn't be wrong all the time, and on this business of therapists and patients she certainly ought to be an expert after as many of them as she had seen.

Maggie felt sore, right in the middle of her chest. Was that why people always put their hand over their heart when they talked about their feelings? Maybe because when they were wounded that's where it hurt. Maggie felt the heaviness come back, that weight attached to her inside, tender parts pulling down like it hadn't done in weeks. She went through the mechanics of ending her day—brushed her teeth, pulled off her clothes, and fell into bed. It was all wrong with Dr. Golding, and finally, she faced that fact. And another one, equally searing. It was all going to end. She lay there in the dark for a long time, unable to sleep, knowing in some part of her that it had ended already.

* * *

There was a light on in the back of the house. Jake went around and tapped on the back door and sure enough, Joe was still up, watching the baseball scores on the eleven o'clock news. He greeted Jake with resignation.

"I've been wondering when you'd show up. Got yourself in over your head," he said, and it was more of an observation than a question. He flipped off the television and motioned for Jake to follow him into the kitchen. "Go ahead and sit down," Joe said, agreeable if not exactly gracious. He opened the refrigerator, bent over, rummaged around, and came up with a covered dish. "You hungry?" he asked.

Jake thought for a minute. "I guess maybe I am," he said.

Joe nodded, got down two plates, heaped them with some kind of chicken casserole, and put them in the microwave. "So what happened?" he asked, measuring out coffee and filling the pot with water. "She find you out?"

"Not yet," Jake answered, already feeling a little better. His older brother had been like a load-bearing wall for him, shoring him up ever since his dad's death. Who does he lean on? he wondered, then answered his own question. On Carol, of course. That realization set off a fresh bloom of pain.

"But you're feeling bad and you don't know how to tell her."

His brother slid a steaming plate in front of him and handed him a fork. Jake could smell the coffee as it began to drip.

"I guess so."

Joe sat down across from him, shook his head. He blew on the bites of casserole to cool them off before he wolfed them down. "You know, Jake, I can't figure you out," he said in between bites.

"How's that?" Jake asked. His brother so rarely gave personal advice, he was curious as to what he would say.

Joe finished off his casserole in three more huge bites before he answered. "I don't know," he said, leaning back and burping behind a closed fist, the discretion definitely a new development since marrying Carol, Jake thought. "Seems like you always shoot yourself in the foot with women."

The coffee had stopped dripping. Jake got up and poured them each a cupful. Maggie had mugs like this. He remembered her sitting right here in this kitchen and saying it, and he felt another twist of pain. He found a little pitcher of cream in the refrigerator—their very own cream, heavy and turning the coffee a swirling brown with only a drop or two.

Joe continued on, apparently deciding Jake's silence was agreement with the charges. "I mean, first you bring that Lindsay around, and no offense, but what were you thinking there?"

Jake slumped back into his chair, too tired to even shrug. His casserole was getting cold, and Joe eyed it. "You going to eat that?" he asked, and when Jake shook his head no, Joe reached over and pulled it toward him with his fork. "Anyway," Joe said. "You'd have been about as happy with a department store mannequin as with Lindsay. And now this."

"Don't you like Maggie?"

"Well, of course I like her." Joe was almost finished with

Jake's casserole now. "But that's not the point I'm making here."

"What is your point?" Jake was beginning to wonder if he'd made a mistake to come over.

"My point is that this time you've gotten hooked up with a perfectly fine woman, but you've gone and screwed things up again."

Jake sat there and stirred his coffee. Joe got up again and came back with half of a pie. Apple by the looks of it. He gestured toward it with the fork. "Want some?"

Jake shook his head and his brother started eating it straight from the tin.

"Well, you got any ideas what I should do now?" Jake asked him.

Joe took a few more bites of pie, then took a knife from the drawer by the sink and carefully cut away the evidence of his bad manners. Jake thought it would have been just as easy to cut himself a piece and put it on a plate to begin with, but he didn't say so. Joe covered the pie with Saran Wrap, sat back down, and sipped his coffee.

"You can bring her here if you want," he offered, his little snack apparently having put him in a slightly more charitable mood.

Jake brightened a little at the thought.

"Bring her here," Joe went on, "tell her when you're with us, where she can be with Carol to talk things through, and where we know you and can tell her you're all right even if you are a little dense sometimes."

"Thanks," Jake said, half sarcastic and half meaning it.

"Anytime." Joe stood up and stretched. His eyes were red from fatigue, and Jake remembered how early milking started.

"I'm going to bed," Joe said. "You know where the blankets and the couch are." He clapped his big hand down on Jake's shoulder as he passed.

Jake poured himself another cup of coffee and sat at the worn oak table looking at the papered walls and waiting for a solution to dawn, watching for it to come up with the sun outside the garden window. He didn't get any new thoughts, but by the time the long, dry night was ending, he felt a little better. A little of the tightness in his chest had eased. He put his coffee cup in the sink and let himself out the front door, opening it as quietly as he could, and he whispered the dogs' names so they wouldn't bark. They raised their sleepy heads and thumped their tails in recognition.

He would take his brother's advice, he decided as he climbed in his truck and started for home. He would bring Maggie Ivey here, tell her the truth, and pray for the right ending.

11
———

Sunday, May 3

Jake fell asleep on his couch for a few hours and felt a little less gloomy when he woke up. He guessed it was because he had finally decided to come clean with Maggie. He got up and showered, and put his trailer to rights, making sure the garbage was out and all the dirty laundry was in the hamper. Just in case he wanted to show her where he lived. It looked all right, he judged, giving it a cold eye in the bright sunlight. Not fancy, but the paint was fresh, the carpet vacuumed, nothing rotting in the refrigerator, and no bad smells.

He called his mother. She was delighted to meet Maggie Ivey, as he had known she would be, and even more delighted that he had decided to tell her the truth.

"I might not get a chance to tell her until after lunch," he reminded her, "so don't say anything that will get me into trouble."

"I'll try not to." His mother sounded doubtful. "Will you make it to church?"

"I don't know. Don't wait for us." He rolled the last word around on his tongue one more time after he hung up the phone.

He hummed as he looked around the trailer one last time and debated whether or not to call Maggie. Things had been a little awkward when he left last night, and no wonder. She must be feeling crazy, with him telling her he was her therapist and then turning around and kissing her. He felt another twist of guilt, but decided to let it spur him to action instead of more torment. He was going to come clean and make things right. Today. Right now. He would take her to Joe and Carol's while everyone was at church, tell her the truth, and if all went well they would walk across the pasture and join the family for Sunday dinner. He shook the truck keys in his hand and again debated whether he should call her or just show up.

He should call, he finally decided. He put the keys back in his pocket, and felt his good feelings deflate when he got the recording, and heard Maggie's voice, with just a hint of a Southern accent, say they were not at home, and to please leave a message. He did, then sat down on the couch, hands hanging limp, suddenly deflated. Now what? He had been primed to get the deception over with, to bring her here and tell her the truth, in a place where she could see what kind of man he really was, but once again, he realized, he had not taken into consideration that Maggie had a will of her own in all this. He was feeling more humbled every day. He gave one more thought to driving to Oakland on the off chance that she was at home, but immediately discarded the option, feeling arrogant even to consider it. If Maggie was at home, she obviously didn't want to talk to anyone. He would respect her by not showing up again uninvited. He felt a lump of disappointment, though, right behind his ribs, and just sat there on the couch for a minute, elbows on his knees, head in his hands. Finally he called his mother and canceled, and asked her to tell Joe and Carol, then got up and headed out the door to find some work to do. If Maggie Ivey needed a day to be left alone, he would give it to her.

* * *

Saturday night's sleep was awful.

Maggie kept thinking about Jeff and how right that had felt, and even though she had Tim now, and nothing could make her regret that, she still wondered about her ability to judge men, the present case a perfect example. She tried to sleep, and did, sort of, but it was the kind of sleep where she knew she was asleep and her mind was whirring and tense all the while. She finally gave up in defeat around five o'clock and paced and prowled around the little apartment like a caged cat. She took herself in hand by going back to her timeworn comfort measures. She'd always said cleaning was less damaging than alcohol or drugs and cheaper than therapy, but just that word made her stomach lurch again.

She dug her supplies out from under the sink and started in the kitchen, scrubbing the sink with Ajax and rubbing the chrome until it gleamed. She swept, and mopped, and washed windows, and even took down her curtains and washed them. She baked a cake, and by then Tim was awake, and he helped her frost and decorate it with some cookie sprinkles left over from Christmas. The phone rang twice, but she didn't answer it. Didn't even listen to the answering machine. She didn't want to talk to Gina or her mother, and didn't think she could talk to Dr. Golding.

After lunch she splurged, and she and Tim took the bus into

Oakland to McDonald's for lunch and then to the weekend children's matinee—actually musty old Disney movies the Bay Theater would trot out on Saturday and Sunday afternoons for a two-dollar admission.

She and Tim walked down to the Oakland Marina and looked at the sailboats, tossed a few rocks into the water, stopped at the park, tolerable in the daylight hours, then came home and played games and read until he went to bed. Then Maggie cried for a while, almost laughing at herself as she did— at least seeing the humor in the situation. She hadn't cried for nearly a year, but had been doing nothing but weeping and sobbing for the last weeks. She always felt better afterward, though, still hurt but a little more calm and peaceful. She'd read an article once that said crying released natural opiates that actually lifted your mood. She ought to have a whole truckload of them coursing through her veins by now.

She finally fell asleep on the couch, her mother's afghan for a cover. Going to bed seemed like making too much of a statement, tempting the part of her that wanted to lie awake again and stare at the ceiling. As long as she just lay on the couch with the afghan she could pretend she was just resting, not really going to bed. But she must have fallen asleep right away, because the next thing she knew Tim was standing over her. She had missed her alarm, and she had barely enough time to get Tim ready, throw together their lunches, and fly out the door, remembering only after she was on the BART and halfway under San Francisco Bay that she had never listened to yesterday's phone messages.

12

Monday, May 4

Maggie's morning was grim. At least the six hours of sleep gave her the strength to trudge through the routines of her day, but the whole time she was typing the minutes to the loan committee meeting, and filing, and circulating memos, Dr. Golding's face—concerned and kind—would bob before her, to the accompaniment of Gina's voice saying, as only she could, that he was a lying scoundrel and a cheat.

At lunchtime she ate her sandwich with Leann in the employee lunchroom, and then the two of them circled the long block. Fortunately, Leann had had a great weekend. She was seeing someone and told Maggie about their date in minute detail, which spared Maggie from any conversation except the um-humm's and oh-really's she was so adept at providing. And as they walked she decided what she would do. It was so simple, now that she'd come to it she wondered why it had taken her so long to use her common sense. Enough of Gina telling her what was and was not okay for a doctor to do, and enough of her threats to bring him down. Maggie would find out for herself.

She said good-bye to Leann at the main lobby, and then took the elevator up to the lunchroom instead of down to the typing pool. She passed a few tellers who lingered after late lunches and those already taking early afternoon breaks. She went into the employee lounge and settled herself at the phone by the couch in the outer room, a little more private than the one at her desk. She searched for the telephone book and after two tries, thought she might have found what she needed—some kind of consumer watchdog group for the mental health professions. The woman was brisk and sounded businesslike.

Maggie tried to sound businesslike, too. "I'm wondering about the ethical requirements for counselors."

"What kind of counselor? Psychiatrist, psychologist, licensed clinical social worker, marriage, family, and child counselor, licensed educational psychologist, psychiatric technician, priest, minister, rabbi, or other member of the clergy?"

Maggie was silent, mentally sorting through the list the woman had reeled off.

"Are you there?" The woman on the telephone slowed her voice, as if talking to a two-year-old.

"Uh, this would be a psychologist, I think," Maggie answered.

"So what was your question?"

Maggie plunged in. "What are the ethics of a psychologist having a relationship with a patient?"

"What kind of a relationship?" The woman's voice sharpened. "Sexual?"

"Oh, no. Just kissing." Maggie felt like she was in high school again, describing a date to her sister.

"That would still violate the code of ethics."

Maggie's tongue felt dry and thick. "What exactly does that code say?"

"Well, let's see." The woman was silent for a minute, then spoke quickly and flatly, as though reading. "Psychologists should never have any type of sexual contact with a patient, including inappropriate touching, kissing, or sexual intercourse. This type of behavior is *never* appropriate, and it is cause for mandatory revocation of the psychologist's license. They may not advertise falsely, act in an unprofessional, unethical, or negligent manner, assist someone in the unlicensed practice of psychology, focus therapy on their own problems, rather than on those of the patient, serve in multiple roles: for example, by having social relationships with patients, lending them money, employing them, et cetera. This confuses the patient and may interfere with treatment—"

"Wait." Maggie interrupted the woman.

"Yes?" Her voice sounded irritated.

"What's inappropriate kissing and touching?"

"It's all inappropriate."

"Really?" Maggie could hear her voice sounding thin and sad.

"Yes. It is." Exaggerated politeness.

"And that part about social relationships. That would mean that it would be wrong for him to have a relationship with me now."

"Now and later on, too." The woman's voice took on a sharp tone. "Who are you inquiring about? Maybe you should make a report."

Maggie hung up the phone without saying good-bye and stared at the ugly orange wallpaper, the corners of the design blurring together with her tears.

What was it about her, Margaret Sarah Ivey, that made men

look at her and see someone to whom the normal rules of decency didn't apply? No matter what she thought about the loving way he seemed to treat her, what Dr. Golding was doing was wrong. She'd just heard the confirmation. And he had to know it. Hurt, like a hot liquid, seemed to fill her chest. She got up and went back to the typing pool, and tried to keep it in through the rest of the day. She didn't let herself think of Tim, throwing himself at Jake and hanging upside down and laughing. She berated herself instead. She had done what she had vowed she would never do—hurt her child, through another bad relationship. Now Tim would have to lose someone he had grown to care about. She worked hard without stopping for an afternoon break, and didn't let herself think about Jake Golding again until she climbed onto the bus that would take her from the BART station to the preschool.

It wasn't enough that he might sincerely care for her, she thought, as the bus trundled along the potholed streets. She remembered the way Dr. Golding had scooted his chair near hers on the first visit to his office. How she had looked up through her sheet of tears to see his eyes looking down at hers with concern. And something else—alarm. She would have smiled if she hadn't felt so wounded inside. Dr. Golding had looked alarmed. Almost as if a patient's distress had never touched him in such a way before. Maybe he did care for her, but the fact remained that he knew his profession didn't allow him to do what he had been doing with her. It would never allow it.

She went inside Happy Campers and found Tim coloring at a table. He was drawing some kind of farm, with black-and-white cows, actually dotted circles with stick legs, lined up to go in the barn. She felt another wave of pain, but oohed and aahed over his picture and promised to put it on the refrigerator as soon as they got home. They walked the four blocks to the Embarcadero Arms, and fortunately Tim didn't seem to notice her quietness. He was describing the plot of a book they'd read at school about a pirate's dog that had a treasure map tattooed on his back.

"Uh-huh. Oh, really? That's funny," she said in between every one of his exchanges, her mind on other things.

She let them into the apartment, feeling another wave of pain as she turned the key in the deadbolt lock and went to make dinner while Tim played with the cat. Another wave. It seemed that everywhere she looked something reminded her of Dr. Golding. It was hard to believe that their lives had become so intertwined in just two weeks.

The two images didn't fit together at all. Dr. Golding was violating his code of ethics and from what Gina said, had other problems as well. But when she actually remembered Jake Golding, the man, and the things he had said to her and done for her, she could hardly believe it. But she had heard the proof herself.

She filled a pot with hot water and put it on the burner, turned it to high, shook in a little salt, and started chopping lettuce for a salad. When the water boiled she shook the macaroni into it. She grated a carrot into the lettuce, listening with only half her attention to Tim chattering from the next room. With the other half she was hearing again the words Jake had whispered in her ear at Angel Island. He hadn't said, *I don't think that would be a good decision to move away and marry a man you don't love,* or *Have you really thought this out,* or any of the things she had expected a psychologist to say. He hadn't even said just *Stay.* She grabbed a napkin and blew her nose and wiped her eyes, and as she washed her hands and splashed water on her face she could almost hear his voice, tender and insistent in her ear, and feel his warm breath. He'd said, "I don't want you to leave. Stay with me."

* * *

The Better Business Bureau had turned up nothing, of course. Jay Golding knew the contractor was crooked, but the clean record surprised him not one bit. From his own experience he knew how these things could be taken care of. A few thousand in the right hands made it seem less important to make a stink about some minor complaint. He ran his hands through his hair, still thickening nicely, and swung his feet over the side of the bed. He was heartily sick of this place.

"Monica, get me that doctor on the phone."

"We've left messages, Jay." Monica had reclined in one of the visitors' chairs, the kind that folded out into a bed for anxious family members. He almost snorted to himself thinking of Monica in that category. She was watching the *Jerry Springer Show* and reading a tabloid magazine, wearing another new outfit. He gave his head a decisive little nod. A lot of things were going to change around here.

Though unplanned, this illness was the best thing that could have happened to him. He realized that now, had realized it several days ago, when the title of a new book dawned on him. *Dying to Live: How Your Life Can Gain New Meaning in the Face of Death.* He had already called his agent, and she was pitching the idea to Random House over lunch today. He had wanted to go with her, but that moron of a doctor said he should stay in the hospital one more day. He shuffled over to the television and looked in vain for the on/off switch, then, because he was annoyed at himself for not turning it off at the bed controls, he snapped at Monica.

"Go get that nurse," he said. "I'm leaving here this afternoon."

"It's not that simple, Jay." Monica pulled the chair into the upright position, losing her hold on the *National Enquirer*. Its pages slithered to the floor, one at a time.

There was that tone again. He looked at her sharply, but her face was as vapid and bland as ever.

"You can't just walk up to the ticket counter and get on a flight," she continued.

Jay narrowed his eyes, annoyed and a little surprised. Monica's saving grace had always been her affability, and it was looking as if her last attractive feature was wearing thin.

"I'll have to make arrangements," she went on, sounding aggrieved. "I probably won't be able to get us on a flight out until tomorrow."

"Well, do it, then," he snapped. Tomorrow was Tuesday. He considered. If he stayed one more day, he might be able to go with his agent on a second call to Random House—the publicity department would want to meet him, of course. It was always better if people met him—after all, he was very promotable. He thought again. Monica was already reaching for the telephone.

"Hold on," he snapped. "Maybe I'll wait."

She looked up at him expectantly, her bangs hanging in thin strands over her eyes.

"Make the reservations for Wednesday," he finally said. "I'll take care of the book while I'm here and deal with that contractor when I get home. We'll go straight from the airport. Catch the bum napping."

That thought cheered him a little bit. He tucked it away, like a big bill in his wallet. He also made a note to himself to call his attorney as soon as Monica had gone out for her afternoon shopping trip, ignoring the loud sighs she was making. Let him get started on the paperwork, and he'd tell her what he'd decided about their—actually, her—future after they were back home. Sitting here in this hospital room, gazing at the vista of the greasy river of traffic on the street below, had convinced him of a few things. He thought of them now and simultaneously envisioned them in bold type on the back dust jacket of his book. LIFE IS TOO SHORT TO WASTE IN DEAD-END RELATIONSHIPS. LIVE AS IF EACH DAY WERE YOUR LAST. He took another look at Monica, engrossed again in *Jerry Springer,* and wondered if she would notice if he made the call now.

* * *

Maggie called Tim to the table and sat down, her mind definitely not on dinner. She stirred her salad around with her fork, and took a bite of macaroni. It sat in her mouth with no more taste or appeal than a wad of paper.

She shook herself out of her thoughts, since they were leading nowhere anyway, and tried to pay attention to Tim for the rest of the evening. They played the inevitable games, Candy Land and Hi Ho! Cherry-O, she read their customary armload of books, and finally Maggie got him to bed.

She was feeling as though she could sleep herself, maybe even in her own bed tonight instead of tricking herself on the couch, when Gina showed up. Maggie's dismay must have shown on her face when she opened the door, because Gina just glared at her and barked, "Well, are you going to let me in or not?"

Maggie stepped back and waved her in, but for once she didn't try to hide her irritation.

"We could have done this on the phone," Gina snapped, "if you would return my calls."

Maggie looked at her friend and sighed. It was obvious Gina was riding one of her swells of emotion. Maggie wondered which one it was this time: outrage, righteous indignation, or sulkiness at some real or imagined slight.

Maggie was fed up with all of them, and no longer willing to pretend otherwise. She was tired of being pushed and pulled by people. She had made a decision sometime in the past weeks, almost without realizing it. She would tell the truth from now on, simply and without pretense, and let the results settle where they would. She would start now.

"Gina, it's late. I'm tired. I don't want to talk to you." She said it mildly, almost absentmindedly.

Gina's face went white, then red. "You'll want to talk to me when I get finished telling you what I've found out about your precious Dr. Golding."

Maggie found herself strangely unmoved by Gina's dramatics. Her own worst fears had already been confirmed. She didn't see how anything Gina added could make her feel any worse. "What?" she asked, her voice flat.

Gina sat down, letting her jacket slide off her shoulders. Maggie stayed by the door.

"Have you got any wine?"

"No."

"Fine." Gina leaned back. Her face lost its redness then, and she just looked—Maggie realized with a start how Gina looked. She just looked mean. Her face had the tight, drawn look of someone who spent hours rehearsing grudges, and her mouth the downward slant of perpetual unhappiness. Maggie felt a rush of pity for Gina, but she still didn't want to take part in this event, whatever drama Gina had planned.

"Okay, fine. I'll just get to the point." Gina sat up and ran her hands through her hair, making it stand on end. Sometime since Maggie had seen her she had gotten it cut into the crew cut again—actually it was more like a flattop. Maggie forced herself to look away from Gina's hair and concentrate on what she was saying. "That investigator I hired to look into Dr. Golding found some things."

Maggie didn't answer. Just crossed her arms.

"You could sit down," Gina said, obviously irritated.

"I'm fine," said Maggie.

"I know you don't like all this, but I felt responsible." Gina didn't look motivated by concern, thought Maggie. She looked angry. Gina went on. "I mean, I'm the one who arranged for this, who paid for it. In effect"—Gina paused, giving her words emphasis—"I'm the consumer here."

Maggie still said nothing.

"Anyway"—Gina shrugged—"the guy's a crook."

"What's your proof, Gina?" Maggie hadn't intended to defend Dr. Golding, but she found herself doing so anyway. "You keep talking about him being a crook, but I still haven't heard anything convincing."

"Okay. I'll break it down for you. My detective started with Golding's business dealings. Found he was overextended, but nothing else."

"So?"

"Just a minute." Gina glared at her. "Anyway, then he called Golding's alma mater. Found out he almost didn't graduate. Right at the end of his graduate program another student says Golding paid him to do his thesis. Seems Golding reneged on the paying part. Anyway, they ended up letting him graduate because they couldn't prove anything, but everybody knew the truth."

Maggie's pulse was loud in her ears.

"There's more." Gina was beginning to look happier. "My detective found out there was a lawsuit filed this year—later dropped. For plagiarism. Golding stole the idea for his latest book from one of his colleagues. The guy told him about the idea at a cocktail party and next thing he knows, Golding's on the best-seller list with it. They settled it out of court. But Golding had to pay plenty."

Maggie was shaking her head. None of this made sense.

"And finally, he's cheating the IRS. He has all the copyrights signed over to a foundation run by his wife, so the book royalties look like they're nonprofit, but he's raking in the bucks and cheating the IRS the whole time. So there you are. Your precious Dr. Golding is a liar, and a cheat, and he scams on his taxes. The jerk is probably going to jail."

One word of Gina's tirade stood up and shouted at Maggie, dressed in red and waving a flag. She walked to the recliner and sat down. "His *wife*?"

Gina stopped for a minute, looking at Maggie with an expression somewhere between incredulity and pity. She shook her head, then said slowly, enunciating each word, "Yes, Maggie. His wife. He's had two and now he has another. If you'd taken the trouble to read his book, you would know that. It's right in the front: *Dedicated to my wife, Monica.*"

Maggie didn't even hear the rest of what Gina said. It had to do with all the ways Gina was going to tighten the noose around Dr. Golding. All Maggie could think about was the way his shoulder had felt against hers, with the warm rock at their backs, and the way he had kissed her, so softly and tenderly, as if he, too, wished he could stay there in that spot forever. She didn't wait for Gina to leave. She laid her head down on her knees, as she had done that first day in Dr. Golding's office, and cried.

13

—

Jake sat at his desk and waited for Ethelda to get back from her estimate. He wanted to at least greet her before he took off for Golding's office for the closing act of this mercifully short-running play. The past two days had been awful. Even now he felt tight and full of dread, but it was finally Tuesday, and this morning he would see Maggie Ivey and put this all to rest. He would meet her at Golding's office, pick up Tim at the preschool, and take both of them to his brother's, and at the old oak table, which had seen its share of drama over the years, he would tell her the whole story. He would tell her who he was, Jake Cooper, contractor, and how he happened to be in Dr. Golding's office that morning, and how he had felt when he had seen her standing there in the doorway, so scared and alone. He would tell her how his heart had softened, and how he had only wanted to help her. He would tell her everything and ask her to forgive him for the deception. And if she did, he would tell her that he loved her and wanted to marry her.

He had done more praying over the last few days than the past few years put together. He had told God that if He would forgive him for the lying, and let Maggie forgive him, too, that he would be grateful all his life.

Jake checked his watch. It was almost time to leave. This would be the last trip to 949 Market, the last time Maggie looked at his face and saw Dr. Jason Golding. After today the little charade would be over, and he didn't think he could wait. He looked around now at the office and felt bad. Things looked fine, thanks to Ethelda's efficiency, but he hadn't been pulling his share lately. Even if you counted the house in the woods, which was nearly finished except for the landscaping, he had done precious little the past few weeks. But all that would change now, he reassured himself. In fact, they had better get moving on Golding's remodel. Now that this business with Maggie Ivey was drawing to a close he could give it some attention.

He decided to atone to Ethelda by greeting her at the door with a mug of the French roast coffee she had bought in response to Jake's house-brand Colombian. He ground up some beans and filled the pot with water. Ethelda came in just as the coffeemaker was starting to make the comfortable dripping sound that he loved and filling the office with its slightly burnt aroma.

She was wearing jeans and a purple silk blouse today, and a red hat that said COOPER-JACKSON CONSTRUCTION. She smiled at him, and he felt relief. Even though Ethelda let every thought fly out of her mouth, she seldom held a grudge.

"I got a message off Golding's voice mail this morning," she said.

Jake smiled. Though Ethelda still objected to Jake's charade often and loudly, she actually had a real talent for deceit when she put her mind to it, he thought. She was definitely the more gifted of the two of them in that respect. She had been religiously checking Golding's voice mail each morning, but up until today there had been nothing from Maggie Ivey. Now she waved the little pink message paper in front of his face.

"I'm glad I caught you before you left for the city. It's from *your patient*." Ethelda said the last two words with sarcasm.

"What's the message?" Jake felt the beginning rumble of a tremor in his delicate peace.

"The message is that she's canceling today," Ethelda said, and handed him the little paper.

Jake looked down at the message slip, as uncomprehending as if it were in Braille. It just said, *While you were out: Maggie Ivey called. Cannot make appointment today.* He looked at it hard, and read it again, as if this time it would yield more information.

"What's wrong?" Jake knew his voice had an edge of panic. "Is she sick or something? Is something wrong with Tim?"

"I don't know." Ethelda spoke slowly and started shaking her head, and looked at him hard. "She didn't say."

"How did she sound?"

Ethelda narrowed her eyes and frowned. "Congested. Look, you're already in this over your boots. Just take the day off."

"Yeah." He didn't say anything more. Just sat there looking at the message.

Ethelda sat down at her desk and began making phone calls. After a few minutes he realized the sounds from her side of the room had stopped, and he looked up. She was sitting still, looking at him.

"What?"

She sighed. "Go."

"What?"

"Come on, Jake. You and I both know what's going on here, and I won't kid you, I think—well, never mind." She paused again and shook her head at him. "Go on. See about it."

He nodded and stood up, shoved the message in his pocket. He didn't know how he felt. Concern for Maggie, fear of the catastrophe that had always seemed to be looming ahead of them, shame for the stupid lies he had led her to believe. He couldn't analyze it. Besides, the time for that had passed. All that remained now was to tell the truth. To do his best to fix it. He hoped Tim was all right. He grabbed his denim jacket, stopped briefly at Ethelda's desk, leaned over, and planted a kiss softly on her cheek.

She didn't say anything smart this time. Just patted his forearm, and said, "God help you."

It seemed to take forever to drive to Oakland. At least this time he didn't have to stop off in the city at that doctor's office. He would never do that again, he vowed, except to do the remodel. He wound through the one-way streets around the pulp mill and plastics plant, and finally pulled up in front of the Embarcadero Arms. There was a fresh pile of broken glass on the sidewalk in front of the empty lot and some garbage that had caught on the tall grass. He took the steps two at a time and stood on the sagging porch, pressing Maggie's buzzer again and again, heartily regretting having told her to keep the front door closed. There was no answer. Her name plate was still there. M. IVEY. He tried again. He could hear the dull grate of the ringer, but still no one answered. Maybe she hadn't been sick at all. He should have gone to the bank first.

He hesitated, then pushed the buzzer for I. WEAVER. She answered right away, remembered who he was, and buzzed the door open.

She came to her door, hair starched in place again today, her veined hand beckoning him in. "I'm so glad you came by," she said. "I'm just worried to death about Maggie."

Jake felt his stomach lurch. "What happened?"

"Come in, honey, and sit down."

Jake didn't want to go in and sit down. He wanted an answer to his question, but he followed Mrs. Weaver into the apartment. "What's happened to Maggie?"

Mrs. Weaver sat down and arranged herself on the couch. She motioned for him to do the same, and to move things along he perched on the edge. "Well, she was here Saturday morning, you know, for her birthday."

Jake struggled not to interrupt, not to demand that she tell him what he needed to know.

"Anyway," Mrs. Weaver continued, oblivious, "Sunday she checked on me, to see if I wanted to go to the movies with them. I said no, it was sweet of her, but my Bible study group comes over on Sunday nights and I had to get ready for them." Mrs. Weaver's face softened at the thought of Maggie's kindness, and again, Jake had to restrain himself. Mrs. Weaver picked up the thread of her narrative after a moment. "Well, she went on to the movies. Then she went to work as usual yesterday. I saw them go out to the bus and I waved at Tim." Now Mrs. Weaver's thin lips pressed together and her eyes teared up, and Jake felt his pulse begin to pound in his ears. "Then last night her friend came over, and then that young man, and then she came down all upset, and said she had to go."

"What friend? What young man?" Jake knew he must be

shouting, he could tell by the alarm that crossed Mrs. Weaver's face.

"That Eye-talian woman. She came over here last night." In her alarm, Mrs. Weaver's native Southern accent became stronger. "They were arguing, and I could hear her, that Eye-talian woman," she clarified, "going on and on. These walls are thin. Well, she carried on so, Mr. Jacobsen went to pounding on the ceiling. Then I didn't hear any more hollering, but I heard that Eye-talian woman leave, come down the stairs like a herd of cattle. I went on up there to see about Maggie. She was crying like her little heart would break. It like to break mine."

Jake felt sick. "Why was she crying? Where is she now?"

"Well, I was fixing to tell you." This was the closest Mrs. Weaver had come to a rebuke. Jake forced himself to sit still and wait. "While I was there trying to find out what was the trouble, here came this fellow up the stairs, Bobby something or another, came right on up to the door. He must have come in when that Eye-talian woman went out. Nine o'clock at night, here he came, bold as you please, and said Maggie's mama had sent him to bring her home. Well, she went to crying again, said she wasn't going anywhere, and he went to shouting at her to get her things together, said they were leaving, just come on. She said she wasn't going to do it and he said he guessed she was. Woke up Tim with all the fuss, then he came out and saw his mama sad, and he went to crying. I brought him downstairs, that fellow still carrying on. I never did get him comforted."

Jake felt as if he would be sick then. He thought of Maggie, alone and facing who knew what from her friend. And the man must have been the one she told him about, who wanted her to come home and marry him. Bobby Semple.

"What happened then?" He felt ruined inside. As if the plates that held him together had shifted. He felt a crevasse open up around his middle.

"Well, finally Maggie came downstairs, and took Tim. Said everything was all right, and that I shouldn't worry. But said in the morning she'd be leaving." Here the old woman paused, pulled a handkerchief from the pocket of her sweater, and pressed it against her eyes. "I asked her was that really what she wanted to do, and she said yes, but I've never seen anybody look so sad. And sure enough, they left. He came back this morning with a U-Haul truck and loaded up her things. They're gone," she finished, and looked at him bleakly.

"Gone." He repeated her last word.

She nodded, and pressed her eyes again. "I don't feel right about it. It just doesn't seem right for him to come and take her off like that."

"They couldn't have just left. Could they?"

Mrs. Weaver shrugged and went to her bulletin board, covered with pictures of missionaries. She took off a piece of heavy paper and handed it to him. One side was an address and the other was covered with blobs of color. Maggie must have used it to blot her brush when she was painting. He felt a sharp pain.

"She gave me this number." Mrs. Weaver pointed to the unpainted side. "Said it was her mama. That I could get in touch with her there in a week or so." Mrs. Weaver started crying in earnest now, the tears following the ridges down her cheeks. "That Tim was the sweetest thing. Hugged my neck and cried like his heart would break. And that fellow that came for them was downright mean. Said Tim wasn't bringing a cat in the truck. Well, I never saw Maggie so mad. Said if that cat didn't go she wasn't going. He gave in then." Mrs. Weaver wiped her face and tucked the Kleenex into her sleeve.

Jake sat still on Mrs. Weaver's stubbled couch for a full minute before he spoke.

"Thank you, Mrs. Weaver," he finally said when he could trust his voice. He copied the telephone number onto the back of his spiral notebook, feeling another stab when he saw Maggie's neat writing, and handed the scrap of paper back to Mrs. Weaver. She placed it carefully in the drawer by the telephone.

"I hope you find her, Dr. Golding."

"I'm not Dr. Golding. My name is Jake Cooper. Here is my card." He handed her one from the contracting business. "If you hear anything else from Maggie, please call me right away." He didn't explain, just left her there with her questions. Then he went down and got back in his car, staring at the smokestacks of Oakland, and wondering where to begin to look.

He finally began at the bank.

"Missed her by about a half hour," the head teller said. "She came in, said good-bye, left an address to send her last check. Had her little boy and a guy with her." The teller looked at him curiously. He thanked her and left.

Jake even drove around to a few motels before he headed back to Petaluma, stopping at all the ones he could find in Oakland and along the freeway, looking for U-Hauls. Nothing. It seemed as though Maggie Ivey had vanished from the face of the planet. She was probably miles away by now.

Fortunately, Ethelda was gone to lunch when he got back to the office. He didn't think he could face her combination of I-told-you-so and sympathy. He went inside and tried the Georgia number.

Maggie's mother gave him no information. She was almost rude when he identified himself as Dr. Golding. Said only that her daughter was coming home where she belonged. She claimed she didn't know where to find Maggie. That she had promised to call from the road, and if he left his number she would pass it on. He gave it to her, without any confidence it would ever reach Maggie, then sat with his head in his hands for a few minutes, and got up and left before Ethelda returned.

He went home and sat in the trailer. He must have sat there for hours, alternating between self-recrimination and desperately trying to think of a plan. None came. The little trailer grew dark around him, and finally around eleven he admitted there was nothing more he could do right now. He would have to give Maggie time to get back to Georgia.

14

Wednesday, May 6

It wasn't like on television. Carson Fuller spent a good fifteen minutes once he arrived at the San Francisco Federal Building just finding the suite of offices designated for the Internal Revenue Service. Feeling triumphant, and flashing his retiree badge from SFPD and his PI license like a victorious banner to the receptionist, he had been asked to take a seat. The first free representative would talk to him. He had taken a seat. That had been twenty-eight minutes ago, and Car was still waiting. He got up, stretched his bad knee, and walked stiffly to the reception desk, where the secretary deftly held the phone between her shoulder and ear, scribbled furiously, and stuck a Post-it note onto a file. She looked up at Carson and held up a finger. One minute. He waited.

"Yes, sir." She hung up the phone and addressed him. She was nothing if not polite.

"Maybe I should make an appointment and come back."

She gave a slight shrug, lifting her eyebrow a millimeter. "It should be only a few more minutes."

He nodded, sat back down, then told himself it didn't matter. It was really no skin off his nose. That Tucci woman would pay for the half hour of waiting at his standard rate. He picked up a magazine, and thought of her again, a little piston, determined to pound the guts out of the doctor, whom Car had actually begun to feel sorry for.

After he finished his business here he'd go back to the office and write his report. He wanted everything typed up nice and neat so the Tucci woman wouldn't give him any grief about his bill, which would be enough to pay his own bills this month and maybe provide for a few days of fishing in Nevada. He thought about all the trouble she was going to, all the money she was spending, and shook his head, though when he remembered the flat glint of those dark eyes of hers he wasn't really surprised. He had seen so much spite over his thirty-year career, it no longer amazed him what lengths some people would go to in order to get revenge.

* * *

Maggie dialed Dr. Golding's number and let the telephone ring three times before she hung up. It had been a long, hard day, and it was late, nearly eleven o'clock. This was her second day of being a virtual hostage in the Motel 6 with Bobby Semple standing guard in the next room, looking out his door every time she went to the ice machine or down the stairs to the laundry room. He had been in such a tearing hurry to leave that she had had to bring a big garbage bag full of dirty clothes, which she had been washing all afternoon. And now that Tim was asleep she was calling, and feeling as though Bobby must be able to see through the walls and know it, so intense seemed his desire to pull her back in line. He was suspicious and sulky, always watching her as if he expected her to bolt any minute.

She felt as if she barely knew Bobby Semple. He had changed from one of the Georgia boys she'd grown up with, who played football and hunted with their fathers, into an unsmiling man who seemed to be on another hunting trip, this time with her as the prey. He felt like a stranger, even though she had dated him on and off through high school, and she had to admit, kept the embers alive since then, as much as a chatty monthly letter could. And he was obviously her mother's choice, having sent him on the errand of getting her daughter and bringing her back home.

That errand had gotten off to a rough beginning and had now come to a dead stall. Bobby had wanted to leave right away on Tuesday morning, but by the time they had packed the U-Haul, gone to the preschool to pay the bill, to the bank to close Maggie's account and say good-bye, had lunch, and gotten the map and a few groceries for the cooler he had insisted on bringing, it had been afternoon. They'd headed out of San Francisco, and as soon as they were north of the Golden Gate, Tim said he had a stomachache. Maggie had felt his forehead. It was cool.

"He's fine," said Bobby. "Let's just get on the road." He seemed to want to put as much distance as he could between the three of them and the Embarcadero Arms right away.

But Maggie, maybe just wanting to be contrary, had argued with him. "I want to wait and see if Tim's coming down with something," she said. "Besides, it's nearly four o'clock. We're not going to get very far today. Let's just spend the night here and get an early start in the morning."

Bobby grumbled about that being easy for her to say since

she wasn't paying for the motel, and then Maggie asked him who *was* paying for the motel, and he had gotten red in the face and admitted that her mother had given him five hundred dollars for the trip home. And that was when Maggie had begun to feel as though she'd been bought and paid for and was now in the process of being delivered.

Bobby said he was too tired to drive all night anyway, seeming to need for the delay to be his idea now that it was inevitable.

"Where are we stopping?" Maggie asked, stroking Tim's forehead.

"Well, we're sure as hell not staying here." Bobby gestured toward the fancy hotels that lined the freeway in Marin County.

"Which way are we going to take to Georgia?" she asked, forgetting until his face turned red again that Bobby took every question as a challenge to his authority.

"Well, Maggie, I'm sure as hell not driving across the desert in this heap."

"You still haven't answered my question." She barely recognized her voice as the sharp one that bit out those words, and realized that whatever else the future held, it probably wouldn't include Bobby Semple.

"We'll go north on Interstate Five and then head east." He glowered at her as he spoke.

Maggie nodded and was silent, and tried not to think about the last time she had seen the landscape they were passing.

"My stomach hurts worse, Mom. I think I'm gonna throw up."

"We need to stop, Bobby." Maggie refused to look at him, and found a plastic bag in case Tim made good on his threat.

Bobby gave in with a huge sigh, turned off the freeway, and was somewhat soothed when he found a Motel 6 in Novato.

Tim had felt better after last night's sleep, so this morning they had piled in the U-Haul again, but when Bobby went to pull out of the parking stall the U-Haul wouldn't shift into reverse. Bobby tinkered and fumed until nine o'clock and then called the company, barely containing his rage. They sent out a mechanic, who worked on the truck for nearly three hours, while Maggie and Tim walked around the strip mall next door and watched television in the motel lobby. By the time the mechanic reached the conclusion that the transmission was shot, it was two o'clock. Maggie paid for another night at the motel and carried her and Tim's suitcases back to their room.

"Just give me another truck," she hear Bobby yelling at the U-Haul man as they passed. "I'll reload the damned thing."

"Got no more." The mechanic seemed to take pleasure in telling Bobby the news, though he did shoot a pitying look at Maggie and Tim, now leaning against the second-floor railing along with the man from the room next to them, who took turns tossing cigarette butts and spitting onto the bushes below.

"Like hell!" Bobby raised his voice to the man and the two of them exchanged words for five minutes or so.

"Hey! You're scaring Tim!" Maggie finally yelled down at them. That made the U-Haul man stop, though Bobby just shot her a glare and went on yelling, now at her.

"Maggie, you get on the phone and find us another truck." His chubby face was red.

Maggie went back inside the room, turned on the television for Tim, found a cartoon he liked, then lay down on the bed and went to sleep.

"I don't understand you" was all Bobby said when she'd admitted to him, hair mussed and still groggy, that she'd made no calls. She hadn't answered that, just closed the door and left him standing outside.

He came back an hour or so later with some dinner.

"Why don't you just leave all this junk?" He gestured over his shoulder at the crippled U-Haul still parked below. "I'll buy you new when we get home." Bobby had been recently promoted at the peanut processing plant, and acted flush.

"They're our things," Maggie said with what she hoped was dignity. "We want to keep our things." She thought of her paintings, carefully packed away in their jaunty frames. She'd wrapped them in newspaper, even though Bobby had been pacing in and out, arms full of furniture and blankets, urging her to hurry. She'd left the furniture and given the plants away to Mrs. Weaver.

She took the Burger King bag from him at the door, not inviting him in. She looked inside. Bobby hadn't even gotten Tim a cardboard crown. Jake would have gotten Tim a crown, she thought, the comparison springing to her mind. No, Jake would have taken them out somewhere, she corrected, probably to one of those pizza places that have the big pool full of plastic balls for kids to jump in, and rides, and games to play. She looked up. Bobby was glaring at her, his face dark.

"I hope you straighten out once we're out of here," he said, in a tone that she supposed was meant to make her repent. "You always was stubborn, but I swear, Maggie, I don't know you no more." He gave an exaggerated sigh, and shuffled off to his own room.

And here she was, still unable to sleep at eleven, and on the phone like an adulteress, calling the office of a married man. Whom she had kissed. And held.

She hadn't told Bobby anything, and she was childishly pleased. She hadn't told him about Dr. Golding, or his wife, or any of the things Gina had said. And she hadn't called Gina to say good-bye. She would send her a letter once she was back home. Maybe. But at least now things were settled. This is what she would do. This would be her life. She would go back home and even though she probably wouldn't marry Bobby, she was realistic that she would probably end up with someone just like him. And that was fine. She would make it fine. She dialed Dr. Golding's number again, waited through the ringing this time, and listened as it switched to voice mail. She looked over at the lump in the other bed that was her son and thought to herself that it was time she quit behaving like a child.

Poor Tim, Maggie thought, and felt another ripple of pain begin in her chest and spread outward. His stomachache had eased once they were out of the truck, but he had asked twice about Jake, if they were ever going to see him again, and could they at least say good-bye. Maggie had tried to change the subject, but there was no easy answer to that question, and she would rather wait until they were settled back in Georgia before she told Tim the truth. They would not be seeing Jake Golding again.

She listened to the voice mail message, a woman's voice, matter-of-fact, leaving another doctor's number to call in case of emergency. Of course, he wouldn't be there. It was eleven o'clock. He was probably at home in bed, and she realized that during all the time they'd spent together Dr. Golding had never given her his home telephone number. She was flooded with shame when she thought about it. Of course he wouldn't give out his home number. He had a wife. She hung up the phone again without leaving a message.

She wrapped herself up in the stiff motel blanket and sheet. A lot of things finally made sense to her, now that she knew the truth. That much was a relief. She had always sensed an uneasiness in Dr. Golding, and every time they started to get closer, it was as if something came between them. The fact that he was married explained everything.

She lay there long into the early morning, trying for the hundredth time to reconcile all of what Gina had told her with what she knew of Dr. Golding, feeling almost crazy when she couldn't. The two didn't mix, no matter how hard she tried to make them. She wondered if he would be waiting for her tomorrow morning. The last day of her *21-Day Overhaul.* She gave a twisted smile and supposed in a strange way she had gotten what she'd asked for. She couldn't deny her life had been overhauled.

"Be ready by nine" was the last thing Bobby told her, just before going to bed. "That's when they're bringing the new truck, and I want to get an early start. We need to get out of here." He had shrugged inside his shirt as if the very air of California made his skin crawl.

She thought of him sleeping in the room next door and laid the thoughts against her memories of Jake Golding. She remembered him in the hallway of the Embarcadero Arms, installing Mr. Jacobsen's locks, hands moving easily between the drill and the door, riding Tim on the bike at Angel Island, and in the backyard of her apartment, balancing his paper plate on his knee at the potluck. She remembered him holding her in the barracks at Angel Island, and feeling, like a strong wall, his desire to come between her and anything that made her feel alone and afraid.

She couldn't sleep. She looked at Tim, and at the kitten clutched in his arms, and thought about picking up the phone again, then just as quickly pushed the idea away from her. She should never have called him to begin with. He was a married man.

15

Thursday, May 7

Carson Fuller got to the Camden Professional Building with time to spare. It was only ten fifteen and things wouldn't start cooking until eleven. He was counting on getting into Golding's office the same way he had when he'd gone through the good doctor's files. The maintenance man had seemed impressed with Car's old SFPD badge, and he'd pocketed the fifty that was wrapped around it without saying a word. This morning Car would get in the same way, take a seat, and watch the show. Showdown was more like it.

He smiled, brushed a piece of lint from his best navy jacket, and straightened his tie. The Tucci woman said she'd called the press, and he didn't want either of his ex-wives seeing him on the front page of the *Examiner* looking like a derelict. He went through the revolving doors and bought himself a cappuccino at the espresso stand in the lobby and an *Examiner* from the newsstand. He whistled as he waited for the elevator.

A few more hours and he'd present his bill and be on his way.

He'd typed it up last night, detailing every charge so the Tucci woman wouldn't have anything to gripe about. He brushed off a slight feeling of guilt with another piece of lint. To be thorough he should have tailed the guy, at least for a day or two. But what the hell? He'd nailed him, just like she wanted.

He strode into the elevator, as jaunty as he could be with the gimpy leg, punched the button, and rode up to the twelfth floor. As it turned out, he didn't even need the maintenance man today. The door opened when he turned the handle, and the woman sitting at the secretary's desk gave him a sassy look when he walked in. She had coppery skin and full red lips, and Car thought he had never seen anyone so delicious-looking in his life.

"May I help you?" She had a voice like honey.

"I certainly hope so." He flashed her his most charming smile. "I'm waiting for Dr. Golding."

"Dr. Golding's busy now." The woman raised her chin and gave it a toss in the direction of the office behind Car. "He's expecting a patient."

Car looked behind him, and his mind flashed onto the photo of Golding in his file—a big, beefy, smooth-looking guy, smarmy expression on his face, a little bald on top. He didn't see Golding now. There was a kid, maybe late twenties, early thirties, sunburned face and short blond hair, looking worried and uncomfortable. He was dwarfed by the huge desk, though Car guessed he was a big man when he unfolded himself. He compared the guy to Golding's image in his mind.

"Look, lady," said Carson Fuller. "I don't know what you're trying to pull here, or who that is." He shook his head. "But I know who it's not. And that's not Dr. Jason Golding."

* * *

Lindsay woke with a sense of movement and finality. Of convergence. She was in touch with her own universe, she knew. She nodded to herself as she looked out over the foggy bay and finished her kasha and peaches. She took another sip of green tea. She had been feeling the buildup over these past few weeks and a few things had come clear. The movement had to do with Jake. That much was certain. She had waited, though, pursuing him ever so gently, waiting until the finely tuned forces around her were poised in the right positions. As they were now. Today was the day.

She sipped her tea with a feeling of determination. She had read it during her morning centering time. Her growth reading for today in *365 Days of Enlightenment* said it in plain language. *You are about to embark on a journey to which you think you know the way and the destination. There are new turns in the road. Go into your being with a new consciousness of its dangers and opportunities.* She became excited when she read that, waiting as she had been for some sign that the universe was ready for her action. Her reading had confirmed it. Obviously. The time was now.

She finished her tea in one gulp, and gathered up her purse and keys. She pulled the phone across the table, punched in the numbers with the tip of her fingernail, and hoped that Jake's partner didn't answer the phone. Lindsay suppressed a little sigh. That woman had never liked her. Lindsay didn't like Ethelda, either, but that was only because the woman had started the negative energy between them.

"Cooper-Jackson Construction."

It was the other one, the young girl with the heavy thighs.

"This is Lindsay Hunt," she said, using the polite tone she always took with subordinates. "Could I speak to Jake, please?"

"I'm sorry, Ms. Hunt, Mr. Cooper is at a job site right now. He should be back this afternoon. Could I have him call you?"

Lindsay gave her head a shake even though the girl couldn't see it. If she left her number, Jake would likely ignore it. No. Today was the day for action. "I need to know the location of that site. This is an emergency. I must get in touch with him now."

The girl hesitated. "Okay," she said finally. "He's in San Francisco at the office of Dr. Jason Golding, 949 Market Street, suite—"

Lindsay cut her off. "Is this a job?"

There was a pause. "Sort of. I'm not sure." Another pause. "Maybe I'd better have him call you."

"No. That's all right." Lindsay pressed the button to end the call and laid the telephone down on the table. It couldn't be possible. All this time she had thought him in therapy, could he have just been doing a job? She thought back to how she had gone to Borders Books and bought everything in print by Dr. Jason Golding, even his newest release, *Celebrating Me*. She thought again how she had reread all his books and listened to the tape series of the *21-Day Overhaul*. Just so she and Jake could be on the same page, so to speak, when they finally entered therapy together. She shook her head and dismissed her doubts. It couldn't be true. He probably just told his secretary it was a job so he wouldn't be embarrassed. But now that the seed of doubt was planted, she couldn't dismiss it.

She sat there a few more moments and remembered her morning reading, then, coming to a decision, left her condo and walked down the stairs to her car, heels clicking a sharp accompaniment to her thoughts. She had no appointments this morning. She would go right now to Golding's office. If Jake was there, she would find out exactly what was going on and where things stood between them. She revved up the car and pulled out of the parking garage with a hoarse burst from her engine.

* * *

The baggage carousel was agonizingly slow. Monica's head hurt. She was weary. She pushed her bangs out of her eyes, and looked around for the rest of the luggage one more time. How perfect that the airline had lost it. The perfect ending to a perfect trip.

"Monica!" Jay shouted at her from where he sat in a wheelchair at the periphery of a little constellation of passengers who waited for their luggage to orbit near them. "Get the damned luggage and let's get out of here!" They had been waiting for over an hour for the flight that carried their luggage to arrive.

Monica didn't answer, just looked at the bags being spit out of the opening and sliding down the ramp toward her. There was lots of black Samsonite but so far no Louis Vuitton.

"Monica!" Jay was turning a deep plum. "Get the damned suitcases, and let's go!"

A few people were giving Jay dirty looks. One mother pulled a small girl away from him, glancing over her shoulder toward him as she did.

Here came her overnighter. Monica grabbed it, and waited for the other pieces. It had really been a hellish trip. She'd booked their tickets on yesterday's flight from New York to San Francisco. It should have taken six and a half hours. But there had been engine trouble or something and they had sat on the runway at LaGuardia for hours. Finally, around six, the airline volunteered to take everyone to hotels, but Jay had thrown one of his fits. He'd changed their tickets to the red-eye on some no-name airline that Monica half expected to fly them into a swamp. They'd had a four-hour layover in Pittsburgh or Milwaukee, or some other godforsaken place, and had finally landed in San Francisco early this morning, barely beating the fog. But the luggage had stayed in Pittsburgh. And Jay had been in one of his snits. Monica hated it when he got like this. He would seize on some small thing that hardly mattered, really, and turn it into a federal case. Her hand tightened on the carry-on bag. This last one coming down looked familiar. She counted the pieces at her feet. One, two, three, and the carry-on. Thank God.

She held the claim checks out for the attendant. Jay was flagging down a skycap. "Over here, for crying out loud! I'm not a well man. Is this how the airline treats invalids?"

Monica sighed and massaged her forehead as the skycap took the bags. She was sick of Jay. Sick of his illnesses, and his ranting and raving. She was sick of always waiting for him. She was sick of being the brunt of all the jokes he thought she didn't get. She looked over at him now, screaming at the skycap as the poor guy tried to load their luggage into a cab. She slipped the man a twenty when Jay wasn't looking.

Finally, they were all loaded in, Jay, the luggage, and her, wedged as far toward the door as she could get. As far away as possible from Jay, who was glowering at the back of the cab-driver's neck. Monica couldn't wait to get home. She had two goals—a hot bath and bed. Jay would have an agenda, of course, but this time he was on his own. She had had enough. She took off her shoes and wondered why on earth she had ever bought them. She looked at them now as if she had never seen them before. They were expensive black leather, with high heels and impossibly pointed toes. No wonder her feet always hurt. She kicked them to the side, and pulled her feet up under her.

"For crying out loud, put your feet down, Monica, you're taking up too much room." Jay had his briefcase open on the seat between them, and Monica had moved it a fraction of an inch.

She ignored him and looked out the window, mentally counting the cash in her wallet. She had about $150 and the Visa and American Express cards. The cab pulled out and headed north. They passed the outskirts and when they entered the city, instead of continuing north toward Marin and home, the driver turned east toward the Financial District.

"Where are we going?" Monica asked.

"We're going to my *office*," Jay told her in that insulting way he spoke. "To my *office*, Monica. That was the whole point of us coming home. So I could find out what the hell was going on *at my office*."

Monica felt her jaw tighten. She looked out the window until the cab drew up in front of 949 Market. The cabdriver got out and began to unload the luggage. Monica didn't care. Jay could have it all. The driver unfolded Jay's wheelchair—he had insisted on buying one and bringing it along even though the doctor said it would do him good to walk. The driver got back in and waited for instructions. She could hear Jay hollering through the closed window.

"Come on, Monica. Don't make me carry all this luggage."

"Call the security guard, Jay," she hollered back. "He'll carry it in for you."

"For crying out loud, Monica, get out or roll down the window. I can't hear you."

"You getting out here?" the driver finally asked, looking at her in the rearview mirror.

Monica shook her head slowly from side to side, and crooked

an index finger in a tiny wave at Jay, who was turning red in the face and yelling her name.

"Take me to the nearest branch of Wells Fargo, and then back to the airport," she told the cabby. "I'm going to make a withdrawal. Then I'm going to take a trip."

She could see the cabby's eyes in the rearview mirror. They crinkled in amusement. She could hear Jay screaming at her from the sidewalk.

"Do these doors lock?" she asked the cabdriver, and leaned her head back against the seat.

He snapped them shut, then grinned at her again in the rearview mirror.

"You had lunch yet?" he asked.

*   *   *

Gina was excited. She checked her watch and drove a little faster. She wasn't angry any longer. The fury that had set all these events in motion was gone. In its place was an almost manic excitement. She was going to nail the son of a bitch. She, Gina Tucci, and the detective she had hired were going to bring down Jay Golding.

She felt a slight tremor of guilt at the thought of how hurt Maggie would be by all of this. But Maggie needed to grow up, Gina told herself, and went back to visualizing the scenario. She had chosen eleven o'clock as the time for the confrontation because she knew that's when Golding would be there. She ignored the twinge she felt when she realized that Maggie would be there, too. To witness the whole thing. The serving of the search warrant. The ransacking of the premises, and the seizing of the files. The whole nine yards. She took another sip from the double-tall latte she had bought at the drive-through near her house. They always made them too hot. Ten minutes on the road and it was just now cool enough to drink.

She checked her makeup in the mirror on the sun visor. Rubbed a glob of lipstick off her tooth and fluffed up what was left of her hair, delicately so as not to disturb the mousse. She'd worn her black suit, white blouse, and tie. There would be reporters.

She had called the news desk at the *Examiner,* and the guy had been eager to talk to her. They'd actually been planning an interview with Golding, since he was such an up-and-comer in the psychotherapy scene, but the guy seemed happy to change angles. It would be beautiful. The fall of a con man, and she had brought him down. Front page news. She swung into the parking garage of Golding's building and took a ticket, tossing it on the dashboard. She got out, pressed the button, and her car alarm chirped. She started up in the elevator. She couldn't wait to see his face.

* * *

Jake waited behind the smooth teak desk. He didn't care anymore. Didn't care that the private investigator, this Carson Fuller, had nailed him. He'd freely admitted who he was right after the guy called his bluff. He'd half expected the man to cuff him and haul him away, but the guy just shook his head, made him repeat the whole story, with lots of clarification from Ethelda, then shook his head again.

"I guess I should retire," he said. "How'd I miss all this?"

"Don't blame yourself," Jake said. "Even I'm confused, and I planned the whole thing."

Carson Fuller grinned and shook his head again, tossed his empty coffee cup into the garbage, and sat down with his *San Francisco Examiner.*

"Are you staying?" Jake asked him.

"Wild horses couldn't drag me away," he said.

Jake had gone into Golding's office and shut the door. He cared about only one thing. He needed to be here, just in case, on the off chance, on the very off chance, that Maggie Ivey was still around somewhere and would show up for her last appointment this morning.

He would give it another five minutes. Then he would have to face the fact that she was not coming. Then he would have to get up and deal with the mess in the waiting room, with the contracting job, with his life. He felt foolish even thinking that she might come today, but he couldn't let this last connection go without at least waiting for her one more time. But he had to face the fact. She was gone. Probably halfway back to Georgia by now. He stopped. No, he counted the hours in his mind and compared them to the states. Actually probably somewhere around Illinois. Maggie was probably in Chicago.

He wondered if Bobby Semple would take the time to show Tim and Maggie the sights there. There was the Sears Tower and Wrigley Field. There might even be a Cubs game today. Jake would have taken Tim to a Cubs game. Bought him a cap. And he would have taken Maggie to the top of the Sears Tower, and let her look all around. "See," he would have told her, "you're on top of the world. The highest building in the world."

But that would never happen now, and there was no one to blame but himself. He accused himself of hubris, that deadly pride that had brought down heroes from Othello to Nixon. The feeling that you were above the rules. That they didn't apply to you. He held his head in his hands and felt grief over how he had deceived Maggie Ivey. She had deserved to know the truth. From the very beginning. Who was he to take that kind of power over her? To think she was too fragile, that he knew better than she did what was best for her. It had been the tears, he knew. He had panicked at the tears. Had felt that he must stop them.

He shook his head, and looked out Golding's window. He couldn't see anything. The entire city was blanketed by a bank of fog this morning. He checked his watch. It was eleven fifteen. He could hear Ethelda in the outer room, probably talking to the crew of plumbers who were going to plumb for the Jacuzzi as soon as he vacated the office.

He shouldn't have been afraid of her tears. He knew that now. He stood, hands in his pockets, looking out at the fog. He could hear the low moan of a foghorn, somewhere out on the bay. He knew exactly what he should have done, now that it was too late. He should have told her the truth. And then let her cry.

* * *

Ethelda leaned back in the receptionist's swivel chair. She had gotten used to this chair in the last three weeks. She'd even adjusted it to her height, and it fit her perfectly now. She swirled around in it, and picked up the clipboard that listed the estimates for Golding's remodel.

"When can we get started?" The younger plumber was anxious, leaning against the side of her desk.

"Relax," the older one said. "The meter's running. What do you care?"

Ethelda looked again at her watch. "We'll give him another five minutes. If the person he's waiting for hasn't shown up by then, I don't think she's coming."

At the feminine pronoun, the younger plumber seemed to get philosophical. "Where's the coffee?" he asked.

Ethelda pointed to the counter behind her, and he trudged toward it, heavy brown boots leaving an imprint in Golding's thick white carpet. Ethelda didn't like to think where those boots had been. She sighed. She felt sorry for Jake. Poor child. She'd seen him this miserable only once before, when Erv had died. But she'd been too sad herself then to be of any comfort to him. They had just gone on the best they could. Ethelda shook her head. She supposed that was what he'd have to do this time, too. From what he had said, that woman was gone.

She still kept looking toward the door for her, though, in between glances at Carson Fuller, who was sitting in the waiting room, pretending to read a magazine, but glancing up at her when he didn't think she was looking. She caught him now, and smiled at him.

She was just about to give the plumbers the okay to go in when someone opened the door from the hall. It took a minute for Ethelda to register the woman's face. She had been expecting Maggie Ivey. But it wasn't Maggie Ivey. It was that other woman. "The Amazon" was what Ethelda called her to Val. She knew her real name, of course.

"Lindsay. What a surprise to see you here."

Lindsay looked down at her from her considerable height. But then again, Lindsay always looked down on everyone. It just made it so much more convenient that she was built for it, Ethelda thought. She shook her head at herself, disgusted by her own cattiness.

"What are you doing here?" Lindsay looked blank.

Ethelda, prone to tell the truth in stressful circumstances, did so now. "I'm just filling in here while I wait for Jake."

Lindsay shrugged. "Is this a job or is he here to see the doctor?"

"Not exactly," Ethelda said, not answering either question. She inhaled to try again.

Lindsay's face was something between confused and hopeful. "Is he in there now? With Golding?" She sounded excited.

"I think you'd better talk to him." Ethelda started to stand.

"Don't even start." Lindsay held up a carefully manicured hand. "I know everything. I know what's been going on here. I'll wait. Just buzz the doctor and tell him I'm here, and that I want to join their session before it's over." She walked over to the seating area, paused before the magazine table, and sat down.

Ethelda thought quickly. There was a back door from the inner office. Maybe Jake would want to use it. She picked up the phone to buzz him. Before he walked right out into Lindsay Hunt. But before she could do it, though, the hall door opened again. A short, dark woman with a crew cut walked in. She looked Hispanic or Italian, and even though she was a full foot shorter than Lindsay, there was something about the way she carried herself that made Ethelda wonder if they were twins separated at birth. She smiled to herself.

"My name is Gina Tucci. I'm here to see Dr. Golding. A friend of mine has an appointment at eleven. In fact, she's probably in there now. Maggie Ivey?"

Ethelda felt her heart sink. She looked toward the closed door of the office and prayed Jake didn't choose this moment to come out. She scratched her head with her pencil. "Actually," she started to say, but she never got a chance to finish her sentence, because Lindsay rose up from her chair, looking more like the Amazon warrior than ever.

"I couldn't help overhearing. Ethelda, isn't Jake in there right now?"

Ethelda nodded.

"That's impossible," said the Italian woman. "My friend told me she would be here today at eleven. It's her last session of the *21-Day Overhaul*."

"Your friend must have rescheduled." Lindsay pronounced it like a verdict. Ethelda nodded. It was so easy really. To deal with egos like these, she just got out of the way.

"I'm sure Dr. Golding will sort all this out, if you women will just have a seat." She did her best to smile. Carson Fuller was grinning, seeming to enjoy it all.

Both women went to the seating area and sat down, eyeing each other over their magazines.

Ethelda picked up the phone. Intercom 1 or Intercom 2? She was just getting ready to press 1 when the door opened again and two business types came in.

"I am Ronald Turpin of the Internal Revenue Service." The tall, thin one spoke. "I have a warrant to search these premises for any and all documents and information that might give evidence of defrauding the government of the United States of its rightful revenue."

This was too bizarre. Ethelda felt a laugh begin to rise up from somewhere in her chest.

Lindsay came over to the desk now. Suddenly Ethelda felt the laughter begin to erupt into sound. Again and again.

"I really don't think this is funny," Lindsay Hunt was saying. The IRS man didn't seem to think so, either. He was asking her where the financial records were kept, and telling her to step away from the computer. Then he began putting tape over the drawers of the file cabinet so no one could open them without breaking the seal. The Italian woman was smiling, too, but more catlike than amused. What could happen next? Ethelda had a sudden vision of the absurdity of it all. It reminded her of a Marx Brothers movie she had seen once, where people kept coming into a stateroom on a ship, and it got fuller and fuller, and each time the door opened someone even more unexpected came in.

Ethelda had to find the Kleenex. She was laughing so hard the tears were beginning to flow. She was up from the reception desk now and the IRS man was pulling files up on the computer, and asking when the doctor was due back.

"Due back? He's in there right now." Lindsay pointed her finger toward the oak door of the inner office.

"Yes, of course he is," the Italian woman chimed in.

Carson Fuller was shaking his head.

Agent Turpin of the IRS gave a little frown, rose from the reception desk, walked over to the oak door, and gave a smart series of knocks.

Jake answered the door, looking as haggard as Ethelda had ever seen him. He looked out at the little crowd gathered in the waiting room, his eyes traveling like pencil lines from dot 1 to 2 to 3 to 4 to 5; from Agent Turpin, to the plumbers, leaning against the wall, to the short, dark woman, to Carson Fuller, with a slight nod, finally coming to rest on Lindsay Hunt.

"Jake," Lindsay said.

"Dr. Golding," Agent Turpin read from a paper he pulled from his briefcase, "you are hereby served notice to appear in the United States District Court, Northern Region of the State of California, to answer charges that you have evaded payment of rightful taxes, and are under notice that any and all property on these premises and others that you own or occupy is seized for evidence and possible repayment of levies owed."

"What are you talking about?" Jake asked.

"He's not Dr. Golding," said Lindsay Hunt. "Where's Dr. Golding, Jake?"

"No, he's not Jason Golding," the Italian woman echoed.

"No." Carson Fuller shook his head, and gestured toward the hallway door, opening a crack to produce the front wheels of a wheelchair. "If I'm correct, that's Jason Golding."

Ethelda backed up as far as she could to make room for the chair. It was stuck in the door. Finally, the man who sat in it, heavy, expensively suited, thinning brown hair, red-faced, and cursing, got up and walked through the door, giving the chair a shove back into the hall with his foot.

"What in the hell is going on here!" he fairly roared. "Nothing has been done at all on this remodel!" His face went dusky, and the artery on his neck pulsed above his tie. "Where is the contractor who's supposed to be in charge of this fiasco?"

"That would be me," Jake said.

Agent Turpin turned toward the red-faced man. "You're Jason Golding?"

"Yes, I'm Jason Golding. Who the hell are you?"

It went on from there. Ethelda finally gathered up her purse and clipboard while the IRS agent was reading the real Dr. Golding his rights. Lindsay Hunt had Jake by his shirt and was letting loose a whole barrage of words at him, like a blanket of bombs on a sleeping city. The woman with the crew cut was on the phone. Ethelda heard her asking where the hell the reporter was. Ethelda sent the plumbers home, telling them the job was canceled. "Send me your bill," she said, "and we'll pay it. I don't think Dr. Golding's going to be finishing his remodel." Carson Fuller gave her a wink on her way out.

The only thing to be thankful for in this whole mess, she reflected, as she let herself into her car and drove wearily up the highway toward home, was that with all the charade with Maggie Ivey, they hadn't done much on the remodel. They'd have been out thousands and would have to stand at the end of what was looking like a very long line to collect from Dr. Jason Golding.

Ethelda wished there had been something she could do for Jake. Not able to think of anything, she had left it all where it fell, and the last she had seen he looked like misery personified, though she couldn't imagine him taking much time with Lindsay Hunt. His grief had another source. She shook her head and breathed a deep breath of relief when she crossed the Golden Gate, leaving the whole sorry mess behind her in the city. She thought back on how it had all begun so innocently, and how it had progressed, becoming more and more complicated and snarled. And how it had ended with today's little performance. She still wasn't sure whether it was tragedy, comedy, or farce. Whatever it was, she thought, they had played their finale to a full house, and the show was finally over. And the only one who hadn't come out to see the closing act was Maggie Ivey.

* * *

Car had never seen such a melee, outside of a hockey game. The room had finally cleared out except for Agent Turpin, who was still looking through files like a madman. He had called SFPD after Golding took a swing at him. They'd sent some young officers to haul Golding away till his arraignment, but at the last minute, they'd detoured to the hospital because Golding said he had chest pains.

Gina Tucci finally left, but only after the cops had threatened to haul her away, too. "I want to see him punished!" she shouted as they escorted her out.

The kid, Jake whatever his name was, had spent a few minutes talking to the tall, shrill woman. She'd finally left, too, madder than hell, and cursing a blue streak. Car couldn't say exactly why he'd waited. The kid, still standing in the door of the inner office, looked at him now.

"You're going to have to leave, gentlemen," Agent Turpin said to them, still making notes. "These premises are closed to anyone but agents of the United States government."

The kid didn't say anything, just picked up a denim jacket and headed toward the door.

"Care for a cup of coffee?" Car asked.

The kid turned back and looked at him for a minute, then shrugged. "Why not?" he said.

* * *

Jake told Carson Fuller the rest of the story. About losing Maggie Ivey, and her leaving with Bobby Semple. The guy just sat there shaking his head.

"She's halfway across the country by now," Jake said.

"Maybe not."

Jake felt hope lurch in his heart. "But she left two days ago."

The old detective shrugged. "Did you try to find her?"

Jake shook his head. "I guess I didn't think she'd want to see me."

Now Car shook his head. "Kid, that kind of thinking will get you nowhere. At least find her and give her the chance to tell you to go to hell in person. Don't you owe her that much? Besides"—Car took another slurp of his coffee—"from what you told me she's probably already sorry she left with the hayseed."

Jake caught the tiny thread of hope and decided to follow it until it broke.

"Shouldn't be too hard to track her down," Carson Fuller went on. "Start at the U-Haul rental places and trace anyone with a Georgia license, then look at motels fanning out from there."

"I'll pay you whatever you charge. Will you help me?" Jake waited, almost holding his breath.

The man looked at Jake, his faded eyes not giving anything away until his whole face creased into a smile. "Sure, kid," said Carson Fuller. "I'll help you."

It had taken hours, not days. Jake prayed for luck the whole time they looked. He and Car had gone to the detective's offices, booted up his computer, gone to the Internet yellow pages, typed in *truck rental* and a search radius. Then they started phoning. Car finally hit the jackpot. Found the U-Haul dealer, and only after five calls. The owner had been extremely helpful once he found out they weren't friends of Bobby Semple. He told them right where to find Maggie Ivey, and she wasn't that far out of town—the Motel 6 in Novato. Jake shook his head in amazement that all this time Maggie had been right under his nose.

He pumped Carson Fuller's hand up and down a few times, then drove to Novato, hoping all the while he wasn't too late. Now he sat parked half a block away, watching Maggie and Tim and Bobby Semple, his thick neck bulging from the tight collar of a work shirt, shift their load from one truck to another.

His only consolation seemed to be that things didn't seem to be going so well between Maggie and Bobby Semple. He almost came out of the truck at one point when the little ape grabbed her arm, but Maggie had taken care of it herself, wrenching her arm away with a twist and then stepping back and saying something to him with a little jut of her chin that made Jake proud of her, just like he'd felt when she told that guy at the bank to leave her alone.

He was almost hypnotized watching Maggie move, so light and easy, and yet so strong, picking up the boxes and putting them down, only every now and then straining at one. He wanted to get out and help her but instead he forced himself to sit and watch.

He'd better go soon, or it would be too late. Finally the moment he'd waited for came. Bobby Semple went into his motel room and closed the door, and Maggie and Tim went into the room next door to it.

Jake bounded out of the car and up the steps, and rapped on the door before he could think or rehearse what he would say.

"Just a minute, Bobby." Maggie's voice sounded harried.

Tim opened the door. "Jake!" He threw himself into Jake's arms. Jake picked him up and held him, and closed his eyes. When he opened them, Maggie was standing in the doorway. She reached her arms out for Tim, who went to her reluctantly. She sat him on the floor and he immediately threw himself at Jake's legs.

"What are you doing here?" Maggie's voice was cold.

"Maggie, I had to find you." He could hear Bobby Semple slamming drawers in the next room, probably taking one last look around before they left.

"I can't see you anymore."

"Please, Maggie." Jake opened his palms. "Please just give me five minutes. Then if you want to go, I won't stop you."

Maggie stood with her arms folded, her neck beginning to spot with large red welts. "There's nothing you can say to make this right."

"Please let me try."

"You can't." Tim was looking back and forth between his mother and Jake, his face beginning to look a little worried. "I may have done some things I'm not proud of," Maggie went on, just as Jake was beginning to suggest they talk outside so they wouldn't upset Tim. "But I've never gone out with a married man," Maggie finished. "You shouldn't have done that, Jake."

"Is that what you think?" He was amazed at being accused of the one thing he wasn't guilty of.

"What else am I to think? Isn't it true? Can you stand there and tell me it's not true?" Maggie sounded angry now, and her whole face and neck were blotched red.

"It's not true."

"Oh!" Maggie almost shouted, then she noticed Tim's face. "Watch cartoons for a minute, Tim." She lowered her voice and patted him on the shoulder. "I need to talk to Jake." She shut the door to the room and motioned him with a quick jerk to follow her down the stairs and across the courtyard to the laundry room. There was no one there. The machines gave off a sweet smell and a hum.

"How dare you! You could at least have the decency to tell me the truth." She was shaking.

"It's not true."

Maggie started to cry, but a different kind of crying than the first time he had seen her. These looked like tears of rage.

"How dare you think I'm stupid enough to believe that! My friend Gina hired a detective to spy on you. And in addition to all the illegal things he found you doing, she also told me what

I would have known if I wasn't such an idiot. You're married. He checked. You're married—not separated or in the process of getting a divorce. I can't believe you're standing there telling me you're not. It's right there inside your book: *Dedicated to my wife, Monica,*" she quoted Gina. She seemed to lose some of her steam then, looked more sorrowful than angry, and wiped her eyes with the back of her hand. "I guess I should have done my homework better," she said. "Then I would have known."

Jake took a deep breath. He reached out for Maggie's hand. She pulled it away from him, back to angry again. He exhaled and with the breath went all the clever plans he had made for how he would tell her the truth. "Dr. Jason Golding is married," he said.

Maggie stood looking as though she'd been turned to stone, a white marble statue with pink spots. The only sound was the hum of the dryers and the wet slosh of a washer behind her.

"But I'm not Jason Golding."

* * *

Maggie went back upstairs, told Bobby Semple she wasn't ready to go yet, and refused to give any explanation other than that. She comforted Tim, who was a little scared to see his mother arguing with Jake, and promised him that if he was just patient for a few more minutes they would leave the motel room for good. She'd fashioned a leash for the kitten from a piece of twine and she found it now and gave him permission to walk the cat to the laundry room and back.

Jake had left. She couldn't believe what he had told her. She wished she had about a week to just think and digest everything he had said. "Go away," she finally told him. And he had. She'd watched him walk to his truck—*his* truck, not his brother-in-law's. She watched him sit there for a minute, then pull away from the curb and drive off. She felt a lurch of something as she watched him drive away, but she hadn't had time to figure out what it was.

Now she went to her suitcase and dug around and under the wadded-up clothes she had piled into it. Bobby had been in such a hurry, packing had been a fiasco. Finally she found what she was looking for—the book she'd slipped out and bought at the Longs Drugs next door just before Jake came. She'd waited until Bobby was busy inspecting the new U-Haul, then she and Tim had run across the parking lot. There it was, right on *The New York Times* Best Seller rack, Dr. Jason Solomon Golding's new release, *Celebrating Me*. She'd had the clerk double bag it so Bobby wouldn't see what it was. When his back was turned she'd tucked it in her suitcase. Foolishness. But she had wanted something to remind her of Dr. Golding, to hold him in her heart one more time.

She pulled out the book, its glossy cover already seeming at odds with the plain, simple style of Jake Golding. Or was it Jake Cooper. She felt the urge to laugh. She read the ridiculous title again, then opened it up to the inside flap of the dust cover. She would have known by the time she had gotten to this, at any rate. Jake could never have written such nonsense. She shook her head, still unsure whether her smile was the appropriate response, or the tears that still were caught in her tight throat. She turned to the back flap of the cover, somehow, in spite of what he had just told her, expecting to see his face again, with the warm eyes, the blond hair and cowlicks, square jaw and jutting chin, the little scar under his eye. Quickly, she held the cover up to the light and looked at the picture that should have been familiar. DR. JASON GOLDING, it said. And there, smiling up at her, was a smooth, handsome face, cupped in a soft-looking hand. The man looked suave and assured, and Maggie Ivey had never seen him before in her life.

She did laugh then. At the whole ludicrous situation. At how she had had her sanity saved. By a carpenter. That was rich. She laughed so hard she could feel herself circle the edge of hysteria.

Tim came back from walking the cat. "Uncle Bobby says he wants to go."

Tim looked sad. She smiled at him, wiped her eyes, and vowed to stop scaring him. "Come here, sweetheart," she said, and held out her arms.

He jumped into them. "Do I have to call him Uncle Bobby?"

"No, baby, you don't." She kissed the top of his head. "He's not your uncle. He's not your anything."

She gave the book a toss. It landed neatly in the imitation brass garbage can. She kept squeezing Tim and looked around her at the cheaply furnished room, with even its lamps bolted down, and at her suitcase, filled to overflowing with all her belongings, gathered up and stuffed inside just because Bobby Semple had told her to do it. She looked down at the top of Tim's head. She thought again, hard, and stayed in that chair holding Tim for what seemed like hours. When she was done thinking, she knew what she would do. She got up and snapped the two suitcases shut, went into the bathroom and blew her nose, then splashed cold water on her face and neck. The hives were beginning to disappear. She shook her head and looked at herself in the mirror. She was finished crying.

Everything was easy, once she had decided. She went out to the truck where Bobby sat there smoking, belted Tim in the middle seat, then told Bobby she'd forgotten her makeup bag. He rolled his eyes and cursed, but she put honey in her voice and said, "Please, Bobby, would you go get it?" and maybe thinking she'd finally snapped out of her snit, he lumbered up the stairs toward her room. Maggie saw him talking to the maid, then watched as the woman unlocked the door and Bobby stepped inside. Maggie hopped out of the cab, opened the back of the U-Haul, and tossed out Bobby's duffel bag, just as he emerged from her room, glowering. She closed the back and started up the truck, Bobby having carelessly left the key in the ignition.

They were her things, her son, her life, she told herself as she drove away. The only thing that could even be remotely considered Bobby Semple's was the truck, and her mother had probably paid for that.

It sounded crazy, but Maggie felt good. She smiled down at Tim, and he smiled back and lost a little of the worried look. "We're going to take a little trip by ourselves," she told him, and headed the car north, by process of elimination. South was Mexico, east was her parents and Bobby Semple, west was the ocean. That left north. She'd heard good things about Seattle. Maybe they'd live in Seattle. Away from everyone.

After Jake had told her the truth, that he was a carpenter and had been fooling her all this time, she'd had a flash of insight, seen her life in crystal clarity, like someone had suddenly snapped on the light after she'd spent a lifetime banging her shins in the dark. She felt as if she'd never been anything but a rag doll, pushed and pulled and dragged along by everyone, having no bones or sinew to hold herself up. But in the last hour she had finally decided a few things. She was a long way from knowing what she wanted, but she knew what she didn't want. She didn't want to go back to the Embarcadero Arms. And she didn't want to go anywhere with Bobby Semple. She would decide everything else later.

* * *

Joe was tired. It had been a long afternoon. He'd just finished milking, and he was ready for supper. He trudged wearily out from the milking parlor, and as he did he caught a movement in the corner of his eye. Somebody was driving a U-Haul, none too skillfully, down the Clover Creek road and signaling to turn into his driveway. Joe stopped to see if the truck would make a U-turn and go back toward town on the highway. But it didn't. It drove up to the barn and stopped. He wiped his face and hands on his handkerchief as he walked over to the driver's side.

"Hi, Joe. I'm sorry to just show up like this, but I didn't know what else to do."

Joe opened the door for Maggie Ivey, and looked across the seat to the boy, trying not to show his surprise.

"Where's Dawson?" the boy asked.

"I guess he's in the house," Joe answered him. "Why don't you go on in and see, and tell Carol that your mom is here." That part was important. The sooner Maggie Ivey, who looked as though she might have been crying, was handed off to Carol, the easier he would feel.

Tim jumped down from the cab of the truck, that kitten they'd given him under his arm, and ran up onto the porch, through the banging screen door, and into the house.

"I don't quite know what to say," Joe said honestly. "Maybe I should call my brother."

"I'd appreciate that." And to his great relief, that was all Maggie said on the subject.

He called the office, but Jake wasn't there. He found out where he was working, though, and feeling a little disloyal, gave the directions to Maggie, who wrote them down solemnly with a crayon on a scrap of paper Carol found for her.

"Let us keep Tim," Carol said, "and take my car. You can leave the truck here."

Maggie just nodded, a red flush starting on her neck. "Thank you," she said. Her eyes filled up, but the storm never broke, and Joe had to admit he felt a wave of relief when she drove away in a cloud of dust.

"I wish there was some way I could let Jake know she's coming," Joe said, realizing he had just set his brother up for an ambush.

"Humph." Carol stood in the doorway, shaking her head, watching Maggie drive away. "He deserves whatever she gives him."

"I guess so." Joe knew better than to argue with Carol when she took that tone. Besides, he had to agree. Jake probably would get only what was coming to him. He'd lived through plenty of those episodes himself, and he'd long ago grown philosophical. Anyway, there was no reason for him to end up in the doghouse defending his brother. "I'm going to wash up for supper," he said, and planted a kiss on Carol's cheek before he left the porch. Carol didn't answer. She was still watching the station wagon turning onto the Clover Creek road, and shaking her head.

* * *

Maggie spread the crumpled paper out on the seat beside her and tried to read the orange crayon. She'd turned left at the Clover Creek road, and then north on Granger Road, took the first right, and passed the walnut grove. Go past town, Joe had said, then turn left just past the gas station grocery. "It's an unmarked road," he'd said, "so you have to watch for it."

She had passed a few familiar places from her walk with

Jake. Now she thought she had found it. There was the gas station grocery, and just past it she could see a gap in the trees that
must be the road. She turned.

The road had been cleared and recently graveled. She slowed
down so the rocks wouldn't batter Carol's car, and for just a
minute she was tempted to turn back. She seemed to have lost
the resolution that had driven her flight from the motel.

She had a fleeting thought of Bobby Semple and wondered if
he had gotten himself to the airport yet, or if he was still waiting at the Motel 6 for her to come back. When she had left him
she had had every intention of going straight to Seattle, but all
the way from Novato, driving up 101 past the familiar scenery,
she had remembered Jake and the places he had taken them and
the things he had done. Little by little her anger had cooled and
by the time she came to the cutoff for Petaluma and Clover
Creek, she'd decided that whatever Jake had done, he at least
deserved a good-bye. And a thank-you. At least that.

She gave a little ironic smile now, knowing what she knew,
thinking about how he must have felt that first day in Dr. Golding's office when she had come in and started crying as though
she would never stop. She remembered the concern in his eyes,
and the way he had leaned forward and listened to her. He had
been so kind. Maggie's nose started to run and she stopped driving for a minute and rummaged until she found a napkin stuck
between the seats of Carol's car.

She blew her nose and remembered how he had talked to her
so gently, not telling her what to do, just listening. How he had
installed the locks, and played with Tim, and taken them places.
She abandoned her thoughts of turning back. She couldn't leave
anger between them. She had to at least say good-bye.

It was really beautiful here. She noticed that fact for the first time. On each side of the graveled road were ferns and small saplings, and beyond them, old oaks, their leaves in twisted clusters. The road wound around to the left in a hairpin turn and when it opened up, Maggie frowned. The landscape was familiar. She squinted up her eyes, looked hard, and suddenly, she realized why. She was approaching it from the opposite direction this time, but she had been here before. She looked around her, nodding. There was the picnic table, the oaks, and the creek from her picnic with Dr. Golding—no, Jake, she corrected herself—Jake Cooper. She said the name out loud. She was positive when she saw the little brown and white trailer, looking lonely in the clearing.

She crossed over a plank bridge, then the road curved again and ended. Right in front of a house that hadn't been there before. It was cedar, with a stone chimney. Maggie felt her jaw drop. She wasn't thinking. She couldn't think. She just kept staring and felt as if she were in a dreamscape, and that the things she was seeing were to be accepted without logic, like talking dogs and flying people. She couldn't imagine what it could mean.

She shifted Carol's car into Park, fumbled with the keys, then got out and slowly went up the slate walkway until she reached the porch. There was a whitewashed swing and rocking chair. She walked past a pot of red geraniums, already in spicy bloom, opened the screen door, and followed the sound of hammering. It was her house, she realized. The one she visited every night in those few minutes between wakefulness and sleep.

She followed the sound into the living room, and looked around at the fieldstone fireplace and the oak floors. It was just as she had imagined. Just as if he had read her mind and translated it into a reality of stone and wood.

And there he was. Maggie realized for the first time that the cloud bank had lifted. The late afternoon sun was streaming through the oaks and making dappled patterns on the floor. Jake, not Dr. Golding, was hammering at the framing for the mantel. He had on a white T-shirt and jeans, and the steel-toed boots. She watched him for a minute, his shoulders moving rhythmically as he pounded. She should have known from his shoulders, she thought. A man with shoulders like that didn't sit around all day. She should have known from the truck, too, and from the way he had installed the locks. And from his hands, callused and worn. She should have seen it all, she realized now. But who would have thought? He stopped his hammering for a minute, and she must have made some slight noise, for he turned around.

The moment Maggie saw his face again she felt awkward and unprepared. What could she say? All her speeches seemed to fade away, like the lemon juice ink she and her sisters used to write notes with when they were kids. She shouldn't have come.

"Maggie." Jake Cooper's brows were bunched into a frown, and his eyes looked as sad as hers must have the first time she'd met him.

"You know me," Maggie said, "but I don't know you."

He didn't answer her right away. His breath sounded loud in the empty house. He put the hammer down on the mantel, and then spoke, as if reciting a speech he had practiced until he knew it by heart. "I never meant to lie to you or hurt you."

"What is all this, Jake?" She didn't respond to his speech, but gestured around her at the house, the trees, the creek, the porch with the swing and rocker. "Did you build all this right out of my daydream?"

"Yes." He took a few steps toward her. She could see the little scar, standing out against his face, which was paler than usual.

"Why? Were you planning on installing us here, and keeping us, like some kind of pets? Was this another experiment on Maggie Ivey?"

He shook his head. "This was going to be the last thing I did for you." He rubbed his head and looked so miserable she felt the small flame of her anger fizzle out. "I guess I made a mess of this, too," he said.

She looked down to catch up to her thoughts, not wanting to see his eyes right now. She focused on his shoes instead, and watched the shadows from the moving leaves play back and forth across them. Those shoes. She remembered the first time she had noticed his shoes. She should have known then, but she had been too lost in her sadness and despair.

Jake began talking again. "This was going to be the last thing I did for you. I wasn't going to give it to you or install you here, or anything like that. I'd have let you buy it, make payments or something, I don't know. I hadn't worked out all the details."

Maggie looked up at him then. His face was so earnest, his blue eyes so intense, that she had to smile. "You've had a lot of details to work out," she admitted.

He smiled back at her, and his eyes crinkled in the familiar way. Maggie felt the blotches begin on her neck. She didn't feel angry now or icy the way she had at the motel. "Why didn't you just tell me?" she asked. "Why did you let it go on so long?"

Jake shook his head and looked a little bewildered himself at her question. "I tried to tell you. A couple of times." He paused. "I've never been very good with words."

Maggie looked into his eyes, and remembered how kind and settling they'd been. She remembered the first time she had looked up from her crying jag that seemed to last a week and had seen those eyes in front of her, filled with concern. She smiled a little, thinking of him leaning over her boss's desk and threatening to put him in jail, and how he had whispered in her ear, insisting that she be the one to tell Mr. Brinnon to leave her alone.

She felt a rush of loyalty then, as if someone else had been accusing him. "How can you say that?" she asked. "You've helped me more than anybody else ever has. You treated me like an adult who could do things, and make good decisions. And you did so many practical things, like the locks, and the outings, and playing with Tim."

"Yeah," he said. "But those aren't words."

Maggie answered him and realized this wasn't the speech she had intended to make. "I'd been alone for so long, Jake. I felt as though I couldn't stand it any longer, and then I looked up, and there you were. And after that I never felt alone again. When I needed someone, you were there." She reached across the space between them and he caught her arm and pulled her toward him. "That's more important than any words you could have said."

"I'm all sweaty," he said, but he kissed her anyway, on the cheeks, and on her splotchy neck, and finally on her mouth. It was all coming unglued, she realized, this icy resolve that had carried her from the motel room, up the freeway, to Joe and Carol's, and now here to him. She tightened her arms around his neck, felt his warm skin and short hair under her palm. She felt his lips, warm and soft, and wet, pressing against her own.

"I'm sorry," he finally murmured into her ear. "I'm so sorry." He tightened his arms around her. "I'll never lie to you again."

"I know."

"Maggie?"

"What?"

"Where's Bobby Semple?"

She smiled into his shoulder. "I hope he's on his way back to Georgia by now," she said. "I ditched him at the Motel 6."

Jake looked down at her. His face had lost the tight, drawn look and was beginning to break into a smile. "So you're not leaving?"

"Not if you want me to stay."

"I want you to stay," he answered quickly, not seeming at all at a loss for words now. "I want you to have this place. I built it for you."

Maggie felt his arms tighten around her waist again, and she pulled his head down and whispered in his ear. "I'll stay here," she said, "on one condition."

16

Friday, July 3

Jake loaded the last of the lumber into the back of the truck—some two-by-fours and siding he'd had left after a job. He'd promised Tim he'd bring home materials to build a fort in the big oak by the creek. They'd spent an hour making their plans the night before. Tim wanted a rope swing and a pole, for quick escapes. They'd have to go to the hardware store tomorrow, but he had enough to get started tonight. He made sure his load was secure, climbed into the cab, and started the short trip home.

He had left Maggie this morning, slowly and reluctantly, as usual. She said she was going to paint and then Carol and Shelley and the kids were coming over for lunch. After they ate, the kids would play in the creek while the three of them made pies and cakes for the Fourth of July family cookout. He and Maggie would have it at their house this year. Their house. Jake repeated the words to himself. He liked the sound of them.

It hadn't taken long, really, to move Maggie's things into the house, and only a day or two to get ready for the wedding. He supposed it just seemed longer. Carol and Maggie and Ma and Shelley, who had all hit it off like gangbusters, went into San Francisco one day, and left all the kids with him and Joe. They'd come back with groceries and dresses, and then he had barely seen Maggie for two whole days. He had taken his mind off of it by seeding the yard at the new house. Maggie and Tim had stayed with Carol and Joe, insisting that they would all move in together after the wedding.

They were finally married at the Presbyterian church in Clover Creek. Jake had to remind himself it was only a week in the making. Maggie looked pretty and sweet as always in a pale-colored dress of some kind. Jake didn't really notice what she had on, though Carol and Shelley made a big fuss about it. Maggie's parents had flown in all the way from Georgia, and never did quite get the details straight, thinking this had all come up pretty suddenly. Maggie's mother wept throughout the ceremony, probably grieving for Bobby Semple. Mrs. Weaver had tried to console her.

After the ceremony Jake's mother had cried, and hugged Maggie and Tim, and said she was counting her blessings to have another sweet daughter and grandchild. Then Carol and Shelley cried, too, and all the women hugged, and Joe and Danny had slugged him on the shoulder, and Ethelda, who was sitting with Carson Fuller, had beckoned Jake over and whispered in his ear that he'd really come out of the outhouse smelling like a rose.

"You are one lucky boy," she'd said. And Jake said he knew it. In fact, he felt luckier every day. Every morning when he woke up with Maggie curled warm and soft beside him, every time someone said Tim looked like him.

Jake turned onto the graveled road, passed the new cedar

sign that said THE COOPERS—JAKE, MAGGIE, TIM, with lots of space to add more names. He drove through the oak grove, and over the creek bridge, and up to the house. He could see Jake the cat sleeping peacefully on the porch, and he was barely out of the truck when Tim came running around the side of the house, looking pretty much as he did every day now. He was dirty and wet from the creek, glasses smudged and barely hanging on, his head bobbing up and down as he ran. He launched himself at Jake from a few feet away, and Jake caught him easily, and swung him up onto his back.

"Mom," Tim called out as Jake climbed the porch steps.

Jake could hear Maggie answer from the kitchen as he opened the screen door and walked into the house.

"Daddy's home," he said.